continued from front flap

she "died." Through this manuscript Caroline discovers a past which she believes she is being forced to accept as her own: a rich, condescending girl friend; a caustic, demanding sister-in-law; an indifferent mother whose poetry came before her family; a husband caught between integrity and the social and financial pressures of his community.

While typing the "autobiography," Caroline also begins to keep a daily journal of her days in the hospital, and gradually the autobiography and Caroline's journal intertwine and overlap, just as their two psyches slowly and painfully merge to form a completely integrated Self.

Mary Jane Ward writes with bite, precision and wit, and even the minor characters —doctors and patients in the hospital—are drawn with sharp cutting realism. THE OTHER CAROLINE is a powerful study of the paranoid schizophrenic personality as created and abetted by the pressures and hostilities of society. Yet it is also a statement of personal triumph, of moral outrage in the face of the emptiness of success, a private plea for sanity in an insane world.

MARY JANE WARD'S *The Snake Pit* was made into one of Hollywood's most successful motion pictures. Since *The Snake Pit*, she has written many books, including *Counterclockwise, The Wax Apple,* and *It's Different for A Woman*. She and her husband, Edward Quayle, live in New England, where Miss Ward paints professionally, in addition to writing.

The Other Caroline

The Other Caroline

A NOVEL BY Mary Jane Ward

CROWN PUBLISHERS, INC. / NEW YORK

13969

The Other Caroline

ONE *The Journal*

*E*veryone at Martin House belongs to a group for psychotherapy but mine is the only one not conducted by a local whitejacket. They say the assignment is by lot, but I wonder. Our Man Friday, a Dr. Leonard, comes from Outside, where he is in obviously lucrative private practice. I am told that he was my doctor before I came to Applewood State Hospital for the Insane. (That's the legal name no matter what they try to make us think—Aggie may be slightly nuts, but she knows things like this. She's my only real friend here, if it is possible to have a real friend in a loony bin.)

If Dr. Leonard was my doctor, isn't it rather a coincidence that I was assigned to his therapy group? Believe me, there are many strange coincidences in connection with my case, but of course I don't dare point these out to staff people. Right away they decide I'm getting very paranoid, and if you go too far in that direction it's back to La Salle for you. And when I say back, I mean *back*. I overheard one of our sappy visitors saying how lovely it is now that there aren't any more "back" wards. Oh, boy, she should see La Salle or just get a whiff of it.

But here we are great ladies and some of us, chosen by lot or by malice aforethought, go every Friday morning to chat with each other while Dr. Leonard listens in and gets a whacking deduction from his income tax, I bet, for his charity work. He wears a vicuña topcoat and drives a ten thousand dollar job that looks like a baby carriage or a toy that shouldn't be out on the road by itself. "How do you know these things?" asked Aggie. It is all right for her to know everything on God's green earth including his zip code, but she sure gets suspicious when I say something she hasn't beat me to.

In a way I can't blame her. I don't know my real age, my real name, or a single fact about myself since coming to, over at La Salle. The point is that although I don't remember anything, I do know a good bit. For instance, when I put my hands on this keyboard, I realized right away that I am a trained typist. Dr. Leonard and my gentleman visitor, Mr. Kincaid, had both told me this, but how am I to know when they slip in a little of my actual history? For months they have been trying to get me to accept Caroline Kincaid's past as my own. Fortunately I seem to be a fairly strong personality, and there isn't much chance, particularly now that I am quite alert, that they can sandbag me with the Other Caroline myth.

Yes, I think of her as the Other Caroline. A person has to have a name. Also, while I was still pretty foggy, I began to realize that, as long as I kept on screaming whenever they called me "Caroline" or "Mrs. Kincaid," my chances of getting out of that hellhole were probably slim. So I stopped yelling and even stopped hitting the horrible old woman who used to try to urinate on me because, she said, she hated all Kincaids. I just had to get out of that place. Mr. Kincaid knew it was bad, but he never knew how bad. The visitors never came on the ward.

At first I blamed him. I figured he had to be in on the plot— what else can I call it? Now I realize that although they would have had to have his permission, he must have been an innocent dupe. He's a Quaker, for one thing. I don't suppose all of them

2

are angels, by any means, but I have a feeling a Quaker wouldn't become involved in anything illegal unless he figured it was something more important than the law. Aggie says the man is putting me on, that Quakers went out of existence long before the horse and buggy. I can't prove that they still do exist, but I believe Mr. Kincaid is an honest man. I believe they must have told him the operation was his wife's only chance for survival.

Did anybody express concern for *me?* Did somebody sign *me* away? Or was I just picked up, nearly dead, on a highway, all banged up everywhere except in the head? Dr. Leonard and his conspirators, call them colleagues if you wish, are going to be in very hot water if I get my memory back. I realize they were careful not to transplant the portion of the brain that carries the memory, or that this would have been their intention. However, since I retain so much of one kind of memory, I have not yet given up hope that the other kind will return. One of these days—I keep dreaming this—I not only will recall the title and story of some book read in the past, but I will remember who I was and where I was when I read it. Some day, as I am pushing a soup spoon away from me as the other girls slop the soup toward them, I will remember the person who taught me a little jingle about sending ships sailing out to sea. I couldn't continue to live if I didn't believe this. The present is a nightmare and the future an impossibility if you have no past.

I have nobody to discuss this with. Dr. Leonard, although acting like butter wouldn't melt in his mouth, is my enemy. He seeks my welfare, sure, but why? I expect he is counting on getting a Nobel for his experimentation on Caroline Kincaid and me, for his making one woman where two existed before. He probably expects Congress to excuse him for having broken a few laws in the process.

Mr. Kincaid comes to see me every Saturday and Sunday. He is really quite a wonderful person. I would guess he married beneath himself, intellectually anyhow. But his loyalty to the woman he believes his wife is unwavering. I believe that I, whoever I was, do not exist for him and that he may even have made himself forget that I ever did. I imagine he thinks of me as a suddenly killed woman who happened to have some vital tissue needed for his wife's recovery. He wouldn't have been the one

3

to decide just when I had died. Or if I had. Even Aggie admits that they probably couldn't let a brain stand around any length of time. But she thinks I am crazy when I speak of being the victim of what undoubtedly was the world's first brain transplant. "It's all right to blow off steam to me, kid," she says, "but go easy on that story around anybody else because it sure is screwy." That's what I meant when I suggested that a person is suspicious of everybody else or at least thinks everybody else is crazier.

I don't claim I am in perfect mental health. I know now that I was a terribly sick woman most of the time I was in La Salle. I remember so little of it. And still, somewhere in my mind, the terror I felt there remains. I had no friends. Even the people who spoke kindly to me seemed to be enemies.

Which is worse, I wonder, to have no past to think about when you are lonely or to be convinced that you have no future? Sometimes I think I could accept my present life as the only one I will ever know, if I could just remember a little something of what it was like before. Was I happy at least some of the time? I am realistic enough now to face the fact that I will never be able to escape from Caroline Kincaid's body. I used to think maybe I could kill her. Then I would be free to find my own body. It was wild thinking, all right. Now I know that, like it or not, I am stuck for life with the Other Caroline's too tall, too thin, redheaded body. I suppose I should be grateful that the face isn't bad.

Last Friday as we were leaving the therapy room, Dr. Leonard asked if I had a minute. Aggie, who answers for everybody and gets to be more of a trial daily, said I didn't have anything but time. Politely enough Dr. Leonard let her know he was speaking only to me and she had to leave. Then he asked how I would like to try brushing up on my typing. I didn't bother to say I had no way of knowing if there was anything to brush up, and anyway he wasn't waiting. He said he'd located a place, in an Administration storeroom where there was a desk and typewriter I could use. I said I hoped this didn't mean they would expect me to do work for the office because I'd be scared to death.

"You don't have to do anything but Now-is-the-time-for-all-good-men if you don't want to," he said. "I just thought it would be something to get you off the ward."

Nobody could object to that. "Well," I said, "I think it's more something about a quick fox these days, but I'd like to try."

He gave me one of those strange looks that I get from Mr. Kincaid, too, when they think maybe I am beginning to remember. But he didn't ask what else I might recall about typing to the tune of quick foxes. He said if I wanted something to copy he could supply me with a manuscript or parts of one if I didn't want to do the whole thing. "It isn't anything that has to be done in a hurry. But why not get your coat and come see if you think you'd like the little corner I've found? It's got a fine view of the campus."

And it does have. Whatever else you say about Applewood, and there's a lot more to be said against the institution than ever has been, the grounds are beautiful. There are many fine old trees even now after the elms have been taken down. Landscape gardening therapy, unjustly limited to male patients, has been responsible for the creation of splendid borders and flower beds. At the moment there's nothing green except the tulip spears. Administration, a hundred-year-old pile of gray stone, is veined with ivy that is still leafless. But there is beauty even in this picture in browns and grays, with accenting slashes of black.

It wouldn't be fair, I suppose, to say the total of the grounds and its dozen or so large buildings, with clusters of smaller ones, gives the impression of a penal institution, but for those of us here against our will it feels like it and pretty much works like it. There have been three escapes since I've started knowing what goes on around me and listening to the grapevine guzz. Two of the fleeing patients were caught and brought back in a few hours; the third was struck by a hit-run driver and left dying on the highway a few yards from the front gates. I don't have the guts to try an escape, but ever since placing my hands on the keyboard of this machine I have known I will be able to support myself when I do get out into the real world.

The girl at the desk just outside the storeroom door is pleasant and gives no impression of being told to keep an eye on me. And there's no trace of that special voice when she speaks to me. I might be just another employe. "Let me know if you need anything," she said. "And coffee's at three, but I'll let you know when it's about ready." Evidently they make coffee in the big office. Maybe that's one of the reasons the room doesn't seem to have the smell I notice when I step from out-of-doors into Administration. It's been fifty years, I am told, since patients were housed in this building, but you can still smell them in the ancient wood and plaster of the wide, cathedral-tall entrance hall. Along the sides of the hall are benches where friends and relatives wait to confer with staff. But Dr. Leonard told me none of those conferences are held in the office adjoining my store-room cubby.

I've hardly more than glanced at the typed pages Dr. Leonard had Mr. Kincaid bring me. But I have noticed that the crayoned-out parts apparently are names. Anyway, names have been neatly printed in above the black deletions. I think I could make the original names out if I held the pages up to the light, but I'm not interested. I would get some kind of kick out of the job, I suppose, if I thought Dr. Leonard had written what seems to be an attempt at a novel, but Mr. Kincaid told me it was written by one of Doctor's patients. Maybe the deletions are a bow in the direction of medical ethics. Like when they put those black marks across the eyes of people photographed in mental institutions.

Now Miss Johnson is calling from her desk to say coffee is nearly ready. I sure hope the other girls will be as casual and friendly. I don't think I'll start on the manuscript until Wednesday. Mr. Kincaid brought a ream of very good typewriter paper but no carbons or second sheets. He said Dr. Leonard would have mentioned it if he'd wanted carbons and so not to bother. But I must remember to check with the doctor on Friday.

Aggie says I am a fool not to have found out what I am being paid. I told her I didn't think anything. So she said, "Then you're crazier than I thought."

6

TWO *The Manuscript*

While Marianne and I were waiting in line at the City Club's check counter, she suggested that we have lunch someday soon. "Just us," she said. "Like old times."

The Family Welfare meeting had run on and on. In the old days I used to think it would be wonderful to belong to organizations like Family Welfare, but now I know that the less like F.W. the better. It's the one that has been most resistant to letting the young women have their own group. The older women brag about how they solved the generation gap by stepping down and letting the younger women take over. What they did was quit accepting jobs, while continuing to say how everything should be done. Marianne's mother is the worst of the lot. While she was sounding off at the last meeting, I distinctly heard somebody across the aisle whisper, "Horseshit," but if Marianne heard she never changed expression. All that stopped her mother's filibuster was her sudden recollection that she had a dental appointment.

I adore Petey Hawes, president of F.W., but she just can't cope with the old tyrants like Mrs. Snyder, Marianne's mother. I shudder when I think of taking the office but wonder if I can get out of it. I know from things the boss has dropped that he is very much interested in the social and clubwork doings of his young execs' wives. This is the kind of thing that is incomprehensible to my highly intellectual, very brilliant, but in many ways dumb husband.

The big hassle between the young and the old gals at the last F.W meeting was the nature of the coming benefit. I admit that last year's was a brawl, but the old hens who were shocked by it can't say we didn't make more money than the organization ever made in one benefit before. The older members left in droves before midnight and so didn't know how much worse it got. Everyone was stoned. Oh, not Jock or me. He never says anything, but I have found it very inhibiting liquorwise to have a teetotaler husband. I never did care much for the stuff but of course was willing to go along with the crowd.

It was easier, really, when people assumed that my husband was an alcoholic. I mean, nobody tries to break an alcoholic's refusals down unless they themselves are very crocked. I suppose it must have been Jock himself who let it out that he's a Quaker. I know it isn't anything to be ashamed of, but in Maxwell you just never hear about the Society of Friends. Our crowd is very integrated, you might say, because if there were any blacks who were our kind of people they certainly would be welcome. We have quite a lot of Jewish friends. But I don't know of any Quakers in town except Jock. And so it does make him seem kind of odd to some people. Of course there are Quakers who don't mind going to war and who drink, but Jock isn't one of these. However, I grew up with parents who sure were never orthodox in any of their beliefs, and so it's easier for me to have an offbeat husband than it would be for most of my friends. Well, Marianne being such a saint, I suppose she wouldn't even think about it if *her* husband was somewhat different. He is, brother, he is, but in a way very easy to take. Bud not only has his family's money in back of him; he's made more out of the Snyder Enterprises than Marianne's father, no slouch himself, ever did.

Marianne has been my best friend since we were perhaps younger than four, but I can't remember her before that. I got a scholarship for a high-priced nursery school operated near our block by an elegant but poor widow. It was years before it dawned on me that the Snyders had arranged this so their only child would have a companion for the trip to and from school. Other than the nurse or chauffeur. She was right when she said we used to lunch together almost daily in the old times but not correct in saying we were alone. We were almost never alone for lunch. Before we ate at school, we were either at her house or my house. At her house some of the help were always hanging around, and at my house there was my mother. My mother never went to meetings. My mother was a poet and different. Daddy wasn't a poet, but he was different—different enough to be fired for disloyalty to the United States during World War II.

He and mother were members of the Young People's Socialist League when they were in college, and later on, although not members, they continued to support the Socialist Party. In Maxwell the majority believes Socialists and Communists are the same, but as long as my folks were the only radicals most of their acquaintances knew, they were considered almost cute, something to exhibit, like now when a Negro is put near the entrance.

I didn't think about the Snyders being rich and the Andrews poor. I thought we had a small house because we liked it, and that we didn't have hired help because we didn't want them around. Wally, my older brother, was the one who disillusioned me. Wally had a network of paper routes by the time he was twelve and eventually he took me on as an assistant. I worked cheaper than any of his boys. I don't think Maxwell ever had a girl newspaper carrier before or has had since Wally sold his business to a buyer who didn't want the kid sister. Under Wally's aegis I never had enough money to buy anything substantial, but I dreamed of someday having a dress that Marianne hadn't had first.

Eventually I did make enough money to buy the things the

folks had had to purchase before. Mother saw to it that I limited my spending to shoes, rubbers, and galoshes. My mother can be far more practical than her fans dream, but she couldn't stuff my feet into Marianne's footgear. Eventually Marianne grew almost as tall as I, but her feet never caught up with mine.

I was an ingrate. I always had far better clothes than most of the other girls, not counting Marianne, and they never looked secondhand. I know Marianne often picked things out with my taste in mind and that she pretended to be tired of garments, when she really didn't care what she wore. Her mother didn't give her much say. You would think parents with only one child would have thought that one perfect and spoiled her, but the Snyders were constantly picking at Marianne. Nothing she did ever struck them as being right.

The result was that Marianne loved our little house and especially the mother who was never too busy to read aloud or do fool things like making popcorn or candy. My mother hated keeping house, but Gran came over every few days to dig us out and to cook. Gran was more the mother to me and to the boys, too, than our real mother, but I believe Mother substituted for Mrs. Snyder in Marianne's eyes. My friend was fond of Daddy, too, but didn't see him so often.

The folks' house is on a lot too narrow for the modern zoning laws. So nobody has bothered to buy the little old farmhouse to tear down. Mother has always said how quaint the house would be if it had a white picket fence and green shutters, to say nothing of a new coat of paint every few years now that Maxwell's near-center has become so dirty, but I doubt if the place will ever get any beauty treatment. Daddy was hired back eventually after it became popular again to be against war, but he's never made much money. What little he can save always goes to publish Mother's books. He brings out a new book of her poems about every two years. The most recent is a slight departure. It's poetry, but an epic alleged to have been inspired by the life of my younger brother Richard, killed in Vietnam.

Since I grew tall very young, I began to baby-sit when I was eleven. This gave me some relief from Marianne's constant breathing down my neck, but I didn't like the work as well as I'd liked delivering newspapers. The kids were all right but I

10

couldn't stand the parents, mostly the mothers. They would tie me up for weeks ahead and then think nothing of canceling me at the last minute. I don't remember a one of them ever offering to pay me when she'd decided against me too late for me to get another job. I never had the kind of trouble with the fathers, though, that I've heard other sitters report. I've always thought most of that was made up. But I must admit that I wasn't much of a dish between eleven and sixteen when I was earning at least some of my clothes and trying to save up for college. It was always understood that we three would go to college but under our own steam, aside from being given room and board if we wanted it.

We were never treated like children. Wally was always very adult. I had Gran when I felt I had to be a child and Richard had the Keanes, shanty Irish who may have had twice the money we had but who lived in Maxwell's version of a slum. It wasn't very slummy in those days, and when I was sent to fetch Richard home, I could understand why he was forever running to the far more neighborly area. Our neighbors' hired help lived better than we did, but my family had a kind of position, a sort of status that the wealthy must acknowledge but which they cannot buy or sell.

Marianne couldn't do this or that because it was something "nice" girls couldn't do; nobody bothered to tell me what I could or could not do. And did I appreciate being treated like an adult? No. How often I went weeping to Gran who would comfort me by saying, "Why, you're still just a little girl, honey, no matter how tall you are."

I was just as boy-struck as any other teen-age girl, but I didn't get the kind of cooperation that led to a roll in the hay. The boys liked me fine and treated me like a sister. They told me their troubles and asked me out when the best girl wasn't available. I reaped a lot of compliments about being a good sport. I was complimented upon having a great sense of humor and sometimes upon the color of my hair. Otherwise, I was just the jolly, very green giant.

The day after my sixteenth birthday I applied at the Rankin dime store for a part-time job until the end of school, with full time for summer vacation. The manager was surprised when I told him I was sixteen. People took me for eighteen. I got the job, my biggest thrill until Jock Dunlop, approaching a chair where I was seated, asked if I was tall standing up.

Daddy and Mother have never been what I would call big

talkers, but at table they are active conversationalists. It wouldn't be right to say they didn't give us kids a chance. I can't remember ever feeling I couldn't have got a word in if I had really wanted to. Wally was almost lost in what I believe really were empiric thoughts, and Richard ate as if working hard though willingly. He never stayed at table a moment longer than necessary. Then he would be up and away to the Keanes'.

"What's the fascination there?" asked Daddy one evening after Richard had fled.

"It couldn't be the girl," said Mother. "She's an appalling little creature . . . looks like a white mouse." Even then she was firmly taking Crystal Keane out of her conception of Richard's life.

If anybody had looked at me the evening I came home with a real job under my belt, he would have known something tremendous had happened to me. Gran would have known. But Gran wasn't there and I was still trying to think of how best to surprise her. What I hoped to do was lure her down to the store and have her see me there, punching the cash register, and saying, "Thank you for shopping at Rankins." I wasn't planning how to tell the rest of the family because I didn't think they would be much interested. But I'd thought they would be pleased at the prospect of not having women calling up all the time to see about sitter dates. I would have liked to tell Wally about my new job that day after my sixteenth birthday, but there was no real opening. Mother and Daddy were busy discussing her forthcoming book of poems, to be edited and published, as usual, by my father. So I didn't say anything and thus Marianne got to be the one to break the news.

Marianne isn't a cat or mean. She's a good, kind woman and she was a good, kind girl. But, as I have indicated, dumb. She wanted to do the right thing. She had no idea I hadn't told my folks about the job. She supposed that since I still had it, after a week, my folks just didn't know what a dangerous place Rankins was. I knew, but had long since forgotten something so silly, that Marianne had been forbidden to enter the dime store which had something of a reputation as a hangout. Lots of high school kids went there for soft drinks and hot dogs or hamburgers. There'd been a good deal of trouble about shoplifting, but by the time I got my job it was quite well under control. We girls had special instructions on the subject and there were security officers on the premises and those large mirrors that assure a potential thief Big Brother is watching.

Most of the part-time and vacation help was supplied by the high school students. None of these came from "our" crowd, but what difference did that make to me? The riffraff fascinated me. The girls wore extreme hairdos and exaggerated makeup, and usually smelled of more than cheap perfume. These girls didn't just go steady. They got engaged. Many of them dropped out of school during their second or third year. Ruth Zabeloni, who broke me in at Rankins, was a black-eyed beauty, engaged with a ring that looked like a Cracker Jack prize. Standing in the little cashier's run with her, I wished she bathed oftener but otherwise I had no complaint.

The manager gave me all of two hours to get the hang of checking, and after that Ruth went back to her post at another register. Having identified her smell, I was aware of it even when she was in the next lane. It was a smell I would have associated with dirty underwear if I hadn't been told she didn't wear any.

On the Friday afternoon of my first week, I felt experienced enough to phone Gran to see if she could meet me at the dime store to help me pick out a pattern. "Keri," she said, "couldn't we go someplace else where we could sit down?"

I said I wanted to get my notions at Rankins and that all I wanted her to do was choose between two patterns I had already picked out. She agreed to meet me. However, my mother showed up first. I didn't see her come in. I didn't know she was there until she came into my lane. She'd selected a few items so she would have an excuse not to rush through. I laughed when I looked up and saw her. "Somebody told you," I said.

"Indeed somebody did," she said. "Did you think I would be likely to come to such a place otherwise? Keri, I am simply appalled."

"What about?" I asked. I wondered if she'd found out about Ruth's not wearing any underclothes.

"This dreadful place," she said.

Then I noticed the racket. It was always this way when the kids were still hanging around on their way home. They were horsing around and smoking and some of them, having left the food counters, were playing records. It was good business to let them horse around like this. They were good spenders and steady. These kids made far more noise than the grade school youngsters, but the younger ones were the shoplifters.

"No wonder the Snyders won't allow Marianne to set foot in here," said Mother. "How do you keep from throwing up?"

I rang up her items, a few notions done up in cellophane, articles which I suppose she chose because she thought they would be the least contaminated of the merchandise. I found myself thinking how little I cared what she said. "Just what *is* the difference between the Socialist Party and the D.A.R.?" I said.

She was either too taken aback or just too nauseated by the aroma to answer. She took the bag I handed her and her change. "Thank you for shopping at Rankins," I said. She didn't answer.

My grandmother came later. I saw her come in and beckoned to the floor girl who had agreed to take my lane while I went on a ten-minute pass. But Gran caught sight of me while I was still checking and she was waiting for me when I left my station. "Why, you little rat," she said. "Your mother isn't going to like it."

"She was in about a half hour ago," I said. "No, she doesn't like it."

"What's that smell?" asked Gran. "I've never noticed it before."

"You probably don't come in this late in the day," I said. "This is when they have to cook an awful lot of french fries. And there's a rage now for a hot dog with a lot of sauerkraut on it . . . instead of pickle. Then the girl at the beauty counter is introducing a new incense, I guess it is."

Gran laughed. "It's like Coney Island," she said, "not that I've been there in fifty years."

Since it was almost closing time, she went to a nearby drugstore to wait for me. She wanted me to come home with her for dinner, but I said if I did Mother would think I was sore or even afraid of what she and Daddy would say. I had to laugh when I said this, because the idea of my caring about what either of them would say amused me. I think Gran saw this and

15

that it made her sad. But I told myself it was great to be so free.

"Don't worry," I said. "They won't say I have to quit, they will leave it entirely up to me." Although I pretended to glory in my freedom, I agonized over how little my parents seemed to care about me. They didn't make a big thing of the dime store. I imagine lots of people would say they handled the situation exactly right. I suppose if they had forbidden me to continue at the store I would have felt honor bound to stay at Rankins. As it was, they went back to their old honor-system evasion of parental responsibility, and I stayed at Rankins only until I got a job that paid more money. Wally got it for me. He had been working at Pickalot since getting a work permit and had become the manager's right hand. Wally waited until I had had time to become quite an expert at checking, which took only a couple of weeks.

It was hard for me to leave Rankins. The other girls had accepted me, and their friendship gave me more satisfaction than I'd ever felt out of the girl-girl relationship. It was as if I had been pledged by a marvelous sorority. I can't explain it because I can't understand it. I was the only Rankin girl from the "right" side of town. My mother didn't belong to the D.A.R. but she could have if she'd wanted to. Although we were probably far poorer than the families of my colleagues at the dime store, we nevertheless were honored members of Maxwell's Four Hundred.

Before Wally got me the Pickalot job, I had been determined to stay on at Rankins for the summer and to continue in a part-time job there after school started. I knew I would have a hard time saving up enough money for college, but I figured the pay was as good as I could expect.

I wasn't sore at Miss Goodie-Two-Shoes for having alerted my mother to what I was doing. It was no secret. If Marianne hadn't told her, somebody else would have. When Mother told Daddy where I was working, he didn't seem to be very upset about it until he realized that she had decided it was a dreadful place for their daughter to spend the summer. Marianne had told her it was a hangout for the "lower" elements of the high school.

I liked the "lower" classes but was enough like my brother to grab a job offering ten dollars a week more. I knew I couldn't pretend Pickalot's ten extra dollars a week in the college fund was less important to me in the long run than being chummy with Ruth Zabeloni and company. The manager was sore when I told him I wanted to quit, but said he couldn't compete with the Pickalot pay. "You'll work a hell of a lot harder," he said.

"I know," I said, "but if I'm going to college I've got to work hard or I'll never make it."

He shrugged and then told me I could quit any time. "It's okay if you want to leave tonight," he said. "I always take on a few extra, figuring some will drop out and frankly I had you figured for it. You really aren't our type."

It made me feel bad. I could see it for myself, though. I didn't have the extreme hairdo, the long, fancy fingernails, and heavy makeup. I was more the grocery type.

At Pickalot most of the part-time girls were married women working as much for the discount they got on their Pickalot purchases as for the hourly wage. The store was one of the largest and busy from morning until closing. Wally made extra money by working overtime, which the women couldn't do. I'm not too sure I would have had the energy to do overtime but would have tried it if given the chance.

Although the Rankin girls spoke to me the following fall at school if I spoke to them first, they weren't especially friendly. It's still the same with the few I see. They would rather not stop and chat, but will if I press them. I used to ask what happened to Ruth. She didn't show up at school that fall. Finally I found out that she'd got married, but not to the boy who had given her the Cracker Jack ring. From the way the girls acted, I decided it must have been a shotgun affair. After I was in college, I stopped to talk with one of the girls I met on the street. She was pushing a baby carriage and leading a toddler by the hand. She said she'd heard that Ruth had got a divorce. "Well, maybe an annulment, being in the Church," she said, "since the baby didn't live."

I'd been working at Pickalot for years before I saw Ruth again. I was a junior in college and one of the Pickalot senior checkers. I could check a customer out almost without noticing whether the person was male, female, black or white. There was none of that "Thank you for shopping" rigmarole at Pickalot.

17

The manager had got the bright idea that it might be nice on Saturday to say, "Have a nice weekend," but we'd laughed him out of it. Saturday was the day we could say the least. If Ruth Zabeloni had come through my lane on a Saturday, I bet I never would have noticed her.

But we weren't as busy as usual and as I turned to give the customer her change, I caught a glimpse of something familiar and did a double take. "Why, Ruth Zabeloni," I said, "I almost didn't *see* you! How are you?"

Her abrupt "Okay" made me think she hadn't recognized me. I was pleased because in my opinion I had improved considerably. I was at least thirty pounds lighter and could do a nice job on my hair now and I'd stopped having skin troubles. So, smiling all over the place, I told her I was Keri Andrews. And she gave me that same dead look. "We worked together at Rankins for a little while," I said. "You broke me in. Remember?"

"Vaguely," she said.

So I handed her her change. It was all right with me. I was tempted to ask her if she was still beating the lingerie racket, but all I said was, "Thank you for shopping at Pickalot."

"Is there somebody to carry my things out?" she asked.

I didn't bother to answer but turned to my next in line. That one had only a couple of items and there was nobody after her. So I put up my Closed sign and told the next checker I was taking a pass. I went to the window where I could see Ruthie beckoning to the boy who helps customers load. She left her cart with him and then went to a white Cadillac convertible. I don't think she could have had anything under her slacks which looked painted on. Her sweater was a matching orange, very fuzzy. Suddenly I realized that she was no longer a brunette. Her hair was a tower of gold. She didn't look like Maxwell, a rather conservative community. I wondered where she lived.

I didn't see her again until a year ago last New Year's Eve. Marianne and Bud always have a dinner that night and then we all go over to the City Club dance. Year before last when we got there, perhaps later than usual, Mrs. Justin Hoover, a rather eccentric woman, was ushering her party in. When she saw me, she grabbed my arm, pulled me over to her group, and said,

"People, I want you all to meet the daughter of Maxwell's poet laureate; isn't it exciting to have such a marvelous poet right in our own town?" She was higher than a kite, of course. "Honey, whatever is your married name? I never could remember it."

"Dunlop," I said.

"Oh, of course," she said, "where's your sweet husband, he's so handsome, people, you must meet her sweet husband, he looks exactly like her, so tall and handsome and that same red hair, I wonder how they ever get on, I mean, two redheads."

"Well, I better be getting back to them," I said. "I think they're through checking their wraps."

Mrs. Hoover hadn't bothered to mention the names of her guests, but Ruth Zabeloni, now a redhead herself, was standing beside a little old fellow I figured must be her husband. "How you doing, Ruth?" I said but didn't wait for an answer and so don't know if she would have spoken willingly under these circumstances. If she danced, I didn't see her on the floor. Whenever I looked at Mrs. Hoover's party, which wasn't often, Ruth and the little old man were just sitting there not saying anything. I asked Marianne if she knew who the man was, and she said she thought Bud had had some dealings with him.

So I asked Bud and he said he had met the fellow. "For a while I thought maybe we could do better on some of our supplies through him but when I began to check, I just wasn't too sure. Mind you, there was nothing definite, but some of his connections troubled me a little. They're all legitimate as far as I know, anyway *now*. But it's one of those things you don't want to mix in just in case . . ." He said the man had a big farm not far from town and a place in Chicago, one of the new condominiums on the lake.

"I guess Ruthie could wear underwear now if she wanted to," I said. If Bud heard what I said, it evidently didn't interest him. He was still looking at the little man.

"What made me nervous," he said, "was when I was in his office discussing a possible deal, a fellow came in to get something or other, a fellow I'd seen in the outer office, and I noticed a sort of bulge under one of his arms."

"A gun?" I asked.

"It could have been a tumor, a deformity, or just bad posture,

19

I suppose," said Bud, "but it made me decide to do some checking around before we closed any deal. So I did and then I wrote
to tell Mr. Manini we had made other arrangements."

"Did you get an answer?"

"Oh, yes, a very polite one that said he would be ready to
reopen negotiations any time I might desire. I'm sure he doesn't
have to run after business. . . . Did you say you know his wife?"

"She went to Maxwell High," I said.

Bud said you would never guess it.

"And she and I worked at Rankins dime store for a while one
summer," I said. "Well, I guess she worked there all summer
but I didn't."

Bud said he'd always thought it was pretty wonderful the
way I'd worked.

"Oh, I didn't have much else to do," I said. "I didn't take
music lessons or anything like that."

"Marianne's always told me how much she admired you. And
I think it took real guts to turn down the Snyders' invitation for
those trips to Europe."

"Guts? All it took was a little thinking. An all-expenses tour
of Europe would have been great, of course, but who would have
been earning my next year's tuition while I was off touring? I
don't know. Maybe it would have been smarter to go once and
then drop out of school for a semester to recoup the tuition
money. I don't know what the great rush was. But I seemed to
think I had to graduate with my class."

"Absolutely," said Bud, "because after all you can always go
to Europe."

Oh, yeah? He and Marianne had been only once since starting their family. It was when they just had two children. They
took two maids along. If they should go now, would they feel
they had to take four in staff?

FOUR

The Manuscript

I was early for the lunch date with Marianne at the new French restaurant in the Village Green. My rich brother's project. It is a huge subdivision-cum-shopping center.

When Wally was a sophomore in college, he was asked to join Faber Enterprises. Pickalot countered, offering managership of a new store, but he took a chance. He turned that down and went with the real estate speculator. Mr. Faber has treated him wonderfully well, not that it hasn't paid him to. But he was either decent enough or shrewd enough to hold Wally's job open while he was in Korea. Now I wonder if Mr. Faber is as enchanted by Wally as he is intimidated by my sister-in-law Bébé, the girl my brother brought home when he returned from the war.

I caught a glimpse of Bébé when I entered the new restaurant. She was with a group toward the rear of the gaudy place. Its decor is very precious, sort of Marie Antoinette playing milk-maid. I bet it won't last if Bébé decides she doesn't like it.

Marianne was about ten minutes late. She said she'd stopped at my mother's to pick up a copy of *The Different One*. It had taken Mother a while to locate a copy. She asked if I couldn't persuade my father to bring out another edition. Marianne never considers the little matter of money that just might keep Daddy from publishing another printing whenever Marianne decides she wants to give one to somebody. She's the only regular customer, and there's a limit to how many copies she can buy without making Mother feel she's being patronized instead of appreciated.

I let it go. I'm not a great fan of poetry. My mother's previous books have been quite orthodox in format and, I would say, content, being entirely comprehensible. The large new book, though, purporting to be based on my brother Richard's life, has what one of its three or four reviewers, all local, called a Joycean flavor. I have read all of Joyce except *Finnegan's Wake*, which I do not propose to tackle. I like some of his writing very much but find it full of what to me seems undisciplined excess. Although Mother doesn't go in for puns, she is inclined to write in the manner I don't consider Joyce's best. However, besides not caring for poetry I know I could be prejudiced against the book simply because I'm the poet's daughter. I don't recall ever feeling jealous of my mother's poetry, but I'm sure it would have been abnormal not to be. We grew up with a working poet in the house, not a mother.

Bébé was leaving when Marianne and I were still waiting to be seated. "Beware of the chicken," she said to us. "It could break a tooth."

"She's so beautiful," said Marianne when we got to our table.

"Bébé?" I laughed a little. Bébé's really quite homely. But she has class, style, dash, and great chic.

"Oh, not in any Hollywood sense," said Marianne.

Generally I prefer not to have a cocktail at lunch, but I was feeling bushed and so decided on a martini while Marianne had a sherry. We ordered crabmeat skillets because Marianne said they couldn't ruin that, but they did. Boy, the salt and garlic! Our waitress had got into the phony spirit of the place by adopting a supposedly French accent. The menu didn't have any prices on it and as soon as she noticed that, my friend said it was her party. That was all right with me. I didn't want to cash a check and all I had with me would just about be used up when I paid Helen Marie, the cleaning woman. Fifteen plus carfare. I can't afford her, but I am away from home so much that I have to have her. I feel as if I am holding my breath until the first of the year when Jock will get the vice-presidency. That should mean thirty thousand. I used to think nothing could be more wonderful than ten. I used to think ten would mean money in the bank for old age. Now it's thirty just to scrape along, at the pace we go.

It's been like in a slick magazine, I guess, or some movie. We went directly from six thousand a year to twenty. But unlike the wonderful story, we've had less in the bank when we've had more coming in. Sure, when we were so happy and so poor! Oh, I don't mean we haven't been happy or that I'd want to go back to that six thousand again, for Pete's sake. We have a lot of wonderful friends now, people who know how to do things and have the wherewithal. The children are wonderful, and we can afford to send them to the best schools. Anyway, as they grow up, Jock's income will surely increase. That's the way it goes in our set. We hope, we hope, we hope. I wonder if any of my friends, not counting the wealthy and never-worrying Marianne, ever feel somewhat haunted by their bills. And I wonder if any of the other men feel under constant pressure.

Jock's job hasn't turned out to be what he expected. He hardly ever gets into the lab. He's too important for that. The young fry, just out of school, have all the fun—though, of course, not the income. Jock takes all of the responsibility of the lab but still is forced to spend practically every minute of the day with Mr. Prentice who is a born go-getter. He's the Big Shot. He talks too loud and is too jovial. I always used to think when a writer described somebody as having unsmiling eyes while the mouth was smiling that he was really pulling the reader's leg. You can't smile without wrinkling the corners of your eyes, and certainly Mr. Prentice's are all wrinkled up all of the time, at least when I see him. But believe me if you look closely at his eyes you get the feeling he is sizing the situation up and wondering just what's in it for him. I don't like to think about Jock's having to be with the man so much, but when I've said this Jock has said only that it's his chance to do some missionary work. Jock doesn't complain. I know he doesn't want to upset me, and I know from the conversation at business parties that the company is getting more government orders all the time. "But as long as it isn't for military use," I say, and Jock shrugs. Does he suspect that some of the stuff is going to the military?

One or two of my friends will say to me, it seems at least every week, that you don't have to be a pacifist to be a Quaker. I say I know. Then they ask if Jock is, and I say yes, that was the way he was brought up. Then they say of course they are against war, especially this one, but they don't see how anyone could be a pacifist, that is, wouldn't Jock defend his home against a murderer, would he just turn his cheek? "Oh, don't be silly," I say. "It's as ridiculous as my asking you if you want your daughter to marry a Negro when you don't know if one would have her. I expect Jock would try to knock the fellow down. I don't know. I hope he would have sense enough not to resist if the person had a gun. What do you recommend for resisting an armed intruder?"

They tell me they didn't mean to make me sore, and so I say all right, if you don't like my answers, ask Jock. He's the Quaker, not me.

I was brought up a Methodist and am still one even though I don't hurt myself working at it. The majority of the people in my church are against the present war but hot on winning it, a position I find more inconsistent than they do. But I was brought up different. People who had seemed to think it was quite darling of Daddy to be what they considered a Communist decided he was a subversive because he didn't want to join military forces with the suddenly noble Russians. He was a bit too old for the draft to catch him but had registered as a conscientious objector and probably wouldn't have been given that status had the war lasted long enough for them to get around to him. Our minister advised him to write a testament of his religious reasons for being against war. "That I could include in a character testimony to your draft board," the man said. The minister played both sides of the fence while straddling it. Nobody seemed to like him even though nobody was able to say just why. They finally had to give him an early retirement to get rid of him. The man they have now is more outspoken about his personal views and probably won't last long enough to get a pension, anyhow not from the Maxwell church. Maxwell is a conservative town. I didn't realize how conservative until I heard by what a tremendous majority Goldwater won in the grade schools' mock election. Which reminds me, during that election I heard Bud Chambers say he didn't care for Goldwater, but that he would vote for his big toe if that was what the Republican Party was running. "Bud, dear," said Marianne, "that isn't funny." Actually Bud isn't very bright, which perhaps is a good thing if he's to live happily ever after with Marianne.

During lunch I was sure she had something special on her mind just as I'd been able to tell at the City Club that her invitation wasn't just casual. When she didn't say anything, though, I thought maybe I was mistaken. Or was it that she didn't know how to start?

"Let's get something large and cool, like watermelon if they have it, to cool off with," I said after eating all I could take of the crabmeat à la hot sauce. "What's on your mind?"

"I beg your pardon?"

"Something's bugging you."

"Oh, no, not at all, nothing, really," she said, all flustered. "My God, this crabmeat is awful, isn't it? Keri, I know what a strain you've been under for a long time, I mean getting settled in the new house and having a new baby practically at the same time and having to do so much entertaining for Mr. Prentice, honestly, the nerve of that man . . . you'd think he would at least ask somebody else."

"Jock's his favorite," I said, "which can't be too bad." Mrs. Prentice is an invalid. Mr. P. speaks of arthritis but we all know the difficulty is more mental than physical because nobody ever gets to see her. They have quite a mansion but never entertain. He practically forced Jock and me to buy our house. I mean, he took care of the mortgage, which I'm sure we never could have got. He was the one who found the house in the first place. He heard about it before it was put on the market, and the upshot of this was that it never was made available to the public. Mr.

Prentice knew that the Gilsons were anxious to get rid of it, almost as impatient about that as they were to get rid of each other. Mr. P. made our minds up for us before we knew he'd decided we must have a house. Not just any house, no, the Gilsons', where Mr. Prentice would be pleased to bring customers now and then.

Soon Marianne was chattering, well, chattering for *her,* about her psychiatrist. She isn't much of a talker, never has been. I've often wondered what she and Dr. Lester do for fifty minutes twice a week, just sit and look at each other? I can't imagine Marianne talking for fifteen minutes, let alone fifty. But she's been going to the man for three years now. And thinks he's the greatest, as evidently people usually do of their psychiatrists if they stick with them. I suppose the ones who transfer their hostilities to the doctor leave him and then maybe never need help again?

I can't remember just what she said about Dr. Lester. I wasn't really listening. Marianne has a rather flat voice and, not being one to say much, has never learned how to make a story interesting. "How much longer are you going to keep on with him?" I asked. "Doesn't it ever come to an end?"

"He will decide," she said, "But what I was thinking, Keri, is about his diagnostic hour."

"His what?"

"He keeps this hour free each week, so he can take people who don't know whether they need help or not."

"I thought he was booked up."

"He keeps this one hour open, for diagnostic appointments. He may decide they don't need psychiatric help, or maybe that he can work them into his patient load or something . . . the thing is it's very helpful when people might just wonder or stew around. It's such a waste of time and worry, too."

"Seems to me if a person is really sick, somebody would know."

"Of course," she said, "it wasn't as if I'd had any symptoms, was it? But Bud and I just decided it was sensible to have a check in that department as well as a physical and we got in on a couple of his, I mean Dr. Lester's, diagnostic appointments and he decided I would be better off if I had a course of psychotherapy, not analysis, just psychotherapy. I can't tell you how much it has meant to me."

"But you were in perfect health before, weren't you?"

"I thought so. Bud thought so, too, but I really think I would have run into real trouble if I hadn't got started with Dr. Lester when I did."

This wasn't the first time I had heard her testimonial to psychiatry. It didn't bother me. Maybe she didn't have enough to do before, or maybe Bud wasn't paying her enough attention. There wouldn't have been another woman, I was sure of that. Marianne's rival would always be The Business. Her father had just about stopped going to the office, and so Bud was carrying almost the whole load. He was loving it. If he hadn't married a business he would have still been a rich man, but he wouldn't have been the only big shot in the Chambers' pickle business. There are two brothers and a brother-in-law and no telling how many more coming on for the pickles. But Bud is *it*. Bud is very pleased with his marriage. He doesn't even seem to mind Mrs. Snyder. Mr. Snyder can be very nice, but he has a terrible temper and frequently blows up. None of this appears to bother Bud. Perhaps it bothers Marianne. Maybe it always has. I don't think she was ever happy at home. I wondered if we had got together for lunch so she could tell me again how great Dr. Lester is. Then I remembered she'd said she stopped by to see my mother this morning. Suddenly that and her mention of Dr. Lester's diagnostic hour meshed. I suppose anybody who goes to a psychiatrist is bound to become a sort of public relations agent for the doctor. I mean, they seem to go overboard. So she and Mother had been talking about me?

"Look," I said, "pardon me for interrupting, but I've lost weight because I've been so damn busy. Anyway it won't hurt me because I picked some up during the summer. You remember how fat I was in High? Believe me I'd rather be too thin. I remember being too fat and never again, thanks."

Marianne was never cut out to be a conspirator. She seemed relieved not to have to go through whatever else she had planned to say before letting me know my mother and she had agreed I should consult a psychiatrist. "It isn't just that, Keri," she said. "It's a combination of things."

"Like?"

"Well, you've mentioned you have trouble sleeping."

"I have pills for that. If I don't sleep the minute I hit the pillow, it's my own stupid fault for being too lazy to get up and take a pill."

"It's something you can't just run down like a list," she said. "I don't mean I think it's anything serious, because I don't. Dr. Lester might say you wouldn't need to do anything but get more rest but the thing is, you could stop worrying."

"Who said I've been worrying? My mother?"

"Keri, you owe it to your family to think about yourself—"

"Listen, if I get a cavity before the first of the year it will just have to wait. I am not going to any psychiatrist, for God's sake. I can hardly afford an aspirin."

"Think of it as a form of insurance," said Marianne. "That's what Bud says. He says he wants all the kids to have psychiatric examinations periodically."

"Marianne, you and Bud are wealthy people."

"He charges according to a person's ability to pay," she said. "I know you would find him very reasonable."

"I can't afford to go to any at all, reasonable or unreasonable," I said. "I am not against psychiatry, Marianne, I think it's probably here to stay, but just now anyway it simply isn't for me."

"It would be just in the nature of a checkup," she said. "All you would get from him would be an opinion."

"But I am not interested in his opinion," I said. I was beginning to lose my temper. It isn't exactly the most flattering thing in the world to be told you should see a psychiatrist. I waved to the waitress since it was obvious that Marianne wasn't remembering her duties as hostess. "They promised to have the new wagon for me to pick up at two," I said.

"Well, you think about it," she said. And when we went to the parking lot, she had the gall to bring the subject up again. She certainly has a thick skin. She told me she would be glad to make the appointment for me if I didn't want to call the doctor's office. I really was on the brink of asking her, and not politely either, to mind her own business. I thanked her for the lunch and said I must dash. Again she said to think over what she'd been saying about insurance for mental health.

"Next time why don't you and my mother just stick to poetry?" I said and got in my wagon and slammed the door. Of course she telephoned later in the afternoon to ask, she said, if I'd got my new car. I said I had and that it seemed to be all right and that the children and Helen Marie approved of it. "It seems that Helen Marie's been mortified about having to ride to the station in the old one." I was sorry I had snapped at Marianne. I'd always regretted it after I'd let her get under my skin. I don't know why I should ever have felt guilty about getting riled at a person who is a past master at exasperating people. Evidently I have a chronic case of guilty conscience.

I was hoping she would have sense enough not to refer to the conversation that had ended in the Village Green parking lot, but Marianne isn't heavily endowed with sense. "I'm so sorry I upset you at lunch," she said. "I just don't seem to know how to be tactful. But I felt it was something I just had to say or I would never forgive myself."

"You mean after my suicide?" I asked. Yes, I'd flared up again.

"Oh, Keri," she said, "don't ever say such a thing, not even to be funny."

So who was being funny? But I told her she was right, that it wasn't funny and that I was just cross because I'd spent most of the past hour with the cleaning woman, who gets on my nerves. I wouldn't have put up with her this long, but the kids are mad about her. Again Marianne said I should think over what she'd said about Dr. Lester, and I managed to hang up without blowing my top again.

After dinner we went for a ride in the new wagon. Since the kids had gone to the station in the afternoon, they were no longer much interested in the car. For them the kick was being in their pajamas for the ride. Karen had Andy diving down to the floor every time she saw a car coming. Finally Jock said now was as good a time as any for them to learn that we don't play hide and seek in a car. "Can you fasten your seat belt, Karen?" he asked.

She said of course she could. "Then do it," said Jock, "and fix Andy's for him. We're all going to turn over a new leaf. Nobody is to ride again without first fastening the seat belt."

Karen was pleased to be given a reason to discipline her little brother. And Andy is so crazy about her that he thinks anything she does is perfect. I have a feeling if I'd been the one to lay down the law about the seat belts, there would have been a big hullabaloo. But the children mind Jock without objecting or arguing. I suppose this is because nine-tenths of the disciplining is left to me.

Later in the evening when Jock and I were alone I told him what Marianne had had on her mind and that I thought maybe Mother had put her up to it. I wonder what he would have said if I hadn't mentioned Mother. Jock thinks anything she's been mixed up in is sure to be worthwhile. "Well," he said, "I don't know much about it, but I imagine that at least some of the people I saw in the hospital where I did my alternate service might not have been there if they'd had treatment early enough."

"So you think I've got a screw loose?"

He laughed. "Cara love, don't flare up at me just because you're sore at your girlfriend."

"But you think I should have a psychiatric examination?"

"No, I don't," he said. "On the other hand I don't see how it could hurt anyone. I wish I could get Mr. Prentice interested. Now there's somebody who really needs professional help."

"And who can afford it."

"Right."

"Then all we need to do is bring him and Marianne together," I said. "She's itching to recruit patients for the man."

"What did you tell her?"

"Not half of what I wanted to," I said. "But I did say it isn't something we can afford."

"We could afford it if it were needed," he said. "I hope you won't ever get the idea we can't afford medical care. If we haven't got the money on hand, I can always borrow."

"We're deep enough in debt as it is," I said.

"It will be easier once we get the house payments down a little."

"And you'll be getting a raise."

"I suppose so," he said and sounded more resigned than pleased. Sometimes he makes me feel as if I'm keeping his nose at a terrible grindstone he longs to get away from. But is it my fault we have such an expensive house with such expensive furniture and all? It really isn't Jock's fault either except that Mr. Prentice thinks that he is so great. Like a son. I wish it weren't such a cozy proposition. I wish I didn't have to entertain for Mr. Prentice so often, but what can I do about it?

It isn't something anyone couldn't do. All it takes is dough. Mr. Prentice sends over a box of fancy steaks and a case of wine and some whiskey and thinks he's paid for the party. Ha!

I was so tired I couldn't get to sleep. I waited until I could tell from Jock's breathing that he was asleep and then got up and took a sleeping pill and read in the bathroom until I began to get drowsy. But the pill didn't take hold right away even though I had begun to be very sleepy. So I just lay there in the dark and thought some more about Marianne. In all fairness I had to admit now that I undoubtedly have been acting rather harried in the past few months. Things seem to have been stacking up. Also, Jock's obvious unhappiness has been getting me down. He doesn't complain, but I know he's worried about the new contracts. I keep telling him it isn't as if the company dealt in munitions, but he says if Prentice electronic devices help the modern army to wage a war, it's just the same as munitions. What he's been trying to do is convince Mr. Prentice that it will be bad for the business in the long run to expand to accommodate the wartime orders. Prentice Products can very well be stuck holding a far bigger bag than it can profitably cope with. There's no use trying to make a pacifist out of Mr. Prentice, although if you could think of a way to convince him there would be money in it, you might get somewhere. But if you could make him see that eventually expansion caused by the government contracts, which presumably won't continue to come in forever, will bankrupt the company, that might convince him. But with a man like Mr. Prentice, a bird in the hand is the important one, especially if it's a very large one.

If we had all the money in the world I wouldn't mind going to see Dr. Lester. I know it was childish of me to get sore at Marianne and really I think it was caused mostly by my exasperation with her seeming belief that I could afford to play around with psychiatry if I wanted to. And it's no disgrace to have something wrong in the head, not something you do deliberately any more than you get a cancer on purpose. The thing is that I

13969

can't afford to be even a little neurotic if it should mean I would have to go to a doctor once or twice a week. Maybe when Jock gets the vice-presidency we can afford it, but our expenses are very steep and I certainly want to attend to the current upkeep of the house and family before I horse around on any health kick for myself. I'm sure the psychiatrist hasn't hurt Marianne any, and for all I know he may have helped her. Maybe what he's doing is showing her how to adjust to being second to her husband's business. Maybe what she wants is help on how to be a better parent than her mother was. I don't know. I don't care, either. It's her business and I would prefer that she would let me have my business private, too.

All the same, I can see that I probably am more nervous than I used to be. I think everybody is. What with the war and everything.

So those who can afford it run to psychiatrists or take tranquilizers. But I'm writing a sort of autobiography instead. It's a whole lot cheaper to tell my typewriter than it would be to tell some headshrinker.

Actually since I've started this I really think I have calmed down some. I expect it isn't because of anything I've written. I have always liked to type and really have missed it. Before I got involved with children and with having such a big house, I used to think I would put an ad in the papers as a manuscript typist. But after becoming a member of the Upper Clawses or the Idle Rich, I put away such childish notions.

One thing I have decided definitely while doing this typing is that I will not accept any office in Family Welfare for next year. They've been hinting around about how great it would be for me to be president. Evidently Petey has decided I'm the one to follow her. How can I get out of it? Can I say I'm writing my autobiography? No, I would have to call it a novel. Then they would approve. They would call me my mother's daughter. And hound me about the publication date. They'd never let me be unsuccessful like Mother.

But Mr. Prentice, damn him, wouldn't like me to turn down a chance at the F.W. presidency. Can you believe it, he calls me up every time my picture makes the paper!

FIVE *The Journal*

"**A**re you finding the job tedious?" asked Dr. Leonard. It had been several weeks since he'd said anything to me except in class and even then he didn't say much. I'm not one of the talkers. I really don't go for this group therapy and also am handicapped by my lack of memory. It's quite embarrassing when people ask if I did so-and-such as a child. Many of them think I'm putting the amnesia on. A woman named Leona especially. She and I just don't hit it off and now that she thinks I am trying to steal her thunder, it's worse. Really, if I weren't so much larger, I would be afraid of her. A very disturbed woman. She reminds me of a fox, somehow. She has a pointed nose and beady, bright eyes. I dread seeing her after Dr. Leonard has kept me a moment or so after class. She's determined to make something of it. Laughing at her just makes her worse.

"No, it's not at all hard," I told the doctor. "Of course when

I proofread I may find I've missed places, but I can do those pages over."

"No need," he said. "I meant to tell you not to worry about writing corrections in. It's mainly to see the effect of the alterations. What do you think of it in general?"

"It's a matter of personal whim," I said. "I've always been annoyed by first-person stories if the author's name is different from the protagonist's."

"You aren't much of a fiction reader?"

"Not particularly," I said without thinking that once again he was trying to catch me in a reference to the supposedly forgotten past. It isn't that he doesn't believe me; it's just that he thinks the memory is there for me to dip into whenever I am able to do this without straining, without being self-conscious.

"I read very few novels until I began to specialize," he said. "Then I had a teacher, a man who insisted upon our analyzing authors by studying their fictional characters. It was a revelation to those of us who had never taken fiction seriously before."

"I've never had any professional training," I said, "but I find myself wishing I had as I work on this manuscript."

He raised his eyebrows. "Yes?"

"You've read it?"

He nodded.

"Of course I'm not very far along yet," I said, "but I keep thinking that if I had had psychiatric or psychological training I could spot what it was that made Keri's friend Marianne urge her to go to the psychiatrist."

"The friend hadn't had psychiatric training."

"She had been in therapy for three years," I said. "She probably noticed things the ordinary layman wouldn't . . . that is, assuming that the story is based on fact."

"There's no doubt in my mind but what some people have a sensitivity that just can't be explained. Granted that Marianne had picked up a little psychiatric know-how during her three years of treatment, would that have been enough to make her feel her friend's mental health was deteriorating when nobody else, including the husband and the family physician, saw anything wrong?"

"The husband was wrapped up in his business worries," I said. "As for the doctor . . . you've surely known medical people who are so hostile to psychiatry that they almost seem to go out of their way never to notice symptoms of incipient mental illness." I wondered as I was speaking. How come I felt so sure of myself? Had I studied psychology in college, perhaps? Or just read popular articles on the subject.

Then I laughed. "If you hadn't given me the manuscript, I doubt if I would have thought this, but since you did, I can't help thinking Keri must be headed for serious mental trouble."

"Possibly," he said.

"Also, if it's fiction, I suppose the author has deliberately planted mental illness symptoms."

"I noticed no such symptoms in the section you have. The mentally ill are the same people as the mentally well but with a bit more here and a bit less there. There's nothing peculiar to such a disease, like some kind of wart or boil, not to be found in the normal condition."

"So maybe she's sick or on the way to being sick, or maybe she isn't?"

"That's how I would feel about it."

"If you didn't already know the outcome?"

Now he laughed. "Mrs. Kincaid, you wouldn't want me to spoil the story for you, would you? I'll ask Mr. Kincaid to bring some more of it this weekend if that's all right with you, since you evidently are nearing the end of what you have."

We had left the room where we hold the group therapy sessions and walked down the hall to the side door he uses because it is closest to the parking lot. Since it was such a pleasant day, I stepped outside and started to walk with him toward the parking lot. Leona, whom I hadn't noticed in the hall, called from the building, "Caroline, shall I tell Miss Hazel you won't be here for lunch?"

I turned around. "I'll be right back," I said and then told the doctor I sometimes wondered if I could endure that woman much longer.

"I don't think you'll have to endure any of them very much longer, do you?" he said.

35

"You are asking me!"

"Why not?" he said. "I'm sure you'll be the best judge of when you're up to leaving."

"Well, thanks for the compliment," I said, "but I bet the powers here wouldn't agree."

"Don't you worry about them," he said. "The main thing for you is that Mr. Kincaid and I are on your team. Don't you ever forget that."

I was touched by that and as he drove away, I felt tears smarting my eyes and a tightening of my throat. Then I remembered what Dr. Leonard had done to me. How much I would have preferred being dead! In this modern age can't you even die, all of you, unless the ultrasmart scientists find no use for one or more of your organs? For the first time in these long, long months I thought about suicide and, surely not without reason, found it comforting to tell myself that if it became unendurable, all right, I could kiss the boys good-bye, as it were, and the hell with their great experiment in joining together two personalities, both doomed, and coming out with a nothing, a real nothing. Oh, on the surface I am not a zombie. I speak easily, mind my manners, and seem to have a fair degree of reasoning ability. But who am I? I am not Caroline Kincaid even though the body I inhabit was once hers. Nor am I whoever I was before I was snatched untimely, I keep thinking, though God knows where I read my Shakespeare.

"I'm going to tell your husband," said Leona as I entered the building. "I have warned you time and again and now I feel I must act."

"Leona," I said, "you're acting all the time. You're a born actress. Let me be the first to applaud the performance."

"And furthermore," she said, "I have discovered that you are plagiarizing my new book."

"Interesting," I said. "How am I doing it?"

"You think I don't know about the wireless you and Dr. Leonard have attached to my brain," she said. "But I know more than you think. And you don't need to think it will do any good to kill me because I have filed an affidavit in Washington D.C. to that effect."

"You think of everything," I said. "Now let me go wash up for lunch, please."

"Don't you come near my table with your poisoned salt," she said.

"Okay," I said.

In the washroom where Miss Hazel was fixing Aggie's hair, I asked the attendant how long we were going to have to put up with somebody as sick as Leona. "Well," said Miss Hazel, "look at it this way . . . when you get out you're going to be thrown with more than one like her and so you might just as well start getting used to it. If everybody we had here in Martin was like you kids, you'd be spoiled rotten. This way you're being toughened up to face the world as she really is, baby."

"That's a real cute way of looking at it," said Aggie. She was smiling, but more at her reflection in the mirror than at what Miss Hazel had said. Aggie is quite pretty and is very well aware of it.

Since I have no recollection of any family, the people in Martin House probably mean a whole lot more to me than to any other patient. The majority are like one called Muriel, enduring and just living for the day they can go back home. Muriel tries to pretend none of this is real, that it is simply a nightmare broken only by her husband's visits. She weeps for her children, her home, her canary. She would rather sit in a corner by herself than have to talk with any of us, because when she acknowledges our presence it is more difficult for her to preserve the illusion that the hospital is only a dream. Sometimes I think I will have to speak to her, to tell her that until she recognizes that this is a hospital and that she is truly ill, her chance of going home to stay is slim. What reality was she unable to face Outside, I wonder when I see her sitting with her husband. Usually she is weeping, begging him to take her home. He is as young and handsome as she is young and beautiful. It is excruciating to watch them, to see how cruelly each is suffering.

Although I suffer, my pain is different. Still, I find myself envying Muriel because at least she knows what she has been torn from . . . her husband, her children, her canary. She worries lest the husband work too hard, worries that the children will play all day in wet shoes. She worries about the canary's getting put in a draft. She knows so many things to worry about. I know nothing. I don't know if I have children, a husband, or a canary somewhere who may be doing well without me. Who may be doing better, let's face it.

I am interested in Mr. Kincaid's children and his various problems because he is a nice, kind man who has been very good to me. But my interest is impersonal. After all, how could it be anything else? I haven't known him very long and I have never seen his children.

I must say for him that he hasn't tried to break down my resistance to becoming the Other Caroline by exposing his children to me, or perhaps I should put it the other way around. Children aren't allowed to visit Applewood. The children previously hospitalized here, scattered through the adult wards, presumably are doing better now that they are in all-children wards at another state institution. I asked Miss Hazel if children had been permitted to visit the hospitalized children. The question shocked her. "This is no place for children," she said. But apparently for years it was considered okay for children to be hospitalized here. I can't help wondering if the new plan is so great. Miss Hazel did tell me they have had a terrible time staffing the place. She says practically nobody wants to be a child psychiatrist any more. "Or even a pediatrician," she said. "You just can't charge as much for the little folks. It's like with cats."

"Cats?"

"The vet can charge sky-high for dogs but, boy, he's going to run into trouble if he charges the same for cats. It's like that with children. Even the rich people don't want to pay thirty, forty or so dollars for a kid's visit to a psychiatrist, do they?"

I said I wouldn't know.

"Half-size, half-price," she said. "Like to the movies or on a plane. But the young docs don't see it that way. They all want to make a hundred thousand a year. Even those squirts you see around here, don't quote me. But believe it or not I've seen worse go farther. If I ever do write a book, I'll probably end up in jail."

That fool Leona has got everybody to writing books, well, to talking about it. Leona mostly thinks hers. Already it's won a

38

Pulitzer and is on its way to a Nobel. I asked her if one of her pen names might by some chance be Pearl Buck. It didn't make her sore. "You'd like to know, wouldn't you?" she said.

Saturday Mr. Kincaid got permission to keep me out until eight o'clock. Whether he ever asked before, I don't know. I wore the knit suit he insisted on buying for me a month or so ago when we went shopping. It's beige. Quite nice. He brought me a set of his wife's costume jewelry, and I had no alternative. It does look fine with the knit, rather chunky beads, dark brown and gold, with matching earrings. He also brought out a pair of bone kid slippers that look fine. He said he thought there was a matching pocketbook but hadn't been able to locate it. I told him not to give it another thought because the white one I have been using is all right and can go with everything.

As usual we drove toward Maxwell. He asked if I had any shopping to do. I said I had been wishing I could just walk around in a dime store to look for some small items. I didn't have a list. Nothing worth writing down. But I hadn't been in a dime store or any kind of store except the so-called one at the hospital, really just a supply station.

"Down home we always went into town on Saturday afternoon and evening, too, if we could manage it," he said. "It was always rather like Christmas or a party. It made the week."

"What did you do?"

"We walked down the street," he said. "The boys whistled at the girls, and they turned their noses up at us and pretended to be highly insulted when we yelled at them. It was great. Now and then there would be a band concert. Once each summer there was a carnival. I'm afraid I started on the downgrade when I decided I would no longer resist the sin of going to a low-down type of entertainment like that. I was entranced by all of it."

"Did your folks find out?"

"Oh, I told them," he said. "It wasn't that I wanted to, but I knew somebody would and so I might as well be the first."

"Did you get a hiding?"

"Much worse," he said. "I got prayed over in meeting until I thought I'd have to run away from home. But of course it came to an end when some other kid got in the limelight."

39

"Prayed over in meeting? What do you mean?" I asked.

"Sorry," he said. "I thought I'd told you I was reared a Quaker. Do you think I ought to be sending the children to Sunday School?"

Why ask me? But I was willing to give him an answer. "Oh, why bother this summer? I expect the churches are closed anyway."

"I never get used to that," he said. "Down home religion was considered a year-round project, even for the Methodists." The way he said this made me wonder if his wife had belonged to that denomination. I wondered if he was trying to make a little joke, but of course I didn't laugh. For all I know I was brought up a Catholic. Mentally I tried to cross myself but couldn't think if it went from right to left or left to right. Not a good Catholic, then. Might I, too, have been a Quaker and run off to carnivals? The idea was attractive.

The D-Alphs weren't the crème de la crème at Maxwell in my time, and I don't think they rate much higher now although some of the alums try to make out that it's in the top four. I would say it's more in the middle and that the Snyders undoubtedly would have kept me from joining it if Marianne had gone to Maxwell. I would have had to be whatever they decided she should be. Without her I could sink to a more comfortable level, where I wouldn't have to pretend that I wasn't working my way through school by checking at the big Pickalot. Of course it was very silly for me to join. What did I need with it? I didn't need a place to stay, and I soon found out I certainly didn't need help with dating. As soon as I got rid of the excess weight, I stopped being everybody's sister.

If I had no reason for joining the D-Alphs, the case was quite different for them. I was a girl who always got good grades, something the D-Alphs needed once they were sure of pledging enough out-of-town girls to fill up the house. Also they badly needed girls who not only could find their own dates but who might provide for a few less fortunate sisters. It was stupid of me not to catch on to the fact that I was throwing my lot in with a bunch of old maids. They were all very nice girls who excelled at hockey. Girls thought they were great. Boys approved of them, but at a distance.

I liked being swarmed over by them, of course. I would have enjoyed anything, because now at long last I could go places and do things without feeling guilty if I hadn't dragged Marianne along or being bored because I had.

Although none of the D-Alphs was rich, they all had more money than I had. But they didn't dress noticeably better. Gran and I had slaved over putting a campus wardrobe together for me, and I looked pretty good. Some of my new friends worked summers, but I was the only one who worked all the time. Maxwell isn't the school to pick if you're going to work your way through. Not unless you can live at home with free board and room.

The D-Alphs worked me as hard as they could, but I didn't mind too much because I really wasn't available too much. I tutored the dumb ones when I had time and got dates for this or that sister when I could. I had a marvelous time, so marvelous that I don't think I could have taken the strain of foreign travel if I'd been able to accept the Snyders' invitation to go to Europe with them. Most of my boy-friends went home, away from Maxwell, for the summer and so I wasn't too busy. I just worked and dated a few of the local boys and was rested up and with a nice bank account again when fall came. Sophomore year was about the same as freshman, except better. Nobody could push me around at the house now. I was one of the pusher-arounders but not one who took much advantage of the exalted position. People didn't seem to be going steady as much in college as they did in high school, and I enjoyed playing the field.

We had a spring tea toward the end of my second year in college. It was a Sunday. Pickalot was open until four. I always worked Sundays when I was in school, Sundays and several nights as well as afternoons and all day Saturday. I made about as much as the full-time people who just worked the more regular business hours.

I've always worn a lot of black. My skin is very fair, the typical redhead's, and is set off by dark colors. I usually had at least two quite plain black dresses that I could wear to work and then fix up with accessories before going out with my date. We wore smocks in the store, but unfortunately not full-length ones. You had to have a dress or at least a skirt on underneath. They have changed now. The checkers and other helpers wear regular uniforms, a great saving for them in cleaning and washing.

I tricked my plain black dress up with some junk jewelry that looked like antique gold with amber stones—I don't know what they were supposed to be but it was an impressive-looking set. I had a sort of bow with a bit of veiling for a hat. The girls had decided that since this was the biggest tea of the year everybody should wear hats. I guess I looked pretty good, but of course the D-Alph competition never was very much. All such nice girls, but I'm telling you a bunch of hockey players who relaxed with archery. We hardly ever had a girl in the chapter who weighed less than a hundred and fifty. I didn't weigh anywhere near that. I was tall, but not in the D-Alph husky pattern. Neither was Lois Geer. Lois was a senior, petite and rather pretty in a sort of petulant way. You always had a feeling she would stamp her foot if you said something she didn't like. I hardly knew her and had no reason to want to further the acquaintance. She was engaged to a fellow named Harlan Bremer, a Sigma Chi, but she didn't wear his pin. I forget if anybody had told me why, but I had assumed it was because they were more than just pinned.

Harlan was a Southerner who had come up to Maxwell on a scholarship, an athletic one—although of course this was sub rosa. He'd got some kind of injury his first year and had dropped out of football. He was a year behind Lois in school but just as old, somebody had told me.

When I went into the sun parlor, Lois, on the tea committee, was in the kitchen. As one of the hostesses, I introduced myself to the attractive, very big blond who seemed to be neglected and he answered with what sounded like a burlesque of a Southern accent. It was Lois's Harlan Bremer. Well, I hadn't had any very thrilling dates in quite a while and I suppose was ripe for getting a crush. I fell hard for Harlan and felt quite tragic about it. I could tell he was more than casually interested in me, and I went home thinking about all sorts of dramatic situations in which Lois and Harlan and I would discuss the tragedy that had befallen us. Of course Harlan and I would feel just awful about poor Lois. And so on.

Well, Harlan evidently got the message in my eyes, or else he just took for granted that all girls fell for him. Anyway he called me up for a date. Perhaps unwilling to let go of the tragic fantasies, I said, "But what about Lois?"

"Why, didn't you hear about little old Lois picking up and shaking the dust of Maxwell from her feet?" he asked.

"I haven't been to the house since the tea," I said. "What in the world happened?"

He said you could search him. "But I do know she was worried about her exams," he said, "and so I guess she figured since she probably wouldn't graduate anyway she might as well go on home right away."

This wasn't what I heard at the D-Alph house. There the girls were saying they'd known something like this would happen. There's nothing like the virtue of a hockey player once she's decided a more favored sister is reaping the harvest of her sins. It seemed that everybody but me knew that Lois and Harlan had been sleeping together. "Why, didn't you know? They always went to a motel Friday or Saturday night when she said she was going to stay with that relative of hers in Chicago," one of the girls said to me. "I don't say I approved but I thought since they were engaged, not just going steady but really engaged, it was different, not that *I* would do it but I don't say it's immoral or anything like that."

"Then what happened?" asked stupid me.

"Obviously she got caught, that's what happened," said the girl with what sounded like real satisfaction. "I mean, these girls who know it all don't always know as much as they think."

Lois hadn't confided in anyone, but her best friend in the chapter said she'd told her she and Harlan were going to be married as soon as she'd graduated. "Then suddenly she was gone. And that's that."

The president of the chapter telephoned the Geer residence in southern Illinois and Lois, probably grabbing the phone every time it rang, answered. "But, Lois, even if we didn't give a damn, we'd have to make some effort to find you, wouldn't we? How did we know you hadn't got killed or something?"

Lois said all right, that now we knew she hadn't got herself killed, that she'd just decided to quit school. She said she was sick of it.

The following fall one of the girls who had known Lois better than most of us said she'd got an announcement of Lois's marriage sometime in August. We never heard just when her first child arrived. For all we knew, she might have got an abortion. Or maybe she wasn't pregnant at all but just burned up at Harlan.

I was prepared to forget him and was well on the way to doing this when he came back to school. I really wouldn't have cared if he hadn't called me up again. But he did and I decided to hear what he might have to say for himself about Lois. He didn't say much. Yes, he'd heard that she'd got married. He thought that was fine. He said she was a fine girl and that they'd been very good friends. "Just like brother and sister," he said.

"Oh, come on," I said. "They got away with that in Egypt in the olden times, but I don't know about now."

He didn't like it when I talked rough like that. He wanted me to be a lady. He also wanted me to go to a motel or a hotel, if I preferred. He said there wouldn't be any reason to worry. I said I guessed Lois hadn't thought she would need to worry, either, and he sulked and said he hadn't expected me to listen to low-down salacious gossip. He liked to use fancy words which he pronounced however he wanted, usually giving them an extra syllable. Salasee-us, accent on the see.

I had never gone with a man who had as much sex appeal or maybe just not with one who had as much nerve. I practically had to use my fists to prove to Harlan that I was serious about not intending to go to bed with him. He moped. He said he just couldn't understand what I had against him. Eventually he accepted as fact my statement that I had never been to bed with any man and didn't intend to until I got married. Harlan said it was real idealistic of me and that he admired me for it.

He said again that I was a real lady and that he certainly admired real ladies.

By now I knew he was quite a slob, but that didn't seem to help much. I was mad about him and went out with him every time he asked me to. The family made fun of him. They all imitated his accent, and Daddy said there was something about a white Southerner that made his hackles rise. I told him he ought to be ashamed of himself, still fighting the Civil War, and he said he guessed he should be but that it was like cats and dogs, perhaps, something you couldn't explain away. I think Mother hated Harlan because he treated her as if she were about ninety. Mother is very young looking and at that time didn't have even a few gray hairs. The lavender and old lace treatment didn't go down with her. She looked ready to kill whenever he began to compliment her on her poetry. "He always makes it sound like something real cute written for a birthday card," she said. "Keri, do you have to bring him in the house? Couldn't you meet him on a corner somewhere?"

I've always been glad Wally was away from home, in the Service, while I was dating Harlan. What the folks said never really bothered me, but Wally's opinions have always meant a lot to me.

Of course the girls at the D-Alph house, especially the ones who had followed Lois Geer's romance, were careful to warn me against Harlan. I told them I knew what I was doing, that it wasn't anything serious and that they didn't ever have to worry about me going off to any motel. Since I was dating Harlan steadily, I didn't realize that a change had been made. I wasn't really aware of it until my senior year, but it set in, for most of the girls who weren't engaged or married, in their junior year. The fellows they had dated before had left campus and the ones still around were dating the younger girls, as they had always done. Where was a junior or a senior, especially, to get a date?

I suppose I would have said I was engaged. I told myself again and again that I should remember Lois Geer, but I was playing my cards differently. Lois might have got him, I thought, if she hadn't given in. Obviously Harlan admired a real lady. I didn't seem to be in any danger of losing him. Oh, he tried, every week or so, to get me to change my mind about being such a complete lady, but he didn't get mad. He would just say to be sure and let him know if I ever changed my mind and I said I would, that he would be my first choice if and when I wanted to be led down the primrose path. He said he didn't think I ought to joke so much about it. "It's a very sacred thing," he said. "I have always thought it was a very sacred thing."

SEVEN *The Journal*

I suppose chain stores are the same the country over
and that I should have expected to find any dime store familiar.
It wasn't strange that I felt as if I knew this place at the corner
of University Avenue and Central Street in Maxwell. I suppose
it would have been odd if it hadn't seemed familiar. "Why don't
you wait here and let me browse around in the bobbie pins," I
said to Mr. Kincaid and he said all right, for me to take my
time. I shook my head when he offered me a five-dollar bill. I
had around ten dollars. "You give me money a lot faster than
I can spend it, Mr. K." I'd fallen into the habit of calling him
that because he seemed to get a kick out of it whereas my saying
"Mr. Kincaid" made him look sad. Of course I could have
imagined this.

As I went slowly through the store I was thinking about the

peculiarly characteristic smell. It wasn't just hot dogs plus trimmings, nor was it just whatever had escaped from the beauty counter or from the clientele. I enjoyed it the way some people enjoy the smell of a stable. It can't be that either aroma is intrinsically pleasing but that it brings some pleasant association. Just what pleases me about a dime store, I don't know. But I liked this one and wished I could spend more time in it. However, not having any excuse after selecting a card of bobbie pins, I rejoined Mr. Kincaid.

He asked if I would like to go try on a dress or two or a hat or some shoes. I told him I didn't need anything and that I wasn't a woman who liked to try things on when not in the market. I couldn't help wondering if the Other Caroline had been one of those compulsive shoppers who will wear herself out trying on clothes whether she needs or wants anything or not.

"I thought we might drive past the house," he said after we got in the car. "The kids are at Gran's and they're all going over to your folks' for dinner. Oh, not Ellen. I forget what she said she was going to do."

Ellen is his horrible sister. I said what I had considered saying before but had decided wasn't any of my business. Of course it was still none of my business, but I couldn't keep quiet any more. "I hope you get room and board from her," I said.

"Oh, no. The understanding is that she helps out."

"If she does, I never heard anything about it."

"Graduate work isn't a breeze," he said, "especially for people who have been out of school for a while and then gone back. Ellen can't loaf on the job."

"You mean on her work at the University, not her job with you."

"She doesn't have a job with me," he said. "If she can give us a hand now and then, fine. But we can get along."

"I have a feeling you could get along better without her, if you don't mind my saying so."

"I certainly don't. Why should I? And you know how I feel about the situation. After all I threw her out once."

He did? "Well, if at first you don't succeed . . ."

"I promise you one thing, Cara, you'll never have to put

49

up with having her live with us again. As soon as we get the word from the doctors that you can come home, out she goes. She understands this."

Something he had said another time made me aware that the Other Caroline and his sister Ellen hadn't hit it off too well, to say the least.

He stopped the car in front of a quite ordinary, ugly but sturdy-looking stucco and frame house. "The yard's still a mess," he said. "I don't seem to know what to do about it."

"It looks all right," I said.

"The grass is cut but that's all," he said. "I'd like your advice on some planting."

So I am supposed to be a horticulturist?

Then he surprised me more. Surprise isn't quite the word. I wasn't exactly shocked, but when he asked if I would like to come in, I shrank back away from him. Easily enough he said he wanted me to see that the house really wasn't a mess. "I know you have a good housekeeper," I said almost without breathing between words.

"Yes, but her daughter wants her to retire. The girl has been helping her out a good deal, but she won't continue, either. She doesn't need the money. It doesn't amount to much, of course, but it's the best I can do."

"I'll bet those two have been taking advantage of you," I said, and again was sorry for him rather than afraid.

However, I knew I wouldn't be entirely comfortable until the car moved on. He didn't start it up again, though. "Do you think the house ought to be painted?"

I shook my head. "I would let it go until spring," I said. "It would be terrible to have the paint looking dingy almost before it's dry, but this near the University you're bound to get their soot, aren't you? Or do they have gas now?"

"Part coal and part oil," he said. "Of course since I'm on the faculty I am not quite so up in arms over the school's pollution of the city. Is there somewhere else you'd like to go, somewhere just for a ride, maybe?"

I left it to him. "I keep forgetting," he said after I told him I couldn't suggest a route to take.

"No, I'm the one," I said. "But if you've forgotten that, you really are losing your memory too."

"Don't worry about it," he said. "Your memory is there. Intact."

"And under double lock," I said. "What's the good of it being there if I can't use it?"

He said then that it was terrible to keep asking me to be patient when I'd already been for such a long time. For a while we parked in a forest preserve where we had gone before, along the river. Then we walked and watched the people who were fishing. I wonder if they ever catch anything. Mr. Kincaid asked a couple of friendly-looking men if they had had any luck; each said, "Not yet." There was an example of patience if I ever saw it. Of course it probably didn't matter much to them, if they went home empty handed. Every day I fish, as it were, in an equally muddy river and always come away empty handed. It matters to me. Mr. Kincaid said he knows it means a lot to me and that it does to him, too. "But Dr. Leonard and the others honestly believe it will come back because it's there, Caroline. Nothing has been destroyed. It isn't as if you'd had shock treatment or any kind of medication that might impair memory in some way."

It isn't as if my brain had been transferred from one head to another? But could I say this? People committed to mental institutions have to be careful what they say. You're damned enough as it is.

I took my sweater into the restaurant because Mr. Kincaid said he remembered its air conditioning being on the cold side. It was a place about ten miles upriver from the city and called the Country Inn, a nice-looking building in the early American style, white with green shutters. According to Mr. K. we'd been coming here ever since it opened. Before we were married, he said. He said he would rent a car sometimes after he came to Maxwell. "Only sometimes, of course," he said, "since that was when I was still working at the hospital."

"What hospital was that?" I asked.

"The Ardmore General in Chicago," he said. "That was where they assigned me for my alternate service."

51

"Oh, yes," I said. I remembered then he'd told me before that he was a Quaker and a pacifist. "Was it a mental hospital?"

"Yes."

"Then it seems like you're doomed," I said.

"I certainly don't look at it that way," he said. "I have always been a very lucky person."

The restaurant was almost empty, but the hostess was off somewhere and so we waited in the foyer a few minutes until she came. When she saw us, she exclaimed that it had been a long time, too long, since we'd been there. Mr. Kincaid should have warned me that people might recognize me here. I suppose she didn't notice anything, but it makes me nervous when people I don't remember ever seeing speak to me as if we were old friends. Like that What's-her-name Pink Lady in the art therapy who kept talking about how we used to go to meetings together. She was forever telling me bits of news about people who evidently were supposed to be mutual acquaintances. Maybe the Other Caroline could endure that type but not me.

The Country Inn hostess seated us at what she claimed was our favorite table and asked Mr. K. if we would have our usual. "What a memory," he said. "That okay with you, Caroline?"

I don't know if he'd forgotten or if he said that deliberately. I am sure that quite often he and Dr. Leonard say things they think will draw a sudden memory from me. I suppose they mean well, but all the same it always makes me feel as if, whether unconsciously or not, they can't believe my loss of memory is total or involuntary. Wondering what the Other Caroline's "usual" was, I said of course. Mr. K. was brought a small glass of wine. What I got was a martini that about blew my head off. Mr. K. said not to drink it if I didn't want it. He said he would order a glass of wine for me but I said no, I would fix it. I drank part of my water and then dumped the martini in the glass. It tasted terrible but not as poisonous as before it was diluted. Was the Other Caroline quite a lush? But from what he said I gather she never had more than one, which relieved me because I certainly didn't want another one, straight or diluted.

As we were finishing our drinks, the hostess brought a waitress over and introduced her. Since she was a new girl, she wouldn't be asking if we would like our "usual," I thought with relief. Mr. Kincaid told me we had always liked the baked chicken here, but I saw lamb chops on the menu and asked for those. We have chicken at the hospital a lot but never lamb chops. They weren't particularly good, but of course were very small, and so the lack of any special flavor didn't matter much. The rest of the meal was marvelous. I had forgotten that food could look beautiful. Or, for all I knew, I hadn't been exposed to a nice restaurant before.

On the way out, Mr. Kincaid bought a box of candy figurines for his children. He said they are both very good about candy and never ask for it between meals.

Although there was no alternative in my mind, I really dreaded going back to the hospital after that excursion into the world Outside. Everything looked drearier than usual to me. Our day-room is supposed to be one of the nicest in the institution and I'm sure it is. But our best is none too good. And if it were? If this place looked like an expensive resort instead of a run-down YWCA, would it be much better fundamentally? Wouldn't Muriel Dawes still be weeping for her husband, children, and that damned canary she worries so much about? Wouldn't Agnes Brush still be pacing the floor as if it were a wild animal's cage?

"And now what have you been up to?" asked Leona. "You and your fancy doctor?"

"Oh, shut up, Leona," said Aggie. "She's been out with her husband."

"That will do to tell," said Leona, "but if you ask me . . ."

"Nobody did," said Aggie.

"If you ask me, she was out with somebody else's husband," said Leona.

I felt like saying that for once Leona had hit the nail on the head. But I just went to the attendant to check my good clothes in. After visiting hours it is all right to sit around in lounging clothes. I got into my nightgown and robe and then went back to the dayroom. It was too early to go to bed and there was nothing else to do. A group around the television was watching a dumb movie, which was interrupted every few minutes by six or seven commercials. Some of the girls were complaining about the interruptions, but it seemed to me the commercials weren't as bad as the movie.

"It isn't that I had such a glamorous life Outside," said Agnes, "but it never was as deadly dull as this. I keep thinking it will drive me crazy." She laughed. "Somehow I can't seem to have much hope it can work in the reverse. What did you have for dinner?"

"Lamb chops," I said.

"With paper pants?"

"Yes."

She sighed. "Sometimes I put myself to sleep by trying to decide what dish I'll never never have if and when I finally get out of this miserable place. I think maybe meat loaf."

It isn't the meat that's so bad, anyhow I like to think it's all right, but they season the meat loaf here with something out of a can, bottle, or package that gives it a flavor you are positive must just mean the cook's hand slipped. But after the first few times you have to see that the flavoring is intentional. "There's something of that same haute cuisine in the beef stew, too," I said.

"With your newspaper experience," said Agnes, "you can tell me how to have it worded in the best Emily Post fashion. How about, Mrs. Agnes Brush of the Wellington Arms, has just returned from a long sojourn at the Applewood State Hospital, where she went directly after her former husband ran off with his secretary."

"You aren't supposed to call yourself Mrs. Agnes Brush," I said.

"How about Mrs. Emily Post?"

"She was professional."

"So I'm turning pro," said Agnes.

"Pro what?" asked Leona who had been hanging near us and stretching her ears.

"That would be telling, dear," said Agnes.

"Just don't ask me for an introduction," said Leona.

And so on and so on until Lights Out.

EIGHT *The Manuscript*

*L*ooking back at my love affair with Harlan I find it hard to understand how it could have lasted as long as it did. I tell myself I wouldn't have married him but I know this isn't true. I would have. I knew we weren't an ideal pair, by any means. I could see so much of what, as far as I was concerned, was wrong with him. But I continued to be madly, wildly smitten. Maybe it shouldn't be dignified by being called love. However it felt like what I had always assumed love would feel like. (And never did before or again for me. I can say that last with gratitude because who wants to be crazy, yes, like crazy in her feeling for a man. The mystery and the miracle of the whole affair was that I didn't go to bed with him.)

He was surely not all that handsome. Good-looking, yes, but his features weren't perfection. He was around six three, maybe a little more, and beginning to put on weight that I could see wouldn't be becoming if it increased. His voice was beautiful, lazylike without any of the nasal quality you hear in so many Southern voices. And he had a courtly way of speaking that may be commonplace in the South, but which was certainly unique in my young life. I remember the girls used to make fun of him, but I noticed that whenever he was talking to them they didn't look anything but enchanted. Well, he was just one great big hunk of sex appeal, and I was hungry, hungrier, I'm sure, than he was. Was it really so mysterious or miraculous that I kept my virginity? Could I have if he'd felt the way I did? I doubt it. I see now that his keeping after me was more automatic and even chivalrous than it was really urgent. I see now that he had a girl or girls off campus. He dated me for when it showed. I was his weekend girl and the girl he strolled through the campus and went for coffee with. But there was somebody else, where she didn't show and where she didn't interfere with campus doings. This never dawned on me then.

Harlan had a job waiting for him in a lumber mill down home. A wealthy man named Crevey had taken a shine to him a long time ago, he said. "He don't have a son and so he kind of elected me," he said. Harlan was to start at the mill directly after graduation, as Mr. Crevey's assistant. He'd already worked some vacations there, doing whatever there was to be done, just to get his hand in. Mr. Crevey was anxious to retire in a year or so.

I did wonder sometimes how I would adjust to life in a small town in the South. My parents seemed to think Harlan was a modern version of Simon Legree, but I'd never heard him say a word against Negroes. Now and then I would snap out at the folks that a lot of Southerners were a whole lot friendlier with colored people than we Northerners were. I said Northerners talked a lot about integration and all, but what did they do about it? How often did we have colored guests in the house, for instance? Wasn't it all just theory with us seldom put into practice? I said that, if anything, we were behind the times and that the South was ahead of us in real human relations . . . probably. Of course I didn't know what I was talking about and I never found out anything from Harlan. Maybe he had a fairly decent feeling for the equality of men, but he certainly kept women in a separate category. He would have said on a pedestal.

He had a lot of easy small talk and more of a loving line than I ever ran into before or since. I was never bored. And I was saving my money like mad because I wanted to buy more and more for my hope chest. I had decided I would let him talk me out of graduating but he didn't try. I admired him for this. I thought it was noble of him to want to work a year and save up before we got married. It doesn't seem possible, but I simply never sorted his sweet talk out to see for myself that he had never proposed marriage. When I said of course he would be coming to Maxwell for visits during the coming year, he always said he certainly would. He said maybe then I would change my mind and stop being so mean to him and I thought maybe I would. I thought after all when it's only a matter of a few months before people are going to get married . . . I was getting into the frame of mind where, if he'd known or cared enough, he could have talked me into weekends or at least nights with him before he graduated. I had added a few items to my hope chest that I had told myself I wouldn't save for the bridal trousseau. I wonder now if the fact that he wasn't pestering me much or very seriously had somehow conveyed to me the message that he wasn't so enamored as I had thought. If so, it was known only to my subconscious. I was bright enough to know that giving in to a fellow wasn't by any means guaranteed to be a way to catch him. Look at what had happened to Lois Geer. Or what the D-Alphs had figured had happened to her.

I had about decided I would give him a very extra special graduation present the night of the Senior Prom. His folks were coming for graduation, which was to be the following Saturday, and I had invited them, through Harlan, to dinner that night. Gran had a turkey in her freezer and we planned to have ham, too. "Southerners always like ham," said Gran, "but since it may be warm, let's not have yams. Let's have potato salad and do the dinner more Northern than Southern style. I won't make biscuits but have Parker House rolls . . ."

Mother and Daddy both said they didn't know how they could endure a whole evening of Harlan and his parents, but Gran said maybe they wouldn't stay long. Gran always did what she could to be on my side. She hadn't been around Harlan much and blamed the folks for judging a man to be a fool just because he had the misfortune of sounding like one. "Can that boy help it he was born where he was?" she asked.

"I never said I blamed *him*," said Mother but let it go at that.

"Never mind," said Gran. "Your grandmother and I were dead set against your father. We thought he was a Communist, and for Maxwell he might as well have been, I mean, what was the difference, after all?"

"There was and is a good deal of difference," said Mother, but Daddy told her to save her breath. He said he didn't think there was any use arguing about anything.

"You either see it or you don't," he said.

I spent more for my Prom dress than I'd ever spent for a dress before. It had a pale green bodice and a white tulle skirt with pale green satin roses caught at a couple of places. It was fifty-five dollars reduced from a hundred and fifty. The clerk reminded me when she gave me the package that the dress wasn't returnable. I laughed and said it sounded as if she didn't think I had my date yet and doubted if I'd get one. She laughed too.

Two days before Prom when Harlan came to the bench near U. Hall where we often met, I could tell from his face he had bad news. My first and only thought of course was that he'd heard he wouldn't get to graduate. It had always been touch and go with him, and I guess he was lucky to have got through a four-year course in five years. Perhaps he wasn't so dumb as he was just not much interested. However, as he had often said, Mr. Crevey not only wanted him to graduate but wanted him to have experience up North. What Mr. Crevey wanted was always very important to Harlan. Small wonder.

"What's happened?" I asked.

"Caroline honey, I'm so sorry I don't hardly know how to tell you," he said, "but I just heard this morning that Ella Mae's coming along."

Ella Mae? I'd never heard of any Ella Mae. I knew his sisters' names, of course, and there was no Ella Mae among them or his nieces.

"All along she said she'd be too busy with her own graduation, but I got a letter from her this morning saying she was going

58

to skip some of the things at Briar and so would come with the folks after all. And there was a note from my mother to see about getting an adjoining room for her."

But why the long face? "Goodness, Harlan," I said, "Gran won't mind us having another person. We're just serving buffet style, you know, and we'll be glad to have her."

"That's mighty sweet of you," he said, "mighty sweet. I always did admire your grandmother so much and you, too, honey, which you certainly know by now. Believe me, this isn't the way I would have had it. I want you to know that, honey."

I suppose anybody else would have caught on sooner that he wasn't looking this way because he expected me to blow my top over having to have one of his cousins or something to dinner. It hit me late that what he was trying to tell me was that this Ella Mae was coming for Prom. "What's her last name, honey?" I asked.

He looked frightened. "Why, you've heard me speak of Ella Mae, honey," he said.

"Or anyway of her father? Ella Mae Crevey, is it?"

"Of course, honey, there isn't any other Ella Mae I know of, is there?"

"No, there isn't," I said. "You know, my crystal ball was a little clouded this morning, but it finally seems to be working."

"I don't expect you not to be sore about it, honey," he said. "But I swear I never had any idea at all that girl would miss her own graduation festivities to come up here for mine. She said right along she wouldn't. I just don't know what possessed her to change her mind."

"I guess it's a woman's prerogative, Harlan, and so now I think I'm going to change mine. I think I am going to be indisposed Saturday and have to call the dinner party off."

"Honey, I don't blame you," he said. "I don't blame you one little bit."

"Now, if you'll excuse me," I said, "I've got to get to work."

He walked to the campus gate with me. All the way he kept saying how terrible he felt and how sorry he was and he sounded as if he meant it. I hadn't even started to shake. I got over to Pickalot before I realized that what had happened to Lois Geer had happened to me. She had invested more in Harlan than I

59

had, perhaps, and maybe deserved to lose out since she'd expected to catch him in such a corny way. Well, my way had been corny, too, and I had been no less certain of it. I saw now that Harlan had been warning me every time he'd spoken of being the same as a son to Mr. Crevey. But I hadn't heard the warning. It had never crossed my mind that Mr. Crevey might have a daughter through whom he could gain a son.

There was no hope of my getting another date for Prom. I hadn't dated anyone but Harlan all year. I took the unreturnable dress to a resale shop and eventually got thirty dollars which the woman said was wonderful. She didn't tell me what she sold the dress for. I would guess from her cordiality that it must have been around sixty. Naturally she liked doing business with people who brought never-worn clothes to her. I was tempted to take her the fancy chiffon and lace gown and peignoir set I had thought I might be using after the Prom.

I received an announcement of the wedding at the end of the month. Everything must have been planned weeks before graduation. We had the turkey for Mother's birthday dinner in July. Daddy said it was the best turkey he ever ate and that knowing it was one he hadn't had to share with Harlan Bremer gave it a special flavor. Gran snapped at him that he wasn't funny, and he said he hadn't intended to be. I said, "Never mind, never mind. Be funny if you want to. It doesn't bother me at all."

I was numb. I never put in such a summer. Daddy had insisted that I do something to start on what he called my career. He had insisted that I leave Pickalot, where I made so much money and was so busy that I couldn't think about anything else. He browbeat me into going to see his friend, Charles Good, managing editor of the *Maxwell Monitor,* about a career-type job. Out of friendship for Daddy and in the interests of my career, Mr. Good made me the assistant of a woman who ran a downstairs office where people could pick up papers, pay their bills, leave ads, or file complaints if they didn't want to do this by mail or telephone or to bother with the stairs leading to the editorial and business offices. There was almost no business in the downstairs cubby. Miss Mildred Whatley, a relative of the paper's owner, was my boss. I think I was hired only because she wanted company. She never stopped talking. Even when she went down the back hall to the john, she left the door open and continued to talk. Daddy spoke proudly of how his daughter was learning newspapering, but all I was learning was far more than I cared to know about Miss Mildred.

For our tenth Christmas, Marianne and I got diaries. Mrs. Snyder, ever the gracious lady, checked with Mother before holidays and birthdays to see that Marianne wouldn't get more than I did. Her pony and fur coat, for example, didn't come on any regular gift day.

Her diary was white kidskin embossed in gold and it had a gold lock with a tiny key on a chain to wear around your neck. Mine was white plastic printed in gilt. I didn't mind that difference. What I minded was not getting a key. Never a child to make like a saint on Christmas, I howled about no lock for my secrets. Wally told me to shut up. "If you don't like what you get for free," he said, "go to work and buy what you want." (Sometime I should ask him how I should have gone about getting Harlan Bremer.)

Finally Mother said, "Keri, for pity sakes stop that. If any-

62

body ever didn't need a lock for their diary, it's you. Absolutely nobody can read your writing."

"Jane," said Daddy, "that's not writing, that's a secret code. Keri, you just stick to your code and you'll be okay."

I stuck to diary writing longer than Marianne did. Marianne used to say she never could think of anything to say once she'd taken care of the weather. The only reason I ever stopped keeping a diary was because I always had more to say than I had time for.

Like me, Marianne had a big love that didn't work out the way little girls always assume it's going to. Hers was Wally, of course. In the world of romance he would suddenly have noticed she was no longer just his sister's friend but a beautiful young lady. I expect the transformation would have occurred while he was off in Korea and that they would have gone into a clinch soon after his return home. But Wally came home with a bride. If he ever thought of Marianne as anything but my chum, it was only as a rich man's daughter and, later, a rich man's wife. Wally wouldn't fail to think about something like that. If she hadn't been underfoot so much, he might eventually have thought of her as a potential date but I rather doubt it. Wally did marry a very wealthy man's daughter, but Bébé had to renounce her claims when she married Wally. All she got from her people were their blessings, not very enthusiastic although they liked Wally in his place, which was not in their opinion as their son-in-law, and some heirloom jewelry. She brought the jewelry in a trunk and some of it on her person. She didn't declare any of it because it was all so very old . . . just old emeralds, pearls, rubies, and diamonds. To customs it looked like junk jewelry, and they probably felt sorry for Wally for getting stuck with such a bauble-struck girl. I have heard my brother say that one reason he works harder than most people is because he has to buy insurance for his wife's trinkets, which ought to be in a museum. Bébé just laughs. She says they aren't so much. "They just look different because the settings are old and Oriental." Now and then she lends a piece or two to an actress who wants to wear something special in a play or movie. If the recipient of such favors can get a fee out of her producer, this goes to one of Bébé's charities. She says not to let Wally kid you that the insurance breaks his back, because several of the pieces almost always earn the insurance for the lot.

You can't compare the way you feel with the way somebody else feels, but I expect that the news about Ella Mae Crevey's existence didn't hit me any harder than Marianne was hit when my mother told her that Wally was bringing a French wife home from Korea. It was our first year in college. Marianne and Bud became engaged a few months later. It was and is a happy marriage and would get along fine without any psychiatrist butting in, in my opinion, that is. However, knowing how smitten she became with Wally when she was just a child, I am conscious of how she looks in his presence. It would be wrong to say she is still in love with him. I'm sure she isn't. But for her Wally is very special. I can't help thinking it's too bad he doesn't seem to have any feeling for her at all. She's just another of the many attractive women he sees during the course of the busy social life his stunning wife plans for his amusement and relaxation and, leave it to Bébé, the increase of his business. Maybe Bébé doesn't give a darn about money. She's always had it and perhaps takes it for granted, the way you do fresh air if you don't live in a polluted community. But she wants what Wally wants.

I think it would be fair if rather silly to say that, until I saw him again, I felt a good deal about Harlan Bremer as Marianne feels about Wally. I had to see him again to get over him. I'm afraid I am sorry it happened. It was rather nice although very juvenile to think about him sometimes, about the way he talked, the way he could make love without going too far but still giving you the feeling what was happening was practically the same thing. I thought a good deal about him during the period of my old maidenhood and even now and then after my marriage. The man I married is loving and I'm sure as passionate as most, but he never cultivated the art of loving the way Harlan Bremer did. As I write this I feel my skin crawling. The thought of the Harlan Bremer I ran into a year and a half ago can make me laugh, but I can never again think with some remembered thrill of how it was to have a date with him. Ye gods!

It was my first trip into Chicago after Andy's birth. We had moved into the big house and got settled before I went to the hospital. I didn't have as easy a time with Andy as I did with Karen. I suppose it was because I had got so tired over the moving and all. However, I made a good comeback and was leading a busy life again in a couple of months. Jock had given me a marvelous mink coat when Andy was born. My mother-in-law, who came up to look after things for us while I was in the hospital although we had both told her it wouldn't be necessary, didn't approve of the coat even though I am sure she had no idea how much it cost. "I'm afraid I wouldn't be able to wear fur without thinking about the animals," she said.

She had been getting on Jock's nerves and this evidently was a last straw. "Are your shoes synthetic leather?" he asked her.

When we had told her there was no need for her to come because if we needed somebody there was my mother or my grandmother, to say nothing of hired help, Mother Dunlop had had answers for us. "Mrs. Andrews is too busy with her poetry," she said, "and poor Mrs. Leffingwell too crippled up with her arthritis . . . and it certainly isn't a time when you'd want strangers in the house." The only reason we hadn't had her on our necks when Karen was born was that Jock's father was ill and she had to stay home with him. Our begging her to remember that we had no room for her hadn't made any impression. She said she could always sleep on a davenport or in a chair, for that matter. Or, you gathered, not at all if Duty called. She is a good and an unbearable woman. Jock left home as soon as he graduated from high school and has been back as little as possible ever since. It is a great pity, because he is devoted to his father, a very sweet but by now very beaten-down man.

It was getting on for spring when I went into Chicago that first time after my second baby's birth. But it was cold enough for a fur coat, especially a mink. Jock was spending the day at the Chicago office, in consultation with Mr. Prentice and some new customers. We planned to meet at the Palmer House, to have dinner and then go on to a show, a comedy that hadn't had very good reviews, but we had seen the only other shows in town before I'd gone to the hospital. I was wearing an old tan wool I'd always liked and a little crest of flowers that set it and my coat and hair off to what I noticed myself was a good advantage. As before, I was feeling very beautiful with my slim figure. Aside from the obvious benefits, it's great to have been awkward as a cow and about as attractive. You experience such a state of euphoria afterward.

I was early enough to look around in the stores a little but I didn't buy anything before going over to the hotel to wait for Jock. I was walking through the lobby and looking for an empty seat when I ran smack into a large obstacle and saw that pinned to it was "Harlan Bremer, Crevey Mills . . ." And then that soft Southern voice said, "I do beg your pardon, ma'am."

"My God," I said, "it's Harlan Bremer, it says there."

"Why, if it isn't Keri Andrews," he said. "How are you, honey?"

I never in this world would have known him if he hadn't had that name tag on.

"Ella Mae, honey," he said to the fat little woman at his side, "you've heard me speak of Keri Andrews who was in my class at Maxwell."

"Indeed I have," lied the little woman. She was wearing the small town woman's uniform for coming to Chicago, a two piece print. Dark background with tiny bright flowers just giving a busy effect and masking any possible spills. You never see these prints except in and near the big hotels. I don't think you could find one in a Chicago shop, unless, of course, on the back of an out-of-town shopper.

Ella Mae could have been any age up to fifty but I knew she must be about the same as Harlan or maybe a year younger. Nobody would have guessed that both of these people were still under thirty or very little over it.

Harlan wasn't bald, but I could see that he would be before long. His hair had lost the shine and his face no longer glowed with the radiance of excellent health. He didn't look sick but he didn't look well, either. He must have weighed fifty or sixty pounds more than he had the last time I had seen him. Enjoy him while you can, I thought as I looked at his dumpy but not unattractive little wife, because you won't have him your whole life and you're not likely ever to get another husband. Still, with all that money . . .

I heard myself telling them that my name was Dunlop now.

66

"Well, of course I knew it couldn't still be Andrews," said Harlan with his charm exuding in a faintly nauseating way.

"Honey, would it be awful if I asked you where you got that adorable little hat?" said Ella Mae. "I been shopping all over this town and do you think I can find me one not the size of a bushel basket? But, honey, I keep telling those girls, I'm not but five foot one and you're making me look like a little old musharoon?"

Harlan laughed. I saw that he considered Ella Mae a very cute little trick and told myself I should have known he wouldn't have married her just for the money. But I wondered if he were at all faithful to her. If not, I would have been willing to wager that he wasn't getting anything free anymore. Not this too fat, dull-haired, sallow-skinned old-looking young man. "Now that would be telling, Ella Mae," he said. "I didn't think you girls would give your secrets away like that."

"What you should do is try the hat bars," I said. "I got this at Field's in Maxwell, but I bet they'd have it at one of their hat bars. Did you look on the first floor?"

"I just looked in the regular millinery sections," she said, "and I never saw such tubs of flowers in all my life. I just gave up and put this little old veil on my head."

I said the little old veil looked fine. She was so pleased that she invited me to come along with them for cocktails, which I don't think delighted Harlan although he said of course, of course. "We're just meeting a few of the business people," she said, "but nobody will be talking business if we girls have anything to say about it."

I told them I was meeting my husband, and so they said when he comes I must bring him along and join them for cocktails. I said I would if he hadn't planned something else. "We don't get in town very often," I said, "and there are a few things we should do before the stores close."

"Dunlop," said Harlan, evidently unable to restrain curiosity longer. "I keep thinking I know that name . . ."

"It's a common enough one," I said. "Jock's with Prentice Products. They make electronic devices and . . ."

"They sure do, they sure do," he said. "I wouldn't be at all surprised if I hadn't had some correspondence with your husband, but I don't think I've had the pleasure of meeting any of the Prentice people. We have installed Prentice equipment, however."

"Good," I said. "I'll have to tell Jock."

"You bring him right over to that little old cocktail place there in the corner," said Ella Mae.

I said I would if he didn't think we needed to do any errands. Harlan said they would have to look us up when they came to town again. He said they were always counting on having a little extra time when they came up for a convention but it never seemed to work out that way. "You do that," I said. "We're in the book."

I didn't say what book and he didn't ask, but although I was sure he assumed we were living in Maxwell, I doubted that I would have to worry about hearing from him. Ella Mae was more interested in me than he was and with her it was mostly my hat.

So that, finally, was the end of my romance with Harlan Bremer. Harlan didn't have anything, not for me, after he'd lost his looks. I've read and heard about men being appalled at seeing former loves later on and finding them fat and homely. Perhaps we girls aren't supposed to be so superficial, but I certainly was about Harlan. When he lost his looks, he lost me. A pity it hadn't happened while the two of us were still in school, so I could have exercised the privilege a woman is supposed to have of being the one to break it off.

At dinner I told Jock about the encounter. "Have you ever seen a girl later on and wondered what on earth you ever saw in her?" I asked.

"You are my first and only girl," he said.

"You know that's not true," I said. "What about that Louise or Laura or whatever your mother's always talking about?"

"Lola?" He laughed. "Why, you've seen her."

"I know," I said. "That wasn't the point. The point was were you disappointed when you saw her again?"

"Why, no," he said, "I thought it was mighty nice for Johnny and for her, too, that she'd improved so much."

"Improved! Jock, you can't mean you call that an improvement."

"But you should have seen her before," he said. "My, it was real pitiful."

"That's not the way your mother tells it," I said. According to his mother there hadn't been a girl in the whole county who wasn't madly in love with Jock and all of them great beauties, marvelous housekeepers and cooks.

The show was amusing if trivial. We enjoyed it. On the way home I said what was hardest for me to take was that now I had no romantic past while my husband had a whole county of beautiful girls to remember.

"Say, maybe you meant Lydia," he said. "Now *she* was a beauty."

"And is she one of those I've met?"

"Oh no," he said. "Lydia married away. You wouldn't have been seeing her down home."

"I bet she isn't beautiful anymore," I said. "It would serve you right to have to see her again. It's a terrible experience. And you know what, Jock? A lot of the movie stars don't look any too good any more, either. I guess what you ought to do is change your ideas as you get older, but the trouble is you seem to keep on being young in spirit."

"Hang on to it as long as you can, darling," he said. "Don't let one fat slob disillusion you."

I noticed then that he sounded tired. "I was so wound up about Harlan that I never asked you how your meeting went," I said.

"It's rather frightening to watch Prentice operate," he said. "I keep thinking he puts me in mind of somebody but all I can think of is the mastermind of some criminal outfit in a detective story."

"Oh, Jock, what a think to say!"

"Oh, he's no crook," said Jock. "He's too smart for that. He's just crooked. There's a difference."

"But surely he isn't doing anything illegal!"

"No."

"Then what's bothering you?"

"He's a man not to be trusted," said Jock. "I realized this when I began to see that he doesn't trust anyone himself."

Although Jock seldom said anything about his work, what

little he did say was highly critical of the boss. Of course I was used to hearing my father lambast management and so I didn't let myself get too upset about it, but each time Jock mentioned Mr. Prentice I felt I had to go more out of my way to please the boss when he asked me to entertain somebody for him. I have become as tired of the man by now as Jock was a few months after joining Prentice Products. But too much is invested for us to think of making a change. The vice-presidency is too near. Sometimes I feel as if I am walking on eggs, as if my least movement will break the thin veneer that Jock has put over his feelings in order to endure what to him is the company's increasing dalliance with the forces that encourage the continuation of violence on this earth.

TEN *The Manuscript*

Although I was interested in Jock from the beginning, it wasn't what could be called love at first sight. He claims it was for him, but I'm sure he just says that. What Harlan and I felt for each other didn't grow. It started off big and seemed to stay that way. Of course he knew, all along, that it was going to end and so for him it perhaps never had quite so much impact.

Somewhere along in the middle of my senior year I began to see that what we'd had was hardly a real love affair. It wasn't a cheap, sex relationship only because of my determination to save myself for our marriage—I really was very romantic on the subject although such sentiment was already considered ridiculous.

I would have been perfectly willing to start dating one or more, preferably more, boys as soon as school started in the fall.

The summer had been more than enough for my mourning. I was still aching but ready to be comforted by just about anybody. However, nobody volunteered. It didn't seem possible that the heretofore glamour girl could go unnoticed but she was, she was. The senior men were chasing after freshmen and sopho-mores, just as the seniors had chased after me in my day. The ones who weren't chasing the young girls were tied up securely, but not always looking too pleased about it. I wonder if boys are ever pleased to be engaged while still in school? The girls, especially the upperclasswomen, are always delighted to be out of circulation, but I'm not too sure that the men couldn't endure waiting a little longer before deciding the future. The freshmen girls have a charm for the upperclassmen that can't be explained. Of course they aren't all prettier and cuter and more fun than the older girls, but they evidently seem to the boys to have a special, irresistible attraction. I can think now of three engage-ments that were broken during my senior year, each because of a freshman girl. I am sure there must have been more.

I all but hung out a sign saying I was again back in circula-tion. I did get a few dates, but they weren't ones I would have accepted Before Harlan. The men were nice enough, I suppose, but not what a girl is looking for even for temporary amuse-ment. However, I knew I couldn't just snap my fingers and have the captain of the football team or the president of the senior class come running.

The more my father talked about my career, the more I saw that I must listen to him. I had nobody on the string who was a potential husband. In fact, I could say I had nobody on the string, period. The few I dated were, perhaps embarrassingly, no more excited about me than I was about them. I think it usually is a two-way street. Even with Harlan. He was crazy about me, in his way in love with me. But Harlan's way of being in love didn't cloud his vision of the future in which he saw himself as the owner of the Crevey Mills. His whole world would have fallen apart if Ella Mae Crevey had married somebody else or died, but not because he was in love with her. But I feel sure he didn't dislike her, that it wouldn't have been possible for him not to care for a girl who was going to inherit a business for him.

Will the day ever come when a college graduate will have the courage to state that in the event of her not getting married she would prefer just to have a job rather than a career? It seems somewhat suspect for a girl not to want to teach school or to be a doctor or, at least, psychologist. But if you want something more glamorous, kiddo, how about journalism? To Daddy and maybe to his whole generation there evidently just wasn't anything more marvelous than working on a newspaper. Except for those who went that way and discovered that it was, after all, just a job. Not everybody goes to war and gets shot up enough to write best-selling books but not enough to be made dead.

What did I want to be when I grew up? Married, natch. From what you read in the papers (and may Heaven forgive my dear friend Dora Benson who contributes to the myth) and in the few slick magazines still in existence, smart gals, always gals, insist upon combining homemaking with careers. Now when you ask a little girl what she wants to be when she grows up, you must tell her she's hedging if she says she wants to be a wife and mother. Yes, of course, dear, but what else? Will some young Keri ever have the nerve to say what she'd like to be is a checker in a dime store? Or in a chain grocery? When my father spoke so romantically of the newspaper business or "game" as he would sometimes say, I was thinking of the wretched summer spent listening to Miss Mildred Whatley in the Service Office of the *Maxwell Monitor*. What price career? I made almost twice the money at Pickalot.

"But of course once you graduate you won't want to work there anymore," said Daddy. I wouldn't want money anymore?

"Even if they made women store managers, which they do not, as I understand it," said Daddy, "it's hardly what we've sent you through college for, is it?"

Well, I'd sent myself through college, not counting the free room and board at home without which I realize I would have found the going very rugged. I couldn't say I'd educated myself so I would be a better checker at Pickalot, but if I had had real guts I'm sure I would have told my father I had no desire whatsoever to renew my acquaintance with the *Monitor*. He told me he'd been speaking to the editor in my behalf and that his friend had promised me I wouldn't have to spend another summer with Miss Whatley who, he admitted, was a difficult person to put up with. (By the time I was back at the *Monitor* nobody was having to put up with her. She'd committed suicide.)

Why is it that there are some things you evidently can't, or shouldn't do if you've had a college education? What about the born bricklayers or carpenters, perfectly bright people who have had college educations but who nevertheless would rather work with their hands than be stuck in some little office with account books the rest of their lives? What is so great about my father's low-pay job other than that it gives him the privilege of calling himself an editor? The couple of years he was away from the printing company they got along without an editor but perhaps had to hire an extra proofreader. They aren't publishers in the usual sense of the word, just job printers. But Daddy is a college man and so they call him "editor" and don't have to pay him a union wage. (And could kick him out for being "unpatriotic" without his having any chance of redress.)

Did I, forgetting my sex for a moment, want to be manager of a Pickalot store? I did not. Did I want to be a checker all my life? I did not. But I certainly liked the money I made in the store and I didn't mind the work too much, either. I enjoyed meeting the public, most of them friendly, decent women and a few equally nice men, and I liked working hard enough for the time to slip by quickly. How it had dragged while I had nothing to do but listen to Miss Whatley!

But I went back to the paper. I was a college graduate. I had to do something now that seemed in line with a proper career for a girl who had done well in college but who for some perverse reason didn't want to be a teacher, a doctor, or a psychologist. (And who, poor soul, had had an unfortunate love affair. "I hear he married someone else, some girl in his home town . . . it so often happens that way.")

My chief job at the paper this time around was to go out for coffee, deliver the letters, spell the switchboard girl, and go along with a photographer when they couldn't spare a reporter and the people who would be photographed would be insulted if they thought nobody but a photographer had come. Naturally the photographer couldn't have known less about reporting than I did, and so he would tell me what to do, mostly hold his camera while he took the necessary notes. Daddy was thrilled when I went out on what he called an "assignment." He refused to admit that what the *Monitor* had done when taking me on was fire the office boy, a kid who was going to quit anyway because of no future.

Charles Good, editor of the *Monitor*, had been Daddy's friend from school days. They liked getting together and arguing, mostly, I think, because they were in basic agreement and so could regard their debates as entertainments. Even while Mrs. Good was still living, the Goods and my folks rarely got together as couples. Mother couldn't abide Mrs. Good, who was a social butterfly type but perhaps not so stupid as Mother considered her. I don't know. I didn't see her often. She was always friendly and quite gracious. She died of cancer while I was working for Miss Mildred in the newspaper's downstairs office. Daddy and Mr. Good kept on as before. Sometimes Mr. Good would come to our house and sometimes Daddy would go to the Good residence, which is now presided over by Mr. Good's old maid sister who came to nurse Mrs. Good during her last days. Even Mother felt that Mrs. Good hadn't deserved such a fate, but I imagine that Miss Good isn't nearly the crab she looks. At any rate Daddy speaks well of her, and Mr. Good apparently is pleased enough with his situation not to consider marrying again.

During my first year on the paper Daddy spoke a lot about my apprenticeship, I suppose in an effort to make me contented with practically no money. I thought that since I was through school I should be paying room and board, but the folks said no, I should wait until I could afford it. I wonder now if this argument of ours, recurring during that whole year, wasn't in reality about something quite different. I think I wanted to pay room and board, so I would feel more respectable about deciding later on to get a place of my own. I believe the folks were determined to have me stay at home. They could face losing me through marriage but not through what is surely a normal desire for a grown woman—to have her own home whether she is married or not. Since my mother took and takes next to no interest in keeping house, I didn't have the problems that I suppose some adult daughters living with their mothers have. I could do as I pleased without getting in Mother's hair as long as

I confined my activities to the parts of the house outside of her tiny study. We had a cleaning woman who came in once a week now, Wally's gift to Mother. He hadn't been back from Korea very long but already was doing well. Although we laughed a little when he told us he was on his way to becoming very rich, we knew it might happen or anyway that it had happened to young men like Wally. Somehow, though, I didn't expect anything dramatic in our family. We didn't seem to be either a doomed or an especially blessed family. But Wally did get rich and Richard did get killed.

And I? Well, I got to be society editor of the *Maxwell Monitor*. It happened entirely by chance. I just happened to be handy when somebody was suddenly needed to fill a vacant chair, that's all. That I continued to fill it until my marriage spoke as much for Mr. Good's friendship with Daddy, and his reluctance to be bothered by the need of a change, as it did for my ability. That is, if so powerful a word can be applied to so really degrading and demeaning a job. It's one that should be paid the very highest salary of any on a paper. What you have to go through! Those awful, awful women. Nobody who hasn't been in the position can even begin to guess what a woman is like when she suspects that the grand crush of wedding news will squeeze her daughter's nuptials out of the paper. Mr. Good had no idea of what we were up against. Often he would complain about my having so few pretty pictures on my page, except in June when even the meanest of my clientele saw that they would have to defer to the brides. And the old clubwomen didn't like their pictures any more than Mr. Good did. They would call up and give him fits about the picture our photographer had taken. Or, if it was a picture they'd had taken on their own, they would blame our printing. But of course it would have been worse if I'd enforced the rule Mr. Good had halfway seriously suggested: The *Monitor* will no longer publish the photograph of any woman over thirty.

Even though Mr. Good was prepared to be tolerant of me and expected the going to be difficult until he could find a regular for the editorship of the society page, I don't think I could have lasted very long without Dora Benson, who had the rest of the women's section of the paper. Dora is and was wonderful. Our only complaint about her is that she is so afraid of intruding that it's difficult for us to get to spend much time with her. She can't seem to understand why a young couple with two small children would be interested in her. We just adore her, that's all. And I hope not only because she has done so much for us.

My predecessor at the society desk was Mrs. Rosselle Maine-Fortune, which I always felt sure she made up, but perhaps not; maybe even she would have hit on something more realistic if she'd been inventing a name. But she did select them or at least two of them from a collection. She had been married three times, she told us, but didn't say what the third or her maiden name was. She came to the *Monitor* from a Chicago paper a couple of years before my time with Miss Mildred downstairs.

I saw her only at a distance that summer. A very good way to see Mrs. Maine-Fortune.

She wore far more makeup than you would have expected to see on a woman so militant about being a lady, but she was just a bit ahead of a trend. You see heavy makeup on middle-aged women all over town now. False eyelashes and heavy green eye shadow . . . the whole bit, without any attempt to make it appear at least somewhat natural. Our society editor spoke in a rather high, extremely affected voice and giggled a lot on the telephone but not to her colleagues. She was never seen in the office without a hat and they were creations that made you doubt your eyes. I never saw her in one that just looked like a hat. They were always productions. Since she couldn't very well write them up for her page, she had pictures of herself in various hats run along with her by-line.

It didn't take me long to learn that it wasn't necessary for me to attend luncheons and meetings. The club- and churchwomen were good about getting their publicity in. Too good, usually, and each one insisting on being given more space than I could allow her. I was invited to many meetings and parties, but after a while the invitations dropped off. Why should they invite me? I didn't wear hats and it looked as if I gave no more space to an organization that entertained me than I did to one that didn't. The only reason Mrs. Maine-Fortune attended so many things was that she wanted to show her hats off and have an excuse to absent herself from the office for a while. I think the free food had something to do with it, too.

Well, this woman, this horror who had been married three times and unmarried twice by divorce and once by death (the man probably killed himself), got engaged. It was incredible. As Dora said, "Look at me and then look at her. This will be her fourth husband and I haven't even had one. The world must be going to the dogs." Of course Dora laughed when she said this, but it seemed like the truth to me. I hadn't had a date in I don't know when, except with somebody's visiting cousin, usually somebody married very happily but stuck in town on business. It looked to me as if I would be another Dora Benson. It was one of those things that just couldn't happen to me but it seemed to. I'd been Marianne's maid of honor and a bridesmaid in five other weddings, and it looked as if that part of my life was over. My friends had stopped getting married. They either were married already or probably, like me, never were going to be. And this fantastic old woman, Roselle Maine-Fortune . . .

Mr. Good stirred himself enough to find a successor for the job, a girl who was moving to Maxwell from St. Louis where she'd been assistant society editor. She was very highly recommended and Mr. Good was delighted.

"I don't know why he had to go and do that," said Dora Benson when I took coffee to her shortly after Mr. Good had announced that he'd hired a new society editor.

"Why, did you have somebody in mind?" I asked.

"Naturally," she said. "Why not you?"

"Me!"

"Are you going to be our office boy indefinitely?"

"Oh, but I wouldn't know how to begin," I said. "Really, I don't know anything about a newspaper."

"The next time you go out with Eddie," she said, "you tell him you'll do the writing. Just say it as if it had been settled in the office before you left. Eddie won't care, not really. It isn't as if he ever got paid for writing something."

I said I would think about this but, actually, I was afraid of our photographer, a very cross old chap. I didn't see any future for myself anywhere and most of all not on the *Maxwell Monitor*.

ELEVEN

The Journal

I finished the chapter that ended with Keri's being coy about not expecting to get to an editor at the newspaper and putting it in such a way that you knew she'd get the job. So although it was a little earlier than I usually stopped typing, I quit. The end of the chapter wasn't exactly a cliff-hanger, though I supposed the author meant it to have some suspense.

I stuck the manuscript and my typescript in the lower drawer, inspected my face in my compact, and then went into the outer office. "Knocking off early?" asked Miss Johnson and I said yes, I'd come to what seemed like a good stopping place.

She laughed and said she'd come to one of those at about twenty to nine this morning. "Well, see you Friday," she said and I said yes and left Administration.

It was a hot afternoon and the few people who were outside weren't moving much. Several men were working in a flower bed that was in the shade and obviously making the job there last as long as possible. I wished I'd stopped at the snack bar in Administration for a cold drink, but I always feel funny about going there alone, as if it were forbidden to patients, which it is not. However, very few ever go there unless they are with a visitor. This may be primarily because they don't have the money. But I think it's something more than that. You can't help feeling you aren't wanted. Like Negroes in some restaurants, I suppose. So you get in the habit of not going rather than to risk that miserable feeling of not being wanted.

Since I was early and had no reason to get back to Martin, I decided to sit on a bench and wait for the girls who would be coming along from art therapy in fifteen or twenty minutes. But I had no more than sat down when the whole deal about the manuscript I had been typing suddenly hit me. I cannot understand why it hadn't before. To me it had been a job of work given to me by Dr. Leonard because, I assumed, he thought the assignment would do me good, would give me some incentive for improving my typing. This seemed fair enough to me and so I hadn't thought further about it. Naturally I couldn't type the manuscript without ever thinking about it, but it seemed to me that often I would go on for pages, and without making mistakes, while not really noticing what the words were conveying or trying to convey. It wasn't anything that could be of more than passing interest to me.

But then I saw what they had done. I don't suppose they would have called it a practical joke. I'm sure they decided to do it on the chance that it would be helpful. So here for weeks and weeks I had been typing, not some attempt at a novel written by one of Dr. Leonard's patients or, possibly, by his wife or even by the doctor himself, but somebody's autobiography. And was that somebody me? It was not. It was the Other Caroline, that's who it was. They hadn't made any great effort to disguise the story. Many of the names were quite similar. And they'd left Maxwell, Maxwell, and the *Maxwell Monitor* had retained its real-life name. Anyone paying half an ounce of attention would have caught on much sooner. I hadn't had even a passing suspicion until, sitting down on this bench, I said to myself, but she's made it obvious that she's going to get the job.

I tried to remember if she'd said something about it in an earlier chapter and decided she had given the game away even before the present chapter. What a way to tell a story, I thought. How odd it was that the *Maxwell Monitor* would have such a turnover in its society editorship, which I had been told Caroline Kincaid had had before her marriage. I mean, there was just too much other similarity when you stopped to think about it.

So I knew that what I was typing was Caroline Kincaid's own story which somebody, I'll bet Mr. Kincaid, had gone to the trouble of fixing up to sound like a novel. I'm sure it was the doctor's idea, though. The doctor wouldn't have had the time to change the manuscript, but poor Mr. Kincaid, willing to do anything, still pushed around by the doctors, did the work. I wondered some about them changing names they knew I couldn't remember anyway, but decided they probably did it because Mr. Kincaid used those names when talking with me. Or might. Still it was her autobiography. And now by typing it as it was written by her, or nearly, I was to accept it as a substitute for memory? How impatiently they must have been waiting for me to see the light, to say something to indicate that I had caught on and was beginning to use it either in the search for my memory or in place of it!

I got up and went back to Administration. I told Miss Johnson that I'd forgotten something. "Haste makes waste," I said and she laughed.

I went into the supply room and, taking out my key, locked the desk which I hadn't been bothering to do in a long time. Then I went slowly back to the bench where I sat until the girls came from their art therapy. Aggie asked what the matter was. "You look peaked," she said. "Aren't you feeling good?"

I said it was just the heat.

The next day I tried to think of some excuse to go to my office in Administration. Now I cared what came next in that story. Now I wondered if I would find out what was eating the Other Caroline before she died . . . or didn't die, however it should be put. By what seemed to me a strange coincidence, but I'm not batty enough to think there's anything significant about it, there was an article in the newspaper about a medical convention discussion of how to determine death. It seemed to me what they were trying to do was establish death soon enough to make a transplant possible or, in other words, to figure out a way to say a person's dead when he isn't.

I wondered if Dr. Leonard would notice anything different about me Friday morning. I had to ask the night charge nurse for a sleeping pill. I told her it must be the heat that was making me so restless, and she seemed to think this was an adequate excuse.

This morning group therapy continued on about some trivial point that had been raised just before quitting time last week. It developed into being quite a wrangle, one so stupid that I didn't even try to follow it. I just kept thinking about the Other Caroline's life story and wondering when I would let Dr. Leonard and Mr. Kincaid know I had seen through their game, plot, or perhaps it would be fairer to call it therapy. I am sure they mean well. It's embarrassing not to have caught on sooner. In fact, I don't see why I should ever let them know I didn't see through the whole thing in the beginning. Why not? As I looked through the manuscript today it all became so obvious to me.

Just before the close of therapy this morning, Aggie said, "Oh, what a tangled web we weave . . ." Since I hadn't been listening to the discussion I didn't know whom she was accusing of deceit. But I glanced at Dr. Leonard and decided he looked flustered as he caught my eye. Yes, I thought, you boys are just about tripping yourselves up in all the traps you've been setting for me.

The best course for me to follow now that I know more about what goes on is undoubtedly the one I have been pursuing without knowing it. If and when the time comes for me to admit that I know I have been typing Caroline Kincaid's autobiography, I'll simply shrug and imply, if not directly say, that I've known all along that they were trying to force me to accept the memoir as my own. I might even congratulate them on the scheme. I suppose many people, bereft like me of personal memory, would welcome the chance to memorize what allegedly happened to them before their amnesia. But how many people have ever been in my situation? Has there ever been another such transplant, to say nothing of a victim of such who survived? If heart transplants are still extremely hazardous, think of the odds against survival from a brain transplant! I take no pleasure, believe me, in betting that I am the only one.

Of course I will get back to the manuscript with more interest now. I can't help being concerned about what sort of person the Other Caroline was when her character and personality are supposed now to be mine. They seem to believe that although the intangibles have not so far come "naturally" to me, they can transfuse these, as it were, by having me type the woman's story. I can't help wishing there were someone in whom I could confide, but there just isn't anybody. Although Agnes Brush is my best friend here, I have to face the fact that she *is* a legitimate mental patient and one rather hipped on paranoia. I'm afraid what she would say immediately would be that I'm having paranoid delusions. I couldn't talk to Dr. Leonard or Mr. Kincaid, of course, because they are against me, albeit in what they must consider a benevolent way. I wonder if there is anyone who would agree with me that although I have Caroline Kincaid's body, I must, absolutely must, discover my own true, real self. I am not so foolish as to believe I can ever have my complete self back again. I know the body must be gone, if not actually reduced to ashes, gone anyhow from the living. Even if brain transplants were to become as common and safe as appendectomies, I see no reason to believe I would be happier in still another outer covering. But I refuse to believe that I must or even that I can become Caroline Kincaid, though apparently her husband is quite willing for me to do this and presumably her relatives and I suppose her children, who of course can't know any better. Maybe none of the relatives knows anything, either. Maybe they think the woman made a miraculous recovery from brain surgery but unfortunately didn't start to function perfectly in the head right away. Who actually cares about what you really are inside? Or who you are!

TWELVE *The Manuscript*

*N*obody but Mr. Good was upset when Mrs. Maine-Fortune announced that she was resigning. Like most of the staff, I was glad that she was going even though her hats had amused me. She seldom had a smile for any of her fellow workers and complained daily about her tea. I made no effort to fix it for her, which annoyed her, I'm sure. Getting the water hot enough to suit her was problem enough. "If you would brew it as soon as I've brought it around," I said, unable to be silent any longer, "you would find it plenty hot enough. If you can't be bothered to do that, why don't you get an electric plate or just relax and use Instant?"

She was so furious that she couldn't speak. I didn't catch exactly what she called me other than a young upstart with no manners. After delivering my comments I had gone about my business of delivering coffees. Dora, who had heard my remarks, had said, quite audibly, "Hear, hear."

The only reason Mr. Good was bothered by the woman's resignation was that it obliged him to get somebody else just before the owner was due in for one of his brief but often very upsetting visits. The man, always called Young Mr. Jack although his father had been dead twenty years and the son was around fifty, was too much the Jet-Setter to live in Maxwell. However, he kept the old home place and came to grace it once or twice a year. He and his fourth wife, a former movie starlet, would entertain for a few weeks and then rush off to another of their half dozen homes.

During most of the year Young Mr. Jack's connection with the *Monitor* was maintained by an affable lawyer who left everything to Mr. Good about running the paper. If he had to take a deduction for Young Mr. Jack in the years when the paper wasn't doing well, the lawyer didn't mind. Evidently he didn't work on a commission and knew that it amused his client to own a paper whether it was one that paid off or not. Most of the time, according to Daddy, the *Monitor* did manage to break even, and that appeared to satisfy the owner who had funds rolling in from his father's numerous successful investments.

But when Mr. Jack was in town he made like a newspaper publisher. He came to the office and snooped around and gave suggestions and recommendations that he seemed to expect would be carried out instantly. Mr. Good quite naturally dreaded the man's approach and didn't breathe normally until the fellow was safely on his way to New York or Europe or California again. However, luck seemed to be with Mr. Good this time when, through a mutual friend, he had heard that an assistant society editor of the *St. Louis Post-Dispatch* was moving to Maxwell because of her husband's transfer. He got in touch with her and she agreed to take old Roselle's job, to start as soon as she reached Maxwell, a week before Mrs. Maine-Fortune's departure. Then everything went wrong. Mrs. Maine-Fortune's marriage was advanced because the diplomat she was marrying had orders to go to Europe sooner than he had expected. There was no keeping the woman from joining her elderly but evidently rather impressive fiancé for an earlier wedding than they had planned. The girl from St. Louis wasn't due yet and Young Mr. Jack was. However, after making a lot of telephone calls, Mr. Good located our new girl in a motel where she and her husband were staying before taking off for Maxwell. She agreed to come earlier than they had planned to do and so would be occupying Mrs. Maine-Fortune's old desk when Young Mr. Jack came to inspect his property. All seemed to be well.

But the girl didn't show up. The hotel where she and her husband were to have checked in knew nothing beyond the fact that they hadn't arrived or telephoned to explain the delay. Young Mr. Jack was due to pop in on us at any moment. Mr. Good was beside himself, because if there was anything that upset the owner it was the sight of an empty desk that couldn't be explained away by quick talk of assignments or illness. "You, Keri," said Mr. Good. "You sit at Roselle's desk today and keep sitting there, you hear, until that other girl shows up and if Young Mr. Jack asks you who you are you just say Mrs. Maine-Fortune's assistant."

Dora, at the next desk, watched while Mr. Good installed me there. Mr. Good turned to explain to her that I was to act as the editor's assistant. "You can give her some typing to do, can't you?" he asked her.

"I certainly can," said Dora who had already been saddled with the responsibility of getting out the society page in addition to doing her own work. "But why not simplify matters by just having her say she's the new editor? Otherwise he's going to badger you about Roselle. He's going to have to know sometime that she's gone."

"Oh, I doubt if he would remember her," said Mr. Good.

Dora said people always remembered Roselle Maine-Fortune although usually they would have preferred not to.

"Handle it however you see fit, then," said Mr. Good. "I expect you're right. Maybe he won't come until after Mrs. Channing gets here, but if he does and you have to introduce Keri, just say she's the new editor's assistant. He'll wonder why we have to have one, of course, but I can tell him Keri does other things."

"And how!" I said. "Am I to keep on?"

"Not while he's on the premises," said Mr. Good. "While he's here keep yourself busy with whatever Dora gives you."

Just a few minutes before Young Mr. Jack arrived at the office, the hotel where the Channings had had reservations telephoned to say they had been called by the Highway Police. The Channings had been in an automobile accident and Mrs. Channing had been killed. Mr. Channing was in a downstate hospital and seriously injured. "Just don't mention it to Jack," Mr. Good told Dora when he called her into his office to give her the news. "Just don't mention it. It's a terrible, terrible thing and he hates to hear anything bad."

She told me about it when she came back to her desk. "You just sit tight and keep your mouth shut. Let me do the talking," she said. "And don't stand up unless you absolutely have to. He's half your height."

Although I had been working for the paper the time he'd most recently visited us, I had missed him by being out on an assignment with the photographer. Now, though, I was busily typing when the little fellow came around. Except for the teeth, which were very prominent, he reminded me some of the Duke of Windsor. He even had a slight accent that may not have been so put on as one might have thought. He had lived abroad more than in Maxwell.

First off he wanted to know what had happened to the woman-in-the-hat. "Very amusing, that," he said.

"She's gone off to marry a diplomat and they're going to be in the Italian embassy, I understand," said Dora. "Miss Andrews has taken her place."

"Howjado, Miss Andrews," said Young Mr. Jack. "Welcome to the family."

"Thank you," I said.

"But you don't carry on the tradition of wearing a hat?" he asked.

"We don't ask her to compete with Roselle in anything but the work she turns out," said Dora, and our big boss chuckled and moved on to the next desk. He didn't hang around long that day and didn't come in every day that he and his wife were in Maxwell. But not knowing when the man might come, Mr. Good had me remain at the desk. He said he was doing what he could to find somebody as good as he was sure Mrs. Channing had been. Although he had never set eyes on the woman and I'm sure hadn't more than glanced at any of her work, he took her death hard and really seemed reluctant to replace her.

So the time passed and Young Mr. Jack went on to California and I just continued to occupy the society editor's chair while Dora did the thinking for me. I typed and answered the telephone when Dora felt it was a call I could handle. For perhaps six weeks, she answered my phone first and never let me talk to the ones she analyzed as being troublemakers or problem children. Gradually, though, she turned more and more of the calls over to me, and after two months I was carrying the full load. Dora Benson went to Mr. Good and informed him that this was the case and that it was time for me to receive adequate compensation. It was another year, though, before I was getting what the paper had paid old Roselle or what Mr. Good said they'd paid her. I never quite believed him about this and neither did Dora. "He was always afraid of her," she said, "and he isn't of us."

So that was how I worked my way up in the newspaper business. You should hear Daddy tell it. Onward and Upward with Keri, news gal. Of course people began saying I certainly took after my mother, and I couldn't blame Mother if this annoyed her. I'd got on to the patter and could dish it out almost as well as old Roselle had done. I was never as popular, or as hated, either, as my predecessor. Not accepting invitations to attend functions I could cover sufficiently at a distance, I didn't become personally involved with the women I dealt with. Although they resented my aloofness, they never had as much reason to get sore at me as they'd had when dealing directly with Roselle.

All I had to do to see my future was to look at my good friend Dora Benson, perhaps twenty years older than I. She seemed to be happy enough. She had a nice little apartment of her own now that her folks had gone into an old people's community not far from Maxwell. She had old maid friends, mostly schoolteachers, and drove a car and went into Chicago quite often. I couldn't say her life was dreary, but the thought of imitating it made me sick to my stomach. I found it impossible to believe that I would never marry and still, how was it to come about when I almost never had a date anymore and when I did they were nothing more than convenient arrangements that led no-where. Oh, there were two men I suppose I could have dangled awhile if I'd felt desperate enough, which I knew I should have been feeling. Both were relatives of girls I'd known in college. Both seemed interested in me but not passionately so, not enough, certainly, to pursue me if I didn't feel like being pursued.

When I was younger I had sense enough to accept dates from boys I wasn't particularly interested in, because I knew that a girl needed to keep herself in circulation if she were to find the boy or boys she enjoyed going with. But now, when I was older and certainly not going to school parties, where was I to go to be seen by potential marriage material? I went where practically everybody was married or, with these not very enthusiastic dates, to the movies. I would have had to stir myself to keep either one of those men interested. Neither was wanting to get married, but both probably would eventually. For a girl like me it would have been a hard pull, I was sure, especially since I didn't care too much for either one. I still couldn't help thinking an unexciting marriage would be better than none at all, but at the same time I wasn't able to bring myself around to working toward such a dreary goal.

Marianne did what she could. She must have pestered Bud continually about getting dates for me. What the poor man offered was, in my view, worse than the pallid cousins I might have managed to catch if I'd put my heart into it. Bud's acquaint-ances probably all had a lot of money. They were unmarried, but some of them had been divorced. They all had good manners in a crowd, but were quite single-minded when you got alone with them. I learned that especially among the "better" classes, it was assumed that any girl twenty-five or over must surely be delighted with whatever was offered.

When Marianne was out of things with a baby, my social life dropped to nothing. The friendly but uninteresting cousins faded gently from my picture. I was making fairly good money, and the folks were rather reluctantly letting me pay room and board.

89

I suppose they could tell what I was aiming for was eventual independence whether I ever got married or not. They are people with progressive ideas in so many areas, but they were unable to believe that an unmarried girl working in the home town would leave her parents.

THIRTEEN *The Manuscript*

*O*ne morning during our coffee break, now enjoyed
or at least endured, in the ladies' lounge where a coffeepot capable of boiling water had been installed with a jar of instant
coffee and powdered cream, Dora asked me if I were going
steady. The question embarrassed me for two reasons, the other
one being that when I'd declined her invitations I evidently had
ed her to believe it was because I had a date with a gentleman
friend. I said no and for pride's sake foolishly added, "Not at
he moment."

"Then maybe I can persuade you to go dancing with me," she
aid.

I couldn't have been more surprised if she'd said bear hunt-
ng. "Dancing?"

"Why, yes," she said, "didn't I ever tell you I dance every
veek?"

She certainly had not. "Usually on Sunday," she said, "because that's when there's a lesson, which I always enjoy even if I really don't need it anymore . . . says I as shouldn't, and because it starts at eight thirty instead of nine, the dancing, that is. The lesson's at eight, which means leaving home at about six thirty because you never can tell about Sunday traffic, can you?"

"Where do you go?" I was thinking of a church group doing square dancing, although I wouldn't have thought they'd be holding such on a Sunday.

"You've heard of the Miramar Ballroom, of course."

"No, I don't think so."

"Really? Of course it isn't nearly what it was in the old days when the big name bands were there. Paul Whiteman, Benny Goodman, Isham Jones . . . their pictures are all over the lobby . . . everybody you ever heard of in popular music has been there at some time or other. Of course most of the name bands are gone now, but we do have good ones, real good, and big, ten pieces or more. And it's the most marvelous dance floor in the world, on springs, you know."

"Ballroom dancing?" I said, still finding it hard to let go of the weird picture of her square dancing that my mind had conjured up for me. Dora isn't a bad-looking little woman but she's on the prim side. Very plain, smooth, mousy hair, no makeup to notice, and plain, tailored clothes. Not a woman anybody would give a second glance if they hadn't got acquainted with her and discovered what good company she could be and, as I had done, what a helpful friend.

"Oh, none of that crazy stuff the kids do," she said, "although more to be funny than anything else, I guess, the teacher did give us several weeks on the Twist. I darn near dislocated a vertebra."

Now it was all right to laugh and I did, perhaps a little too much. Realizing this, I was caught short when she repeated that she wanted me to go to the Miramar with her. I had turned down her invitations so often before and so easily, but interrupted while laughing at her rather than with her, I guiltily said I saw no reason why I couldn't. I told myself I would think of a reason, though, before Sunday came around.

Later in the week she told me she didn't mention the Miramar to "the girls," her cronies I had also avoided when not getting more involved with her. "They seem to think there's something rather indecent about it," she said. "They're very romantic, aren't they, and I suppose they've seen movies about dance halls. I'm afraid they would be quite let down if they ever did go to the Miramar, but believe me I am never going to ask any of them to go again, not after the way they've acted, the silly things. By now they assume I have mended my ways and if I mention that I'm busy on a Sunday when one of them has something up her sleeve, I do believe they think it's some church affair." She laughed. "I sometimes wish they could see my tango . . . when I have a good partner, that is."

"And do you usually?"

"Usually," she said. "I manage not to get stuck very often with the poor dancers. Actually they don't come around much. The people there go for the dancing more than for anything else. I've been seeing many of the same ones for years, and I don't know where most of them live or work or even remember what their last names are. Of course people who want to make it more personal than that probably can. Two of the people I've known there in the past ten years did get married."

"Just two?"

"I mean to each other. Other people have married away from the Miramar, as it were, or brought a spouse they met outside. The point is that it isn't a lonely hearts club or matrimonial agency by any means, it's just a place where you go if you like to dance."

I couldn't recall ever having told her I was so mad about dancing. Although Marianne usually saw to it that I went to the City Club every New Year's Eve, it was an unusual year when I danced any other time now that I was out of school. But Dora was taking for granted that she had me sewed up for the follow-ing Sunday. She would call for me at six thirty, she said. She said she always wore what she called a dance dress. "A short one," she said. "You'll see a few long ones, but they're such a nuisance and don't look good on the floor anyway."

"You mean it's formal?" I was appalled. I'd always thought

93

everybody dressed very casually on Sunday nights, no matter where they were going.

"Just the girls," she said. "The men wear business suits. Oh, now and then a stranger turns up in a dinner coat, but none of the regulars put on the dog like that."

"But the . . . girls do?" I'd never thought of Dora as a "girl," let alone one who went dancing. But now I had an out. "Dora, I'm sorry but I don't have any kind of formal, long or short."

"Never mind, dear. Just wear a little cocktail dress or whatever you want. There's always quite a variety of ideas, of course, about what constitutes a dance dress."

I couldn't get out of going. I put on my best dress, a black basic, not an expensive one, but it didn't look too bad after I tricked it up a bit with costume jewelry. Still I wondered if Dora would approve of it, especially when I got into the car and saw she was wearing gold slippers. It was snappy weather and her coat covered her dress.

The man in the parking garage office spoke like an old friend to Dora and hardly noticed me. The girl at the checkroom counter, though, was interested and Dora introduced us. She told me she wouldn't have to give me a check because she would hang my coat next to Dora's. "Any friend of Dora's is a friend of mine," she said. I was wondering if she would call me Ker but she didn't call me anything.

Dora didn't let me linger in the lobby long enough to look at many of the photographs of the famous musicians who had autographed their pictures to the Miramar. She said it was time for the lesson to start and that since it was going to be quite a new wrinkle in the cha-cha she didn't want to miss it. We went up a palatially curving gilded staircase whose red carpet was rather tattered. At the top of the stairs a woman dressed a good deal like Dora greeted us and told us to hurry because the class was starting. Until we went toward the ballroom I really hadn't had a good look at her; she'd been too close to me.

It was beyond laughter. The plain, old-maidish Dora was just as plain and old maidish from the neck up as ever, but below she was done up debutante style. Her tulle skirt billowed out from a tight bodice that was a darker pink than the voluminous tulle. If I hadn't seen the woman greeter and now several other obviously older women in similar doll dresses, I would have been in an agony of shame for Dora. As it was, I was just stunned. "No," I said to her, "I'm going to watch. Since I don't even know the first thing about a cha cha, how could I learn an advanced step?"

"She always gives a review," said Dora, but I shook my head and hurried away. I walked around the side of the ballroom where there were large upholstered chairs and large individually lighted oil paintings. The whole thing looked like a movie set to me, but I would have hated to have to dream up the appropriate story to fit that decaying elegance in which a dozen or so aged butterflies and a half dozen equally old men were dutifully responding to the orders of a yellow-haired woman who was addressing a microphone. "All right, kiddies," she said.

I sat down in a thronelike chair and decided I would stay there all evening. From the dimness of my retreat I got a splendid view of the large oval ballroom with its colonnade separating it from the promenade where I sat. Overhead twinkled a few stars in a quite blue sky where clouds drifted in rather precise formation. On the stage a pianist and a drummer were obeying the instructions of the woman with the microphone who, incidentally, was not dressed as for ballet but as if her gown had been painted on. I'm sure she couldn't have sat in it but it had slits that enabled her to demonstrate a kneebend which she was requiring the class to incorporate into their cha cha. She clicked castanets to indicate when she wanted action to start and stop.

When I could tear my eyes away from her, I began to watch a tall red-haired man who looked to be much, much younger than the others, surely no older than I. He was having a terrible time with the cha cha which, I decided, served him right for being so foolish as to try. Then I looked back at the teacher who had clicked for the class to halt. When I looked for the red-haired man again he was gone.

Since I hadn't heard anyone approach and wasn't looking in the direction from which he had come, the man's voice startled me. "Are you tall standing up?" he asked.

I turned and saw that it was the redhead who had not been able to perfect the knee bend. "Yes," I said. Huffily, as I recall. "But no taller than you."

"Too bad," he said and pulled a small gilt chair up close to mine and sat down. "I purely hate the cha cha cha," he sighed, "or is it just cha cha?"

"I wouldn't know," I said. "I never saw it before."

"I knew I hadn't seen you before," he said. "I noticed you just as the lesson was starting when you came in with Dora."

"Oh, you know Dora?" I said. Brilliant of me.

"Everybody knows her," he said. "I'm not at all sure she would say she knows me, though. But I'll ask her to introduce us if you'd feel better about it."

"I'm not in the least bothered," I said. "I just came along with Miss Benson, that's all."

"Well, I'm glad you did," he said. "Will you have the first dance with me if it isn't a cha cha, a rhumba, twist, or tango?"

I couldn't help laughing. "You've outlined my limitations, too," I said. "But I'm not so sure I can waltz or fox-trot any more, either."

"They don't mention the fox-trot here," he said. "They call it the jitterbug."

"Really? I didn't know they were the same thing."

"They don't allow the Lindy Hop," he said.

"But isn't it the same thing as the jitterbug?"

"No," he said, "I think it's the one where you throw the girl over your head . . . sort of."

I laughed again. By the time the lesson was over and Dora came in search of me, the young red-haired man and I were talking as if we'd known each other for a long time. He stood up when Dora came. "You wouldn't remember my name but maybe you'd introduce us anyway," he said. "I'm Jock Dunlop."

"Mercy, I remember you, Jock," said Dora. "Keri, may I present Mr. Dunlop. Mr. Dunlop, this is my good friend Miss Andrews." She turned now to wave to a man who had given a piercing whistle. "Coming right away," she called. "His manners aren't perfect but he keeps very good time. See you later." And off she went to the arms of the whistler.

"Will you risk it?" asked Jock Dunlop.

"Why not?" I said. "We can always stop if the going is too rugged."

Actually it wasn't at all bad until the band, evidently thinking everyone wanted to keep on practicing the cha cha, repeated the number they had closed the lesson with. Mr. Dunlop and I retired to the sidelines where I was able to ask him some questions without seeming too nosey or so I hoped. I learned that he was working at a state hospital for the mentally ill, located not far from the Miramar. He was from the southern part of the state, a country boy, an electronics engineer at present doing his alternate service as a conscientious objector. When I told him what I did, I caught a look of surprise in his eyes.

"I don't blame you for being surprised," I said. "It wasn't as if I'd been an understudy. It was more as if I just happened to be passing the Metropolitan Opera when they decided they needed to fill a space that had fallen vacant unexpectedly. But the sudden promotion delighted my parents, anyway my father, and there didn't seem to be anything else much. And Dora Benson was determined that I should get to keep the job . . ."

He said Dora was a very nice person and that he was glad she'd brought me along tonight. The music began again. Dora hadn't come to us during this intermission. I'd caught a glimpse of her in a large group some distance away. Mr. Dunlop said it wasn't right for him to monopolize my time, but that if I would dance with him again he would take me during the next intermission where I would have a chance to dance with other men. I told him I hadn't expected to dance at all.

Compared to the people swirling, dipping, and fanning all around us, we were miserable dancers, but we did manage to keep time together. I was sorry when he took me to the large group where presumably you milled around between sets if you were willing to dance with more than one person. The married people, a few couples, seldom came to this side of the ballroom. It seemed generally understood that if you didn't want to dance with people you might not know well or at all, you could go over to the other side of the room.

Although I am no giant—five nine—I do of course always seem taller than a man who is the same height. I have never worn extremely high heels but I don't care for flats, either. There were maybe three men definitely taller than I, not counting Jock

Dunlop. Only one of these asked me to dance and we didn't do at all well. His steps were very fancy and I simply could not get on to them.

I was chosen by a half dozen quite little old men who seemed not to mind pushing me around and then finally Jock Dunlop returned. I told him I was almost too tired to get myself to a chair and that if he wanted to sit one out with me, fine, but he should feel free to go ask somebody else. He said he was glad not to have to dance.

"I come just to get to talk with a few people who aren't sick or professionally engaged in taking care of the sick," he said. "My folks considered dancing a sin and so I used to think it was great to sneak out to a dance and lie about where I'd been. Made me feel like a man of the world, I guess."

So we were just sociable, off in a dim corner, until Dora came hunting to see if I was ready to go home. She said she would give Jock a lift to the hospital. He said this wouldn't be necessary as it wasn't far, but when he was convinced it wouldn't be out of our way, he came with us. It wasn't a long ride, but it was further than I would have wanted to walk after all that dancing. We spoke of meeting again the following Sunday, which, for some reason I didn't care to examine, disappointed me. But I needn't have worried. He called me at the office the next morning.

"Is it all right for you to get a personal call there?" he asked. "I should have waited until evening but I didn't want to."

I told him it was all right. "After all," I said, "I am head of the department, that is, I am the department."

He wanted to know if I would have dinner with him if he came out to Maxwell some day that week. He was working an early shift and could come any day convenient for me if seven o'clock wouldn't be too late. He had looked up the train schedule and found that one reaching Maxwell at seven would be the earliest he could make.

I didn't know how much conscientious objectors got paid but was sure it couldn't be much. I knew from what he had told me Sunday he could eat free at the hospital and so I suggested that he come after dinner since catching the seven o'clock would rush him. The next train during that nonrush-hour period would

98

get him into Maxwell at eight fifteen. But he evidently suspected my motives in trying to change the date from dinner. "When I don't have enough money, I'll tell you," he said. "I have spent almost nothing the whole time I've been on this job."

So I told him I would meet the seven o'clock. When I hung up I noticed that Dora seemed to be trying very hard not to look my way. "Hey," I said, "that was your friend Jock Dunlop."

"Well, what do you know?" she said.

FOURTEEN *The Manuscript*

Would a psychiatrist expect me to probe deeply and intimately into my memory of Jock's and my love affair? I hardly know what to write about it because it was so very ordinary and so without memorable ups and downs. First of all we liked being together. We became good friends before we fell in love, I would say, and the falling in love wasn't anything sudden. Still, I was instantly more conscious of Jock's sexual attraction than I'd been of Harlan's. Perhaps this was simply because I was older and more able to figure out what was happening to my emotions.

It wouldn't be true to say it was easy for Jock and me to "save ourselves." However, if we'd been wanting to fall into the evidently widely accepted pattern that makes it routine for engaged couples to sleep together quite as a matter of course, I don't know just how we would have managed. It really does take some money. Jock had worked at two jobs, both pretty good, before being inducted into his alternate service program at the hospital, but he'd had to pay his college debts back, which hadn't left him with much. And of course what he got from the alternate service job was hardly more than his keep. Our dates had to be inexpensive. When he had paid for his transportation to and from Maxwell, he'd spent all he should have, and a bit more, for a date if he were to have many of them.

We walked a lot and did a great deal of talking. When we spent an evening at my house, it always seemed to me that the folks stayed with us a great deal longer than necessary to show goodwill, but of course I was glad to see that they were becoming very fond of Jock whom I certainly planned to marry as soon as I realized that our friendship had changed and that we were in love.

He claims he must have proposed somewhere along the line, but I insist that a girl would remember. Girls remember exactly how a proposal was worded and all of the surrounding circumstances and I remembered nothing of any such with Jock. I couldn't even say exactly when his speaking of the future would include, as if an afterthought, ". . . but of course we'll be married before then."

If either of us proposed, it was me. One night when we were discussing what we would do the following weekend when he was to get a little more time than usual off, I said maybe we should consider ourselves formally engaged.

"Formally?" asked Jock.

"Yes."

"But is there a difference?"

"When people are formally engaged," I said, "I should think they would feel pretty much about their financial things as they do after they get married."

"I don't quite follow."

"Well, don't you believe that after people get married, what each has is the other's, too?"

"Of course."

"So, why not before, once you're definitely engaged," I said, "why not consider what is yours is also mine?"

"But of course it is," he said and then laughed. "Oh, no, you don't turn me into a gigolo, if that's what you have in mind. I will not be bought, ma'am."

"But when I make such scads of money," I said, which was the first time I had ever thought of my mean salary as "scads," "why shouldn't I rent a car with it if you're willing to drive it for me free?"

However, Jock continued to be unreasonable and very old fashioned, and we continued to walk places or to go by train or bus. It didn't hurt us and I didn't mind. All I'd wanted to do was help out some on the expenses. My living such a distance from where he worked and lived added tremendously to the cost of dating me. He said if he weren't so near the end of his hitch it might be different. "But I'll be back on the job before long and then we'll be rich, I would say almost too rich to keep it confined to a formal engagement."

Maybe that was the proposal. Anyway, I began to make plans and we were married the following June, two months after he had gone back to his old job at the Chicago Mirex Laboratory where he did experimental work in electronics. The wedding was at the Maxwell Methodist church. Fortunately, I guess, Marianne wasn't very pregnant at the time and so could act as my attendant. Wally stood up with Jock, which I later learned annoyed his mother since she had decided upon one of Jock's friends from near his home. Later Jock said he never would have thought of the fellow whom he'd known all his life but had never considered a special friend. "I wouldn't have felt right, putting him to having to spend time and money on my wedding," he said. "Mother overestimates some of my childhood connections."

Mrs. Dunlop is a woman who sighs a lot and speaks as if all hope is lost. I don't know what she's so down-in-the-mouth about. Jock says she isn't, not really, but that somehow she must have got the idea that showing pleasure is sinful. "Dad never pays any attention to her sighing," he says. Well, now and then I have wondered if that self-preserving attitude of Mr. Dunlop's may have been what has compounded Mrs. Dunlop's dragging around with a long face. She appears to be in good health although it wouldn't hurt her to lose a few pounds. The Dunlops are hard pressed, like all of their neighbors, to make a profit on farming, but they manage to save for their old age, Jock tells me, and to be somewhat more prosperous than you might think from the way they live. But their house is modern and comfortable, and they have all the needed gadgets for modern farming. I adore Mr. Dunlop but seldom get to be around him except in the, to me, inhibiting presence of his wife. It is quite true that he doesn't seem depressed by her perpetual depression. He seems to bear that cross with good humor if, indeed, he is aware of a need to bear anything.

Jock's two older sisters, Florence and Jessica, take far more after their father than their mother. They, like Jock, have his tall thin figure and red hair. Jock and his father are striking, if not handsome, men. The girls have a somewhat raw-boned look I don't notice in the men but they aren't unattractive. Their husbands are pleasant enough. Florence's teaches school in Rena, fifteen miles south of the home place, and Jessica's has the automobile agency, garage, and filling station in that same village.

Norma, the youngest of the family, is another cup of tea. She is tall, thin, redheaded like the older girls but doesn't miss being attractive as they do. She is nil on personality, though, as far as I am concerned and I shudder every time I hear her say she's thinking about coming to Maxwell U. for her doctorate. She teaches school in Rena and lives at home. I have sometimes wondered if the reason both of her sisters continue to live in houses that they have outgrown may be because they're afraid that if they had room for her, Norma would move in on them. I feel sorry for her parents for having to put up with her but am more concerned about keeping her away from me. I couldn't help feeling a possessive attitude in her when she saw our guest room. I know that I have to put up with Norma and her mother whenever they come to Chicago for a few days. I can't say I don't mind. I do. But I know it's something you have to do and that relatives are relatives and so stop bellyaching. But two or three days of Norma and her mother and I am practically ready for the loony bin. They do nothing but complain complain, not so much about the service I provide—even Norma hasn't quite got the nerve for that, but nothing is ever the way they think it should be. If you say you're having scrambled eggs, Norma will say never mind, never mind, she can take them any way. If you say you will be glad to do them another way but had remembered her saying she liked them scrambled, she will say scrambled is probably no worse than any other way. And what would she rather have? Oh, she isn't interested in breakfast, really. Nevertheless she comes to the table and tucks away a hearty meal. Her mother is more consistent—she doesn't eat much, anyway not at table. I figure she must make up for it when helping to get the meal or in clearing the table. Or perhaps she never eats much and is one of the unfortunates who seems to gain weight by doing no more than look at something fattening.

These people were not sprung on me. I visited Jock's home before we were married. You might say we were given the opportunity to vote on each other. I refrained from voting on Norma and Mrs. Dunlop. I doubt if they were so reserved about giving their opinions to Jock. Mrs. Dunlop did what she could to make me think Jock had been engaged to a neighbor girl who was still suffering cruelly from a broken heart, but when I met the girl she seemed delighted to make my acquaintance. "I always had a soft spot for Jock," she said, "and I'm sure glad he's getting such a nice girl." She got married soon after we did. Naturally Norma and Mrs. D. informed me that it had been only because of her grief over losing Jock. But the next time I saw the woman she seemed as jolly and pleased with life as ever. Jock said her marriage to a former schoolmate couldn't have surprised anyone but his mother and youngest sister. "And it couldn't have been much of a shock for them, either, but of course they would never admit it." He said he wondered what they would have had to say if he had so much as looked at that Carter girl. "I never knew them to fancy her before they found out they were losing me to you." To him this was all a ridiculous joke, a sort of game his mother and sister played because they had nothing else to think about. He said he laughed about it but that actually he was sorry for people who had so little on their minds.

The last time we were at the farm (I recall Mr. Good's futile effort to make us write "most recent" unless it really was a "last"), Mrs. Dunlop began on "poor Angie Carter." "What's so poor about her now?" asked Jock.

"She's having another baby," said Mrs. Dunlop as if this would be the girl's tenth.

"Her second, isn't it?" asked Jock.

"Yes," sighed his mother as if this were the worst thing that could happen to Angie Carter. She rarely mentioned Angie's married name and often even pretended she couldn't think of who it was the poor child had married.

"Mother," said Jock, "those two became the same as engaged while we were still in grade school."

"That will do for you to tell, I reckon," said his mother. "In your place maybe I'd try to believe the same myself."

"Well, of course there's no doubt but what I am the world's greatest lady-killer," said Jock. "How Keri ever caught me is a mystery."

The look of agreement on his mother's face was really too funny. "Some day I'll write a book about it," I said. "I've always liked mystery stories."

I know, though, that being smarty around my mother-in-law is being stupid. It may give me some momentary satisfaction but I know later on that I not only have been childish but short-sighted. I have no hope of ever winning her over, but this doesn't mean the only alternative is to alienate her. I do have a feeling that she might change her mind about me if I were to die. That would be the one thing I could do that wouldn't earn her automatic, sneering sigh.

But I am not about to oblige. As my chum Marianne has so subtly suggested, I may be sick in the head but I'm rugged in body. I count my blessings after adding up my bills. The children are healthy and bright or anyway normal if not so brilliant as Jock and I are inclined to believe. Jock has never been sick, and the only times I've been hospitalized have been for childbirth. We have a beautiful home with a gigantic mortgage, but our prospects are rosy. If Jock doesn't make vice-president the first of the year, it will be a great surprise to me but perhaps no terrible blow because I know nobody else is going to step ahead of him. Mr. Prentice adores him. Actually it's a bit much and I am afraid the father-son slant gets rather on Jock's nerves. It will be all right, though, if Jock can just ride out the war. He has a good sense of humor and an ability to be sufficiently detached, I think, to endure Mr. Prentice's possessiveness without having it get him too far down. The war, however, is another matter. He seems to take it harder than most people do. He doesn't talk about it, but I know it is continually on his mind.

Sometimes when I think how long it's been since Jock laughed much, I almost wish we'd stuck with the old job. But even his former boss felt he should jump at the chance to go with Prentice. He told Jock he didn't know when, if ever, he could meet what Prentice was offering and that the chance for professional advancement would be far better, too, than Mirex could offer. He was a good friend whom we don't see nearly so often anymore as we would like to. He was right about the financial opportunities Jock would have at Prentice—already he's making three times what he made at Mirex. But I'm afraid the chances for what Jock could call professional advancement are about nil. Almost at once Mr. Prentice decided Jock was far too valuable a man to keep cooped up in a lab, where Jock was wonderfully happy, but I'm afraid Mr. P. doesn't think about so small a point. Prentice Products has a great laboratory where very bright, very talented youngsters work for relatively small salaries. Mr. P. didn't think it was any place for a young man to whom he had taken a great fancy. He began asking Jock to go around to meetings with him, to explain the technical details which he said, and I expect rightly, had got beyond him. Jock said it was as if he'd become a teacher. "Which wouldn't be too bad," he said. "I always considered going into education. But usually the people I am trying to reach haven't had even basic preparation in the field and so it does get a little frustrating."

But he isn't an impatient person, and he said he could see that it helped if the potential or the already sold customer had a general idea of what equipment he was buying. Jock says far too many companies have bought far too many pieces of electronic equipment, not because these are things they need for improved production but because it has seemed to them to be the modern thing to do. They are keeping up with the Joneses in this respect, he says, as much as any woman trying to outshine her neighbor is doing. "It's fair enough, though, for them to expect to be told something they could read for themselves in our literature if they wanted to," he said. "The literature is dull. Maybe what I tell them isn't exactly breezy, but I can hold their attention better than the printed word does and this pleases Mr. P."

I don't know why we both thought the period of his having to go places with Mr. Prentice would be limited. We kept thinking he would be sent back to the lab quite soon. He said he could see that Mr. Prentice wanted to educate him as well as the customers. "It doesn't hurt for the lab man to know something of what's going on outside. Pure research is all very good and naturally I would prefer that, but there's no crime in working toward a definite goal provided it's a socially useful and constructive one."

We had moved from the hole-in-the-wall apartment in Chicago where, perhaps as we shouldn't have been, we were tremendously happy. It was small, dark, and in a filthy neighborhood, but we were so delighted to be together without Jock's having to make that tiresome train trip from the hospital to my house. He could walk to Mirex. He came home for lunch. I have heard some women groan at the idea of having a husband home for lunch, but I certainly enjoyed it when I was a bride. Maybe I would think it excessive now when there are the kids to feed and perhaps a luncheon or an early afternoon or late morning meeting for me. I don't suppose it would take Jock any longer to drive here from the plant than it used to take him to walk to the apartment from Mirex, but we don't consider the possibility of his coming home for lunch now that it isn't financially necessary. And, of course, we are no longer bride and groom. I guess you have to face these things. You seem to get to a stage where it just isn't practical to keep on being romantic, practical or even possible. The outside world kept its distance for a while, but then the moratorium was over and also the honeymoon.

A man Jock met while still in college had gone into an executive placement agency. He got in touch with Jock about an opening at Prentice. The chance to interview for the job, which paid quite a bit more than Mirex intended to raise Jock to within the coming year, came along with the doctor's confirmation of my suspicion that I was pregnant. Jock wasn't thrilled about leaving Mirex, where he had been happy, but he didn't like the idea of rearing a family in a neighborhood where the air seemed to be getting more polluted all the time. He took the Prentice job and we moved to the Maxwell Arms which we thought the most elegant apartment in the world. We had five rooms and they were nice big ones. The building was old fashioned, with a big sun porch and a wood-burning fireplace (that smoked like fury and was best left untouched) for each unit and a large recreation room in the basement where tenants' children could play in bad weather and where adults could have parties or meetings. We made good friends in the building quickly and easily and lost them, I am sorry to say, when we moved to Elk Run. We tried to keep on with some of them, but it just didn't work out. Our new home alienated them and perhaps Jock and I struck them as bending over a little too far backward in an effort to be unchanged. I truly believe we were unchanged and that we're still the same people who lived quite happily in a slummy section of Chicago for a while and who were ecstatic about the wonderful apartment at the Maxwell Arms. But people simply weren't willing to believe we could be unchanged by what seemed to them to be overwhelming good fortune.

We were saving our money toward a house. We loved the apartment but certainly didn't want Karen to be an only child. We had been talking and thinking house for some time and really just waiting until we could swing a down payment, when Mr. Prentice sprang his suggestion about our taking over a property he knew a good deal about. Although he wasn't well acquainted with the present occupants, he had been very friendly with the people who had built it and had advised with them a good deal during the process. After the woman died, the man was no longer interested in keeping the house, which was then sold to a couple who broke up very soon after buying it. They sold at a loss because, like the first owner, they wanted to get rid of it. The next owners got a divorce, too, and the pattern was repeated. As Mr. Prentice said, the place was going for a comparative song.

However, it was far more than we had any intention of paying. Jock told the boss what we had in the bank, and he seemed to be impressed at how well we had done on what he called a minimal salary. He'd already taken Jock out of the lab though he'd said he was to feel free to spend as much time as he wanted there. Then he saw to it, maybe not consciously, that Jock didn't have time for the lab. And even if he had, he knew that the boss's man wouldn't have been very welcome if he came popping in to be one of the boys whenever he had an odd moment. As easily as he had lifted Jock into a position Jock hadn't sought, Mr. Prentice now increased his salary to what completely staggered us. We didn't dream we would ever have twenty thousand dollars a year. Jock was no Wally and the big salary boost just didn't seem real.

What was happening to us didn't happen to real-life people. We accepted as fact the undeniable existence of people like my brother Wally and his partner and Jock's boss but we were not that kind.

The house in Elk Run struck us as being about as suitable for us as Windsor Castle would have been. We saw that it was big and beautiful and in an area of big, beautiful homes. We admired what we saw but couldn't see ourselves in the setting, not even when we could believe that Jock actually had been raised to twenty thousand.

Mr. Prentice showed us through the house as if he were a realtor. He talked about the carpets that were being included and the draperies and the kitchen equipment. He made it seem as if we couldn't afford not to buy it. He brought an interior decorator, to whom Jock and I both took a completely unfair, quite unreasonable dislike, into the picture and said she would spare us the pain of having to knock ourselves out to furnish the place. Mrs. Brewster adored the house, natch, and the idea of relieving us of nagging little nuisances like buying several thousand dollars' worth of furniture and lamps for each room. I don't exaggerate much. Mr. Prentice said we could just turn the whole thing over to her and she would see to what we would need in addition to what we already had. She was very sweet about what we already had and probably got a better price for it than we ever could have done. As it worked out it "just so happened" that what she called "absolutely precious" in our "dear little apartment" just wouldn't do for Elk Run.

Of course you get so you don't really see your own home after a while, but it took a long time for me to see the rooms as mine rather than Mrs. Brewster's. I still cringe when people, coming here for the first time say, as if believing this to be a compliment, "Oh, how wonderful, do tell me the name of your decorator."

The house has been photographed inside and outside for *Beautiful Homes* magazine. Mr. Prentice arranged for this and we had no alternative. Really it has always seemed this way. He had decided we should have this house, where he could entertain quite a lot more comfortably than at a club or hotel, before we knew anything about it. He took the mortgage, of course; otherwise we couldn't have done anything about such a high-priced property. It is true that it was a steal at sixty thousand dollars, but we'd been looking at places in the twenties and wondering if we could manage to buy one of them. Houses no better than this one go for around ninety thousand in this area now. Believe me, more than once I've wished we could sell the place, get ourselves cleared of debt, and move back to the Maxwell Arms. But it seems to be true that you can't go home again, you can't do anything again, perhaps, but repeat stupid mistakes.

Nobody in her right mind could hate this beautiful house and I do not hate it. But I don't have a warm homey feeling for it and don't think anybody could who wasn't brought up in a mansion. Jock's home was much larger than mine and I don't think he feels so much as if we were rattling around as I do. And I'm here more than he is, here and going up and down and down and up from morning until bedtime. I would like to throttle the architect who considered it artistic, I suppose, not to have two contiguous rooms on the same level. So far nobody has broken a neck or leg while the house has been under our aegis, but I always feel it's just a matter of time.

"Thank you," I say and, if pressed, "Yes, we like it, too." Well, I'm sure Jock doesn't think about it one way or another. I'm the keeper of the household accounts. I keep him informed about our financial status, but I don't think it has seemed quite real to him ever since Mr. Prentice said, "Oh, by the way, Jock, you're down for twenty now."

Jock told me later he hadn't known what the man meant. "I kept wondering what, twenty what. All I could think of was twenty lashes. I thought maybe he was kidding me about some dumb mistake I'd made."

But of course when Mr. P. began talking about the possibility of our moving to Elk Run, I knew he had to be planning a big raise for Jock. I suppose I am an ingrate. Mr. Prentice has done a great deal for us. He pays our dues at the country club and at the City Club and gives me embarrassingly expensive presents along with costly trinkets for the children. I know we are all working for him, even the children if they are told to greet the company when the Old Man is entertaining here. Maybe we don't earn all that we get but I would sooner not have the trimmings and be given our independence. I don't complain to Jock, though, because I know he is so unhappy about another aspect. He seems never to mind our having to have the business functions at our house; what disturbs him is Mr. Prentice's increasing interest in government contracts. "Even if one were all for the war," he says, "wouldn't you wonder what's going to happen to the plants all over the country that have expanded to accommodate war contracts? Are we to hold our economic breaths between wars? I tell him to forget about my being a pacifist for a few minutes and just study the future possibilities. But all he can say is he'd be willing to forget it if only I would. He keeps saying, of course, that he's against this war and that all good Americans are. In the next breath what he is saying about the draft evaders and resisters is frightening. He would like to kill them personally for not wanting to fight a war he believes is wrong."

"Darling, he isn't unique," I said.

"I know," said Jock. "Nor am I," he added awhile later.

I didn't ask him what he meant. I was afraid he would tell me. I was afraid he would say he just can't take it much longer. But he has to. We're too deep in this to get out of it. Our friends are people now who either are quite rich or in a bind like us and living rich without being really that way. Our daughter goes to a private nursery school that costs more than I used to pay tuition at Maxwell. She loves it and does very well. Our son will be going there too if we can manage and of course we must. We have payments on the house that have to be met, payments on the fancy furniture the decorator hooked us for, payments on the cars. . . . Is there anything we own outright? I sat thinking for a while and then began to laugh. We paid the hospital bills and the doctor bills pronto and so the children are all ours.

Daddy and Mother prided themselves on not trying to force their political, religious, or ethical views on their children, but Wally and I couldn't help being sharply aware of our father's pacifism when it was popular to be all for war. Now, of course, his opinions no longer alarm anybody, even though so many who now call themselves pacifists seem to be in favor of speeding the war up in order to end it.

If my brother Richard ever had an opinion on anything other than sports, I never heard it. He was a handsome, husky, good-natured boy. He had a hard time in school but scraped by. It must have been hard for him to have to hear continual references to what brains his older siblings had been. Once, at a doings at the high school for old grads, undergraduate students, and parents, I overheard Richard, in conversation with one of my old teachers, say, "No, I'm the different one."

I don't know if Mother heard him or if the title of her book is just a coincidence.

Although Richard may have been different from Wally and me in school and in zeal for making money, I really don't think he was a very different sort of person. He was an average boy, interested in sports and bored by school. He was healthy and husky but not very energetic. There may have been psychological and even physical reasons for this. Anyway I suppose there usually are. But maybe he was the most normal of the lot. Maybe there was something abnormal about Wally and me always being so bright and shining to make a dollar.

I've mentioned that as far back as I can remember in Richard's postbabyhood life, he hung around the Keanes' house more than he did ours. Although the Keanes live only two blocks from my folks, it's an important two blocks. As you walk you can see the neighborhood deteriorating. By the time you get to the Keanes', it is obvious that the people who live in the houses aren't just short of money; they don't give a damn. They don't do the things to their houses that do not cost anything but labor. They rarely mow their lawns. They sit out on unscreened porches, drink beer and pop, and yell back and forth to the neighbors and the passersby. I can't deny that I haven't felt envy of these sloppy, carefree, and careless people as I have passed their houses.

As soon as he could and as often as he could, Richard fled the formal beauty of our neighborhood where children weren't allowed to run barefooted or to stay dirty very long. Daddy never knew how seldom Richard was at home during the day when he didn't have to be in school. Mother had to know, of course, but Mother could and can know things without being very aware of them. She knew that Richard had become more the Keanes' boy than ours. She must have. But Richard was safe and happy at the Keanes' and it was quieter at our house if his playmates convened elsewhere, wasn't it? Later, when it was natural for a boy to think about a girl, or, sooner, for a girl to think about a boy, Mother must have known that the Keanes would certainly have a girl somewhere in the appropriate age group. I think there were thirteen in the family then. For all I know, Mrs. Keane is still producing. But when Mother's women friends spoke of girl-and-boy-trouble in connection with their offspring, Mother said she guessed that Richard's interest in sports would keep him from thinking much about the girls. She knew he went to school things with Crystal Keane but felt he was just being thoughtful. "It's very nice of you, dear," she said one time when he mentioned he would be needing a new suit because he was taking Crystal to the prom, "because I don't suppose the poor child would get to go otherwise." Mother always spoke of the Keanes as very deprived people, but apparently didn't worry about the number of meals Richard had under their roof. Probably she would have shrugged and said what could one more at the table mean.

The Different One is dedicated to the memory of Richard Leffingwell Andrews and is about a young man who is drafted when he elects not to go to college and who is killed in Vietnam a month after his arrival there. The young man's description sounds like Richard and he comes from a home like ours and a city like Maxwell, but there is nobody like the Keanes in the book. The young man goes with several girls, three of whom are described in some detail. None of them could be based on Crystal Keane.

The book's protagonist does not get married. We weren't in on Richard's marriage, but by the time Mother wrote the book she certainly knew about it. Keeping it a secret, said the Keanes afterward, was Richard's idea, not theirs. He had said he wanted to wait until after he got back home. My folks believe, and I suspect rightly, that Richard would have preferred to postpone the marriage. Crystal and her mother went out to the West Coast where Richard was stationed. We weren't told anything about the trip until after Mrs. Keane telephoned to say she was afraid she had bad news for us. Daddy, naturally confused, asked why the Army had notified the Keanes instead of Richard's parents, and then Mrs. Keane had said well, she guessed we would be hearing later on, but that what they probably did first was get in touch with the boy's wife. "Crystal's too upset to talk and so she asked me to call you," said Mrs. Keane. "But I feel real bad about it, too, because he's always been like one of the family. And after they got married he was, of course."

Wally was furious. He wanted to do something about it. What, I don't know. He claimed Daddy and Mother could have the marriage set aside because Richard wasn't twenty-one, but they wouldn't listen to anything Wally said. "It's only money," said Daddy and meant it. To Wally, Richard's insurance was blood money and he begrudged every penny that Crystal Keane got. Crystal never called on my folks and they never made an overture toward her. She married again six months after Richard's death. She works now while her husband attends Maxwell University. They have a nice little house in a new subdivision, a house, says Wally, paid for by Richard. Of course he's right but wrong to feel that Crystal and her mother as good as stole the money. I can easily believe that Richard married Crystal so she could get his insurance if he didn't come back. I don't think he was against his own people, but that he simply preferred another family. It may be that far more people than we'd ever think feel the same way, but haven't the nerve or the opportunity to make a free choice. I don't see why there should be any reason why blood should be thicker than water. Once you are able to navigate on your own, you might very well choose quite a different family if you had the chance.

Sometimes I wonder if Crystal has read *The Different One* and, if so, what she thought. But I don't think she's a girl who would read an epic poem, even one written by her former mother-in-law. Now and then I run into her in a store or on the street and we speak. But I'm never quite sure if it's Crystal or one of her sisters. There are three of them who all look alike to me, and it may be that half the time I'm saying hi to an older or younger sister. They are moderately attractive girls, especially when they aren't smiling. They have bad teeth.

My other brother's marriage was, in a way, a greater surprise to us. We knew when Wally got married. He'd written at great length about Bébé and her family. It is hard to believe that he could have told us so much about the Dumonts without once mentioning that they weren't entirely French or, for that matter, hardly at all. It just doesn't seem possible that he could have just overlooked mentioning how these people had come by their name. It went back to a French trader, all right, but about two hundred years ago and the one infiltration of white blood was the one and only until Wally came along.

He wrote a lot about how lucky he was. His assignment in

Korea was extremely boring and until he got acquainted with Bébé almost unbearable. She took pity on him and introduced him to her family and from then on their house was always open to him. They are very wealthy people and live in what sounds like a great palace. They also have a home in France, just outside Paris. Bébé's first language was French and she was educated in French private schools. Wally's letters told us about all of this and naturally after he and Bébé were married, we talked a lot about when he would be bringing his French bride home. We certainly were not prepared for the girl we met at the airport. It wasn't just that Bébé was so definitely Oriental; I think if she'd been little and pretty in the traditional way, or what we think of as being traditional for those people, we wouldn't have been quite so taken aback. But Bébé was tall and definitely not pretty. It takes people a while to realize that she is stunning.

I remember Mother and Daddy saying they supposed Richard would bring a Vietnamese girl home. They laughed about it and I think hoped he would. They seem to enjoy feeling they are part of the one-world trend. But their liberalism about interracial marriage didn't hold for what you might call interneighborhood. Marrying one of the Keanes was their idea of definitely marrying down. Mine, too, I guess. "Well, at least he didn't turn Catholic," said Mother, the great believer in freedom of religion and in each child's exercising his own choice. "Even though they were married by a priest, Richard didn't let them turn him into a Catholic."

It was somewhat consoling to them, I'm sure, that neither of the boys enlisted. They would have preferred them to ask for CO status but neither would consider this. If either boy thought serving in the Army his patriotic duty, I never heard him say anything about it. Wally griped a good deal about the time he would lose from business and complained that he should have had the foresight to go in for medicine. Richard got a summer job at Daddy's printing company directly after graduating from high school. What he was looking for was a job that might give him military exemption but he didn't find one. The folks were prepared to finance him through college since obviously he wasn't going to go if they didn't foot the bills. But Richard's grades were so poor that Daddy had begun to speak of Junior

Colleges. Then the notice came for Richard to appear for his physical. And that was that.

You know people are bound to get killed in wars, but somehow, like highway deaths, you don't think it's going to happen to you or yours. You know it can, of course, but still when it does happen it is a terrible shock. I don't think any of us has ever quite believed Richard really is dead. It isn't as if he'd got sick and died among us. You keep thinking maybe they made a mistake. Well, I guess Crystal didn't bother thinking about anything like that very long.

She had practically to be carried to and from the church and the cemetery. But her recovery was rapid. One of my friends saw her at a nightclub in Chicago a few days later with the man she subsequently married. Actually my only thought about that is a wondering why people will tell such a thing. Why couldn't my so-called friend have kept that bit of news to herself? But she seemed rather huffy when I said, "I wonder if you'd mind not mentioning this to my mother if you should see her."

"As if I would!" said my friend. "But it seemed to me something that you ought to know."

Why? Did she think we could get the insurance money away from Crystal because she went dancing a couple of days after her husband's shattered remains were buried?

Christmas is a time I sure could do without. Jock's mother seems to believe there is no real Christmas in Maxwell and that her grandchildren will grow up without knowing anything about the holiday unless they always spend it at the farm. Jock has explained to her that it's too great a distance to go for just a weekend or two days, when Christmas falls in the middle or the early part of the week, and that he can't get away any longer. His mother is convinced that he could get away if he wanted to, and I suppose she's right that he wouldn't be fired or even called down. She can't seem to see that the more important his job is the less he can step out of the line they expect of the workers. I know she thinks I am determined to have my children grow up not knowing any relatives but mine. I prefer mine, but would be perfectly willing to alternate if the matter of distance weren't a factor.

Karen is old enough to like the idea of having Christmas at home the way most of her friends do. Andy doesn't care. He likes wherever he is as long as he isn't interfered with a great deal. He seems to be a rather self-sufficient child and can play quietly and happily with a few toys just about indefinitely. Karen, extremely sociable from babyhood, enjoys people but even so seemed afraid that we might go to her grandparents' farm for Christmas. "But then we wouldn't have our own tree," she said. She has also requested that we have a menorah. I don't think she is prompted so much by the brotherhood-of-man idea as she is determined to keep up with a couple of Jewish friends who have informed her that they have trees and menorahs. We have told her of course she can have the candles if she wants them. Jock says he will read up in an effort to be in a position to explain a little something to her. I asked if he also expected to explain the custom of the Christmas trees and about the pagans who originated the, to me, pretty bothersome business of bringing a tree into the house. He has promised to do what he can to represent all sides. A fat chance we would have of talking about any such things at the farm. I can remember hearing my mother-in-law speak critically of the marriage of a Jew and a Christian. It isn't that she would even imply that one is better than another but simply that they should not intermarry. She says her attitude is the one held by the most admirable Jews, which I know is true but which doesn't make me think any better of such pigheaded narrow views.

I am tired. Jock is tired. His voice sounded bad when he was talking on the phone to his mother to tell her again that we wouldn't be there for Christmas. I heard him say no, he didn't have a cold and then, yes, that he had been working hard. She evidently could hear the weariness in his voice. All the same, we were looking forward to Christmas here with the kids, our first one at home. Always before we had to drag ourselves down to the farm. Jock had to keep part of his vacation for the project because his mother made such a fuss about it. "She's a woman used to having her own way," he said when he finally came from the phone. "My guess, Dad has always found it easier just to ignore her than to argue with her. And when she can't kid herself into thinking he's done exactly what she's told him to do, she just ignores that. The secret of a happy marriage, perhaps, but not always so easy for the children."

Jock read up more about Jewish customs than he needed to have done to satisfy Karen. Her interest in Christianity was very limited, too. Like the pagans, she worshipped the tree and Andy followed suit.

Bébé had the whole family for Christmas dinner at two o'clock and all of the children behaved quite well considering that by then most of them were bushed. Everybody was ready to fold up by five o'clock. Jock and I were in bed and asleep by nine. We'd had several invitations from people who either have iron constitutions or no children. They weren't RSVP parties, just open houses, the kind of social activity Jock definitely does not care for. He says he hates just milling around. Although he doesn't say so, I'm sure he must also dislike being with a throng of people who are all drinking too much. Ordinarily the people we see most like to get together in small or fairly small groups and don't drink any great amount. But these same people seem to change during the holidays and to regard it as a time for getting absolutely plastered. They act as if they were home from college, rather than married men and women at the head of households. I suppose I have become self-conscious about liquor on account of Jock, but I find I am drinking far less than I did before my marriage, which wasn't much. Of course I notice the drunks more than I used to when I was somewhat pickled myself. I'm just not satisfied with our friends. They are wonderful, that is, they've got everything you could want in friends, marvelous educations and all sorts of special cultural backgrounds, but they do seem to be getting more and more interested in things that don't interest Jock and me very much.

I must say our crowd is much to be preferred to another one somewhat contiguous to ours, that is, we get together with them for the big parties but seldom see each other at smaller events. I have wondered how these sheep and goats get separated. Certainly we all look pretty much the same and have houses and cars that are about the same and the children are all very young. The only difference, certainly a major one, is something I find hard to believe. But I have heard it from so many different people that I have decided it must be true that the other crowd does trade husbands and wives quite a lot just like in some chi-chi novel. Jock refuses to consider that there is a grain of truth in it. He says some practical joker has made it all up and a few eager gossips then spread the word. I am afraid, though, that Jock is mistaken. So far there have been only three divorces that I know of, a rather small number considering how large the group is and how common divorces are. I suppose some modern thinkers would say the divorce rate is low because these people don't have to get divorced and married again in order to change sexual partners. Maybe there is something in that.

But the whole thing is incomprehensible to me. I don't mean that I never think another man is attractive, but I certainly have no desire to go to bed with anyone but Jock. What's wrong with those girls? Or is it something wrong with me? I suppose men are more or less inclined to be promiscuous or at least to have the yen to be. Are women basically the same but have just been inhibited in our culture? I know I'm not a glamorous woman but I swear I would have to be darned hard up before considering going to the trouble, the nuisance, really, of getting together with somebody else's husband. Maybe with the pill, you don't have the worries that kept clandestine amour down in the olden days, but a certain amount of secrecy surely would still have to be practiced unless you wanted the children and the hired help and the neighbors in on the deal. To say nothing of somebody like me, kept informed by several very busy little bodies who may, for all I know, be sore because they aren't in any of the sophisticated games of Post Office with a Purpose.

Jock would be more fun, really, if he could be persuaded to believe that at least some hankypanky is going on. But he won't believe it or anyway won't talk about it. So I tell Gran what my little catbirds tell me, and we have great fun talking about who may be having whose child next. At least Gran always claims you cannot depend on the pill for sure. Just how she knows is not clear. But Gran is a circus. She is a fund, a great scrap box, storehouse, and treasure chest of the damndest so-called information. She's a woman who remembers what she read in the medical column five years ago. Or she almost remembers it. Anyway, she remembers enough of what you never knew, or have long since forgotten, to force you to accept what she says, at least while you are still in her company and under the spell of what to me has always been a rather hypnotic personality. I have been fortunate to have her. Although I can say in all honesty that I was grossly neglected by my mother, I would be lying if I moaned very much about it, because Gran filled in admirably and she still does. I don't think my children can understand that she is a great-grandmother. She's the typical grandmother. My mother not only seems and looks too young, but she simply isn't interested in accepting the role the children don't offer her, not as long as they have Gran. They gravitate naturally to Daddy who is a better grandfather than he was a father. I think he would have been a splendid father if he could only have had the job on a part-time basis. Maybe it was due to Mother's paying us so little attention, but I know that Daddy got more of us than he really cared for. If he finds his grandchildren more interesting than his children were, it could be because he isn't with them for any great lengths of time.

Wally's and Bébé's children—four at present count—are an interesting combination of their parents. Each has a definitely oriental look but something of Wally, too. The two youngest and our two play together just fine for sometimes as long as an hour. Then everybody gets tired and begins to want the same toys. A family get-together becomes strenuous toward the end of the party. But Wally's house is enormous and Bébé has the charm, and the money, that enables a woman to keep excellent help. I suppose I should have the dinner next year if we don't go to the farm, which I hope we will not do, but I can't compete with my brother's wife.

Although I would have had plenty of time to write on this apparently endless venture in self-given psychotherapy, I broke off at the end of the above paragraph and just didn't get back to my desk, except for writing thank-you notes to Jock's family, until now. I skipped most of the daytime parties during the holidays and got us out of all but two of the evening things. Maybe I wouldn't have thought about it if Marianne hadn't put the bug in my ear in the early fall, but I began to suspect that Jock and I were both headed for mental breakdowns. It seemed imperative that we stop going to parties for a while. I didn't have to say anything to Jock. He always leaves the social planning up to me and doesn't know from one day to the next where we're going unless I tell him. And then he usually forgets and has to be reminded when he comes home from the office if we're going out to dinner or something.

I expected him to wonder why the sudden unpopularity, but he said nothing until I asked how he was liking a vacation from Christmas festivities. He hadn't thought about it, he said, but if he had, just would have assumed that people were finally beginning to get some sense. When I told him what parties I had declined or, I should be ashamed to say, got us out of after having accepted them a long time before, he said he was really grateful. "I've been a little tired," he said.

"Isn't the pressure ever going to let up?" I asked.

"Keri," he said, "I don't think I can stick it much longer. It just isn't my kind of outfit. Prentice isn't my kind of person."

"He's not my kind either, really," I said, "but, Jock, he could be worse, don't you think?"

"Why, yes, of course he could be. He has many fine characteristics. He doesn't scream when he's confronted by an unreasonable union demand, as he often is. He keeps his promises, anyway most of them and has a good excuse when he doesn't and . . ."

"But, Jock, he's going to make you a vice-president the first of the year," I said. "He practically told me so."

"But can that change anything?"

I wanted to say it certainly could change our income, could make the difference between day and night in my bookkeeping if the old man came through as handsomely as I thought he would for vice-president. But since Jock is a person who doesn't seem to think about the financial aspect of a thing until there's nothing else to think about, I hated to mention money. I have always been critical of the women who push and push their husbands until you think they shouldn't be surprised if the poor guys drop dead at fifty. But we're in a situation now where we just have to have more money. Often, late at night, I think how we could get out from under so easily by selling the house. Prices keep going up. We could pay our debts and go into an apartment or find a cheaper house. But Mr. Prentice wouldn't like it; he wanted us to have this house. If we don't string along

123

with him, can Jock expect to continue to hold an important job at the plant or to go up higher in rank and income?

I am sorry, deeply sorry, that Jock can't have what he wants. I suppose we never should have gone with Prentice in the first place. We should have stayed with the Chicago lab and been poor as churchmice all our lives? And had our children stuck in the miserable Chicago public school situation and all of us caught in a deteriorating neighborhood? Why don't the research people get paid more? Jock says because you don't have to shower happy workers with money, because they like their work, I suppose because they are dreamers first of all.

The Prentice lab isn't what it was cracked up to be when Jock took the job. He had great hopes of developing it into a major facility and was started on this when Mr. Prentice suddenly decided he was "far too valuable a man to be left stewing in the sulphuric." So Jock was snatched from the lab and made a kind of general assistant to the president. Jock says it translates into being office and whipping boy. In this job he is finding out how business becomes Big. A fellow like my brother Wally would glory in the opportunity, but Jock finds it more than just dull. He was sour on the job even before Prentice began making a grab for and getting government contracts. So it isn't just the war part that has got him down.

Is it my duty to urge him to look around for something else he would like better? Is it up to me to decide to give up the house and all? Jock's the one with the brains, the one who can make it in a big way in business if he wants to or who can bury himself in research the rest of his days if he would rather. Recently when he was talking about a program Maxwell University has set up in which people can teach part of the time and spend the other part in research in the school's new, largely government financed laboratories, I wondered if he might be thinking about applying for a place in it. I wondered if maybe he was just sounding me out. Or perhaps all he was doing was what was obviously natural for him to do, simply commenting on a plan he found interesting in an entirely impersonal way.

I don't know. I go around feeling guilty all of the time, feeling as if I'd been the one who got us into this house deal and all and as if I should do something to get us completely out of it. But if Jock is made a vice-president he'll have more independence and won't have to be so constantly in Mr. Prentice's company, which should perk him up considerably and believe me if he gets the raise that should go with such a promotion, I'll perk up, too.

*L*ooking at my calendar's final page for the year, I got to wondering if Jock might bring news of his promotion the afternoon of New Year's Eve. But when he came, he didn't look like the bearer of good news. The plant had closed early. Mr. Prentice had decided against the New Year's party, as well as the Christmas one, and had given everybody a bottle of liquor instead. (There'd been a terrible accident on the highway on the way home from the Christmas party last year. Although it hadn't been the Prentice man's fault, the fact that he was quite drunk didn't help his side of the case.)

Reminding Jock that we would be going to the Chambers' for a late dinner, I suggested that he try to take a nap. A high school girl, a senior and very level-headed, was coming to stay with the children and all night, since we would be very late. "I'll give the children their supper around six," I said. "It will be so late before we have anything but snacks that I think you and I should have some soup and salad."

"Okay," he said.

"But if you can sleep longer than six, I wish you would. We aren't due there until eight-thirty and so you can have your supper as late as seven-thirty or so, if you like."

He said okay again and started down the hall. Then, turning, he said, "The Old Man decided now wouldn't be the time to change my status."

"Oh, Jock . . . I'm terribly sorry," I said. I was crushed, of course.

"He says having it come now might give some of the others ideas and that we'll sort of ease into it. I don't know just how he means. Maybe put only one letter at a time of the title on my door?"

"I don't see how he can do that to you," I said. "He practically promised me . . ."

"Oh, I got the raise," said Jock.

"My God," I said, "why didn't you say so? I'm having heart failure. What do you mean, *the* raise? Just *a* raise or really *the?*"

"Thirty," he said.

"That's *the* one, boy," I shouted and threw myself into his arms. "Why didn't you tell me first thing! My God, honey, you'll get the title later on and so don't be so down about it. It's wonderful, just wonderful."

He didn't push me away but he certainly didn't return my hug. "Yes, it's a lot of money," he said.

I let go of him and he went on into the bedroom. I started to follow him, but suddenly I felt shy and almost afraid. Although it seemed ridiculous, I became ashamed of the enthusiasm I had shown. Was it that Jock had become so sophisticated about money? Or was it that he was feeling more and more trapped in a job he neither liked nor felt he could be proud of?

But I was the one keeping the family books. I was the one who knew so well that without a substantial raise we couldn't keep on in our present way of living. Was it foolish of me to have banked on that raise? But what alternative had I had? I'd had either to get a new wagon or keep on paying more and more upkeep on the old one. I couldn't take Karen out of her school because the tuition, already sky-high, had been raised, could I? Not when everybody else was going along with the raise and saying how important a good foundation was and what all you got at private school that you didn't get at public.

But now I would be able to pay the extra tuition without having to put other bills off. And I could send Andy to the school next year. I could get the damn furniture all paid for in a couple more months instead of humiliating myself by asking that dreadful woman if I could pay every other month. I know the kind of pride I have is not admirable and that Jock doesn't understand it at all. I don't blame him, but I don't blame myself, either, for the pickle we got ourselves into by going way over our heads when we came to Elk Run. It was Mr. Prentice's fault. But the Old Man was coming through and would continue to look after Jock if Jock would just let him. *That,* I could see now, was my big problem. I could do all right on what Mr. Prentice paid Jock. I could live the way Mr. Prentice wanted his favorite employe to live and could provide him with a showcase house for his business entertaining. However, how long was I going to be able to keep Jock in line?

At what point would Jock simply say he'd had it and walk out on Mr. Prentice? I told myself he couldn't do a thing like that. I told myself when it came to choosing between his family's welfare and his principles, if it should ever come to such a drastic pass, Jock would simply have to decide in favor of his wife and children. I told myself that but didn't feel too sure.

Really, by the time Jock came to the kitchen for a bite to eat, I'd got myself quite down in the dumps. Here my husband had brought home the news that he'd been raised to thirty thousand a year and I was feeling as cast down as I would have if he'd said he'd been fired. I told myself I needed a drink but of course I didn't have one. I would later on. Maybe more than one.

I answered the telephone when it rang, because I was closer. It was Norma. After wishing me a Happy New Year, she asked to speak to her brother. She talked to him for a good ten minutes. What he said didn't give me an inkling of what the conversation was about. It ended with him telling her to wish the folks a Happy New Year's Eve. He said he would call them sometime tomorrow. Although he always calls them on holidays when we aren't at their house, I thought his mention of calling tomorrow meant that Norma had been telling him something about their folks. I decided one of them must not be well, but when Jock hung up he said he supposed it was a miracle Norma hadn't had a fight with the school people before.

"What school people?"

"All of them, I guess," he said. "First she had a run-in with the principal. So she took her grievances to the school board and got them to call a special meeting last night. I gather what she was after was to get them to oust the principal, but instead she evidently got them all so mad at her that they took his side. At which point she told them they would have to choose between them." He shook his head.

"So I suppose she quit when they didn't choose her?"

He nodded.

"Well, where do you come in? Does she want you to find her a job?"

"She's decided to come to Maxwell to work on her doctorate," he said.

I had warmed his soup up and now I put it back at his place on the kitchen snack bar. The doorbell rang and Karen shouted that she would go, that it was the sitter and so I didn't leave the kitchen but just called hello to the girl as she came into the house. "She isn't planning to stay *here*, by any chance," I said.

"Not by any chance," he said. "Wait a minute, honey . . . it would be only until she finds a place."

"Then I'll find her a place," I said. "I'll start working on it right away."

Jock said I wouldn't need to because the reason Norma had called was to let us know she would be coming to look into the arrangements for herself. She would arrive the following Monday so she could start interviewing people about the courses she would be taking. "*She* will be interviewing *them?*" I said.

"She will," said Jock. "So I wouldn't take it too seriously. If she starts telling the graduate school how to run its business, she probably won't be coming to school here after all. The amazing thing is that she lasted as long as she did in that teaching job."

"Well, let's forget her and celebrate," I said. "I don't know about you, but it's certainly going to take a load off my mind to get the furniture paid for, to say nothing of some other bills that have been hanging around too long. Jock, it's so wonderful, I mean, for anybody actually to get such a salary . . . it just doesn't seem real, does it?"

He said no, it didn't.

We went to the Chambers'. Most of the people were those we enjoyed being with and, as usual, Marianne had planned a marvelous dinner. It was eleven thirty before we got organized to go to the City Club. Then everybody began to rush around so we would be sure to make it by midnight. Two couples decided to leave their cars at the Chambers' so Jock could drive them home. "That way," said one of the girls, "we don't need to be nervous about what we drink."

And that way, I knew, it would mean that we would have to stay until the last dog was hung. So, looking at Jock's weary face I said I was sorry to spoil any of their fun but that we weren't going on to the dance. "We've got just a little high school girl with the children and so we have to be getting on home," I said.

Before they could do more than start to protest I found Marianne, told her I was sorry we wouldn't be able to round the evening off with the rest of the party, but that we had had the best of it, of course. She wasn't feeling any pain and although she protested, she didn't seem to mind too much.

"But didn't you want to go?" asked Jock on the way home.

"I got tired and sort of bored," I said, although this wasn't true.

"Yes, it was duller than usual," he said, "but I thought you wanted to dance."

"Not with drunks," I said, and he said we would have to go to the Miramar Ballroom again soon.

We're always saying this and always telling Dora, whenever we see her, that we're going to join her for sure some Sunday soon. But we never do. There's always something else or we are too tired or don't have a sitter. Something.

"I won't say I'm not very glad to get back home," said Jock

after we'd put the car up. "Thanks a lot, Keri. I appreciate it."

I said not to give it another thought, that I'd just been thinking of myself. I suppose I could have added that I had also been thinking of Norma.

I look out of the window a good deal. Directly south is the parking lot where I can see some activity, although when I am occupying the storeroom in Administration none but staffers are driving in or out. Beyond is Martin House, my home from home. (And where might home have been?) To the west is the group of buildings where La Salle is. I don't know which one it is and don't want to. I haven't walked in that part of the grounds since being transferred. I'm sure nobody would ever want to go back there, even just to look around. It would have to be your job before you could go willingly to such places.

Miss Hazel told me when she got her twenty-five-year citation she informed the superintendent, not the present one, that if he wanted her another twenty-five years he would have to guarantee she wouldn't ever have to work the back wards again. He said he couldn't promise a thing like that and spoke of the challenge of the back wards. "I told him I'd been challenged enough and that now I would take my licking like a man and retreat to where it's easier. He made like I was kidding, but they never got me back out there again. Oh, they're disciplining me a little right now." She winked when she said that. She pretends that she prefers being in a men's building. "They don't chatter around so much. Here it's just gabble, gabble, all day long and half the night." But she doesn't fool me. I know she doesn't care who is listening just so they are capable of absorbing her words or at least able to give her that impression.

The nurses and attendants are like crowned heads among their subjects. None but the miserable Leona dares tangle with them. Most of the staff people have learned to protect their pride and dignity by ignoring Leona, but I would be willing to guess that Hazel has tried often to get the woman sent back to La Salle. There's evidently some pull. Leona speaks of a relative in the state government, and I think maybe for once she is telling the truth. But whoever is influential enough to have her in Apple-wood's best facility isn't going to spring her, evidently, while she is still a headache to those around her.

I speculate a good deal about the people I live with. Some tell you their life history, but of course you can never be sure that it's true. I am not asked many questions about my past but when I am, I just say, "But didn't you know I've got amnesia and can't remember anything that happened before I came to Apple-wood?" I wonder if Dr. Leonard and Mr. Kincaid are waiting for me to begin to dish out fragments of history gathered from the manuscript they have provided?

I do not say I am not sorry for Keri, or the Other Caroline, but she just isn't a type I care for. I know you can't feel very sorry for people for whom you have no real sympathy, but I am trying to make myself always remember that nobody would be like Keri on purpose. She was going downhill mentally when she started the book now in my hands and is in pretty bad shape, in my opinion, where I left off a few minutes ago.

I get so disgusted with her that I have to start working on something else or just look out of the window. Now and then I dip back to previous chapters to see if I remember correctly about something or other she's said. It's fair enough for a woman

133

to be leery of single men who apparently have no good reason for not getting married and so why not vice versa? Of course Keri was no ancient when she and Jock met, but she wasn't a career-minded girl and she was twenty-five. She'd attended a coeducational college and so wouldn't Jock wonder how come she wasn't engaged or married? If he did, he showed no signs of it, anyhow not as depicted by Keri. He was lonely and in a difficult job that is discriminated against even when held by people who have sought that kind of work. But he had the count of being a pacifist against him, too, as well as that of being a mental hospital worker. Miss Hazel has told us how it can be. She says it's practically the same as with patients and so we shouldn't think we're the only ones. "They say you must be crazy to want to work in such a place and I say well, of course it helps." Then she laughs in a way that sounds crazy enough, all right. Well, I guess Jock was a little touched or he wouldn't have gone for Keri the way he did.

Of course he was homesick and she reminded him of his sister. He didn't know this girl was really desperate to catch a husband. She admits it. She admits she would have married Harlan Bremer if she could have got him and I think they would have been a good pair, both ambitious for the Big Buck. But Harlan wasn't going to marry anybody who didn't have a dowry and so that was that.

I don't say Keri is unique. I know (although how I know any such thing is a mystery to me) that the suburbs are full of young women who are driving young men onward and upward to heart attacks. Keri can't see this. All she sees is that she, too, is the victim of a big-business boss who wants them to fit into his picture of the ideal young executive and wife. All along Keri's been pushing Jock toward bigger things. She has to get him away from a small potatoes job in Chicago and then away from an apartment into a lavish house in an exclusive area. She blames Mr. Prentice but is working hand in glove with him. She's about to die of disappointment when Jock says he didn't get the promotion, but recovers the instant he mentions that he got the raise. So who cares about anything else? And they actually want me to accept this woman's past as mine!

"What's eating you?" asked Aggie as we walked toward

134

Martin after meeting at the fork in the Administration sidewalk. "You seem so blue all of the time."

"Pardon me if I've stopped turning handsprings."

"But, Caroline, you'll be going home soon."

"So will everybody."

"Not Leona. Not me."

"Don't classify yourself with that one."

"I don't. She'll be staying because she's still too sick for her family to endure. I'll be staying because I don't have anybody and can't go back to teaching right away . . . if ever."

"What do you mean, if ever?"

She shrugged. "I try to face the possibility."

She's a big, homely woman, maybe thirty-five. I like to look at her strong face and I imagine the kids in her class did, too. But whether the teacher shortage is acute enough for them to overlook a mental illness history I wouldn't know.

The attendant who checks us in was on the front stoop at Martin and we told her we would sit out on one of the benches for a while. It was all right with her. We, even Leona, all have ground privileges, but you aren't supposed to wander off without telling where you're going and when. Leona finally got it through her head that she must stay on the grounds if she doesn't want to be bounced back to La Salle again, which used to happen to her regularly whenever she would run away. Now she stops just short of the fence and gates and stares out at the highway. I suppose she gives passing motorists quite a thrill. "Look quick," they probably say, "there's one of them now."

Sitting on the bench with Aggie, I was greatly tempted to tell her about myself, about the manuscript, about the transplant. I knew I could trust her to keep the story to herself. But could I trust her to believe it? In her place, would I? Just because you yourself are a mental patient doesn't mean you're going to believe everything another patient says. Indeed, you are less likely to believe everything you hear, I suspect, because through long exposure to myth you know that's more what you're likely to get. No, Aggie would try to pretend, but she wouldn't be able to believe what I cannot prove. I could easily convince her that Keri's story is, in actuality, the Other Caroline's, that is, she would soon see for herself that Keri Dunlop and Caroline Kincaid must be one and the same. But the rest of it, no. There wouldn't be any use in trying and it would just make our relationship difficult.

Still, that particular afternoon, I was very near to confiding in Aggie and I think I would have if she hadn't quite unexpectedly begun talking about herself, something she rarely does. For the first time she told me about getting a letter from one of her former apartmentmates, also a teacher. When they had been unable to waken her one morning, the roommates had first called the school doctor and then, since he thought it was attempted suicide, the police. It was awhile before the case came to the attention of a doctor who recognized the catatonic trance. Then she was transferred to the psychiatric ward of the hospital to which she had been taken and then later on brought out to Applewood. She heard nothing from the roommates until she was transferred from La Salle to Martin. The letter came from the older one who told her the younger one had got married and that she herself was moving to another city and so must clear out the storeroom. What did Aggie want done with her things? She said the place would have to be cleaned out before the end of the month and closed the letter with best wishes.

Aggie took the letter to the young doctor in charge of her case and evidently something about it got under his collar. Anyway he said for Aggie to telephone the roommate from his office. So she did. "She nearly fell dead when she heard my voice. I hadn't thought much until then about not hearing from the girls before. If I'd thought about it at all I would have decided the hospital had told them it would be better for me not to get letters or have visitors. I mean, you don't see people you've lived with for five years and liked a lot just washing their hands because what hit you was a mental illness. . . . Well, I told her to call Good Will and ask them to pick the things up and she said all right, she would. Said it as if this would be doing quite a big favor. After we hung up, I got to thinking about the things that weren't in the storeroom and I mentioned them to the doctor, my mother's silver service and flatware that we girls had been using. Well, he looked down at the telephone number he'd copied onto his desk pad when he'd got it from Information after I'd said I just couldn't be sure of it . . . and he called it and while I was sitting there told her I had changed my mind about giving the things to Good Will. "You just ship it all out here," he said, "and then she can decide for herself what to keep. And be sure to see that the silver is adequately insured." Aggie laughed. "I could hear her when she said, 'The silver!' He said yes, the silver service and all the flatware and she said she didn't understand because I'd given that to her. I think if he'd asked me then if I'd given it to her I probably would have said yes, I mean, it was so embarrassing and when you've been mentally ill how can you be sure what you've given away or said or done? But he didn't ask me, he just said he was sure she was mistaken and so would she please send all of my possessions to the hospital. 'I have a list," he said. I guess she hung up on him. However, the only things that were missing were quite small, I mean, nothing really worth mentioning and so I didn't tell the doctor or his wife—she helped me sort and repack the stuff. Some of it could be used by the hospital and some we just threw away, I mean, people save things that will never be of any earthly use. But I'll have all my mother's good silver when I set up housekeeping again."

"All but what that woman stole."

"Oh, well, it wasn't too much. And anyway, just think what would have happened if the doctor hadn't bothered. She would have had all of it. Or—it sort of haunts me—do you think that just before I got sick I might have given it to her?"

"I do not," I said, "and even if you had, she would have known later on that you weren't in any condition to be giving away heirlooms."

"I get a card from the doctor's wife now and then," said Aggie. "He's in private practice in Cleveland now. I want to leave the silver to them."

"Then you better talk to a good lawyer. If you don't have it spelled out in your will, some cousin's going to turn up and claim everything."

"I don't have any relatives anymore," she said. "I did have cousins but not anymore."

"When people are in mental hospitals, they're forgotten. Maybe their friends and relatives can't actually forget them but they sure make a good stab at it. Look how few of the patients

137

here have any visitors. Is it possible for so many to be without kith or kin? Of course not. But you can be sure there are always heirs when there's an estate to be divided up."

But, knowing Aggie doesn't have anybody very close, I've been wondering if after I got a pretty good job I might rent an apartment and ask Aggie to share it. She could look after the apartment while getting back on her feet enough to look for another teaching job or some other position in case they won't take her back in teaching. I think we could get along all right.

I wish I could discuss it with Mr. Kincaid. But he seems to see my future as definitely as he sees the Other Caroline's past, and expects me to accept it. I see him every Saturday and Sunday, as usual. I don't know if it's a habit I could break even if I tried; that is, could I get the hospital to tell him not to come any more? They would just think I'd slipped a few notches, that's all.

But I don't feel so trapped by the present pattern, by Applewood, Dr. Leonard, and Mr. Kincaid as I do by my inability to create a past for myself that would be my ultimate successful defense against the Other Caroline.

NINETEEN

The Manuscript

It's been weeks since I've written anything but checks. Since I'd got pretty far behind and since the new money of course doesn't descend all at once, I don't feel quite so rich as I'd thought I would. Helen Marie hit me for a raise almost before I'd been able to figure out approximately what Jock's paycheck would be. I told her quite frankly if she could manage the work in two days instead of three it would be one thing, but that I simply cannot go any eighteen dollars a day three times a week. She seemed startled when I said eighteen dollars and said I must not have heard what she said. I reminded her that on top of her pay is her train fare, with bus at the other end, and her social security. Actually it would come to a few cents over eighteen. "Well," she said, "I don't know if I can do it all in two days. I only come Fridays when there's so much extra. I'd a whole lot rather stay home and do my own work on Friday."

For a couple of weeks she did stay home and do her own work on Friday, or anyway she wasn't here. But then Trouble came, meaning Norma, and since then I have not been in any position to tell Helen Marie she ought to get her work done in two days. I keep my fingers crossed. Helen Marie isn't a woman who is going to take any pushing around. I keep telling Norma we have to tread gently there, that Helen Marie is a very sensitive person and can't take criticism. But Norma continues to criticize. She says I spoil help and don't keep them in their place. I asked her what she meant by "their place," was she suggesting the help are inferior persons? This made Norma very angry. She preached me quite a sermon about all persons being born equal. It seems that she and Helen Marie were born equal, all right, but then Norma got ahead, not through any of God's doing because He, of course, wouldn't favor one of His children over the other. Norma got ahead on her own. I condense and naturally make my sister-in-law sound even stupider than she is, but I haven't gone too far afield from her general line. "It doesn't have anything to do with color," she said. As Gran would say, "In a pig's eye."

When Norma first came we had no idea it would be for anything but a few days. I think she thought this, too. It may be that somewhere in her subconscious she had decided not to be satisfied with anything she found near the campus. I can't say she didn't try. She was off looking for rooms or small apartments for a good part of each day for a week. Nothing suited her. She had got herself accepted in the graduate school and all signed up and was beginning to sound frantic about no place to live. She said it would be foolish to take a place where she couldn't even breathe because how could she study if she couldn't even breathe? Jock didn't say anything. I am not sure he heard. He was deeper and deeper in his shell since his sister had come.

We didn't offer. To anyone else it would have been obvious that we didn't want her to stay with us. Norma isn't stupid, not really. She just doesn't give a damn about the other fellow. I think the only reason she looked as hard as she did for a place on or near the campus was because the children get on her nerves. When I said something about how convenient some of the places she had looked at would be, she said since she intended to keep on using her car there was no reason why she had to be walking distance from classes. Realizing that the children were the fly in her ointment, next to me, I couldn't help rejoicing when they obviously drove her nuts. Sometimes she would break her rigid silence during their roughhousing and say, "That's hardly the way little ladies and gentlemen behave." She kept her mouth shut when Jock was around, that is, about the children's racket. On other subjects she was voluble. When Jock was at home she acted like a hostess nervous about any pause in the conversation.

She talked about brushing up before school actually started, but although she would hold a book while spending an evening with us, she didn't give it much attention. The guest room, the apple of the decorator's eye, has a lovely desk and good lamps and chairs, but does Norma do anything but sleep there? And throw her clothes around.

I get so sick of her that I turn on the television even though I know Jock would rather have it off. "I'm sorry if this bothers you, Norma," I said, "but you wouldn't notice it in your room."

"Oh, I don't mind," she says. With her martyr's sigh copied from her mother.

Jock buries his nose in the newspaper, a magazine, a book, until ten o'clock when he joins me for the news program. After the weather, we go to bed. Or, sometimes, we take a walk around Elk Run. The first time we did this, after Norma's arrival, Jock said, "Norm, I suppose we can count on you to call the fire department or the police if we should wander a little farther away from the house than usual?"

She said she thought it was shocking for parents to go off and leave little children home alone at night. "But you're here now, remember?" said Jock.

She can't get out of being "sitter" during our infrequent evening walks, but she sure turned me down the two times I asked if she would stay with them while Jock and I attended a meeting. In each case I told her we would be home before ten thirty and in each case I just happened to hit a time when she herself would be out, at the library, until ten thirty. Tough luck for us.

After three weeks of Norma, Helen Marie gave notice. I was

out the afternoon the two came to verbal blows but gather that Helen Marie said she was tired of cleaning up a hog wallow. My sympathy was with the maid even though her airs have always given me something of a pain. She's a very slick chick and looks more like a nightclub singer than a houseworker. The children adored her and are moaning around about her absence. Andy put a nice question to the subject. "Why can't Helen Marie have the guest room instead?" I told him Helen Marie isn't his aunt. He said he would start calling her aunt right away and wanted me to telephone her to say so. Karen's view is more mature, naturally, but she agrees with Andy that Helen Marie would be a more desirable person to have living in. So do I.

Norma had no compunction about being the cause of Helen Marie's departure. She speaks of modern appliances and of what a breeze keeping house is. Also she speaks frequently of the importance of a mother being with her small children all of the time. In other words, I shouldn't go to meetings. Also, Karen shouldn't be going to nursery school. Thank heaven, Norma doesn't know what the tuition is.

The domestic problems, chiefly Norma, hold me so fixed that I haven't even hinted at the family's Big Event, the major aspect of which is that it just might lead to our getting Norma off our backs.

For years Daddy has submitted Mother's books to the Wirth Foundation contests held every other year, which is about Mother's production schedule. The contest isn't open for manuscripts, but there is no objection to vanity publication since trade publication of poetry is scanty. Up to this year, all Mother got in return for Daddy's trouble in filling out the applications and sending the books has been rejections, sometimes just printed with a word or two of personal comment and sometimes with a nice letter. These have always pleased Mother but infuriated Daddy. Mother has never been humble about her work. What pleases her about a personal rejection is it indicates that somebody has perhaps got a faint glimmer of her art.

Well, this year, just as Daddy was about to wire the Wirth people an indignant request for an explanation about why they hadn't returned Mother's new entry, *The Different One*, here came their telegram announcing that she'd won their fifteen hundred dollars. You would think it was fifteen thousand. Daddy has done everything but telephone the news to the President. Mother takes it in stride.

Unfortunately (well, it depends on the viewpoint), she expressed her attitude when interviewed by telephone by a reporter for one of the national news weeklies. His call was probably pretty routine for him until, after he asked if she had been surprised, she said not at all, that all that surprised her was not having won the award eleven times. Evidently this tickled the reporter enough to feel a trip out to Maxwell might be justified. So he came. Before his story was published, the other big magazine sent a girl out to cover the suddenly successful poet, and Mother gave that reporter a piece of her mind, too, on the generally deplorable state of American letters, primarily poetry. She says that by taking many of her comments out of context they gave a distorted picture of her opinions but it is true that she has seldom had a good word to say for Sandburg, Frost, and other poets known to if not read by the American public. Both stories made her sound quite fierce. *Look* magazine came in late but is doing a long story with many photographs. The day *Time* and *Newsweek* came out with their stories, three New York publishers called up. Well, they don't need to think they can bamboozle the Poet Laureate of Maxwell; her big-business son has taken over. Yes, Wally speaks easily of Hollywood contracts. Mother and Daddy have promised not to lift a finger toward signing any contract until Wally has given the word.

I gather that generally the Wirth Foundation doesn't make any fuss over bestowing the award but when this year's recipient got such a lot of publicity, they decided to throw a banquet in her honor. Wally and Bébé went along, as if Mother might be kidnapped or perhaps they thought Daddy would lose the tickets if they weren't along. Bébé forced Mother to buy a dress that would set off some of her, Bébé's, jewelry, and I must say the effort was great and that Mother didn't look at all like the radical the news magazines had painted her. They didn't exactly call her a hippy but that was certainly the implication.

More trade publishers got into the act at the banquet held in New York City. Wally hasn't made up his mind yet. One thing he is insisting on is that Mother retain all motion picture, theater, and television rights. As of yesterday, he was conferring with book club people and the *Reader's Digest*. My guess, however, is that the fifteen hundred has been spent by now.

As soon as the folks got back from New York, the Kermits had a party for all of us. Dr. Kermit, now retired except for an occasional lecture, had Mother, Daddy, Wally, and me in college. His students were generally interested in writing careers but I took a course under him because I needed another English credit and had heard his class was more interesting than the others. It was interesting but it didn't give me any desire to become a professional writer. Evidently Wally was similarly affected. But we all like the old guy and his rather scatterbrained wife. They live in a wreck of a house near campus and take in grad students who are supposed to help out around the house and yard in part payment for their room and board.

Norma was invited, too. I wonder how long she will feel she should be included in all our invitations. I've quite frankly told her it isn't as if she were just passing through town and, too, that many of our friends are under the impression that she would prefer not to attend parties where all the other guests are young marrieds. Marianne is the only one who has persisted in including Norma. But after a couple of times, when I felt obliged to pass the invitation on to Norma, I told Marianne she would be doing us a favor not to include my sister-in-law. I told her Norma's on our necks every minute we are at home. I even feel she's lying awake listening at the wall between our room and hers, in the hope that she may catch a word or two or hear a spring creak. Oh, yes, if I was a little batty before she came, I probably am more than a little now.

Well, we took her along to the Kermits'. Among the guests was David Alstaire, one of their grads. He's a tall, thin, not exactly homely but not handsome Englishman with an accent that sounds like a movie meaning to be funny. Norma was wearing one of her two-sizes-too-small minidresses and looking like a masquerade party. Her hair is quite beautiful and does have enough wave in it to keep from falling entirely over her face. But it is very long and I certainly think she's too old to be wearing it so high school, just parted in the middle and hanging loose. She wears quite a bit of eye makeup and white lipstick and really gives me the creeps with her general, death-warmed-over appearance. But evidently David was attracted. He and she vanished while another roomer, one of Dr. Kermit's special pets, was reading a short story to the assemblage. I was sitting where I could see a reflection in a French window of a corner of the sun porch. I simply could not believe my eyes when only a few minutes after David and Norma vanished, a flickering in the window beside me caught my attention. And in that window I saw a clear reflection of David and Norma in a clinch I simply couldn't believe. It was the kind you see in movies for adults only, although the action is far from that. The young man's hand was under that miniskirt, which hardly covered what you might call the essentials, I suppose.

I moved the window just enough to cut the light from it. I had seen more than I cared to and I certainly didn't want anybody else to get an impression of Norma that was a new one on me. I have since wondered about her leaving the teaching job and just what might have been doing between her and the principal. But the chief thing is that now she's out of our hair occasionally, although not so often as I would like. David has taken an apartment. He told Mrs. Kermit he had to do more studying than he could manage at her house. I have no doubt whatsoever that he took the little apartment in order to have a place to sleep with Norma. Why he hadn't found a willing girl before is a question I ask myself but do not answer. I consider us lucky, that is, if Norma is able to pull it off. I don't think it's the way to catch a man, but of course I am very old fashioned and was even in my day.

On the chance that David might otherwise get the idea he can be casual about Norma, I have him to dinner or to Sunday lunch. It took Jock a while to catch on but one evening after David and Norma had left, presumably for a movie, he asked me what I was trying to do. "I think it's clear that David's interested in her," he said, "and so why are you acting like a marriage arranger?"

"Well, he's a foreigner, for one thing," I said, "and I don't want him to get the notion that American girls are an easy make. I want him to be very aware that she has people who are keeping an eye on him."

Jock laughed. "David!" he said. "Why, he's as big a stuffed shirt as Norma is an old maid."

But at least his laughter had sounded spontaneous. Even though the laugh was presumably on me, I was glad to hear it. I thought maybe things were going better at the plant, maybe Mr. Prentice was seeing that if you expanded on war contracts, you might be caught later on with far more men and equipment than you could do with.

TWENTY *The Manuscript*

*A*gain it's been a long time since I have had either the time or the inclination to work on my autobiography, my self-applied psychotherapy. I suppose one of the chief reasons, if not the main one for going to a psychologist or a psychiatrist, is that when you have an appointment you usually keep it, especially if you might be charged anyway if you failed to show up. But when it's something between you and yourself, it's easily put off.

Marianne has picked at me on the subject of my mental health several times in the past few months. Finally, in exasperation I asked her if she considers herself a psychiatrist now. This hurt her, as I would have known it would if I'd bothered to think before speaking. She's always got on my nerves. I say things to her sometimes that I don't really mean simply because I have got so tired of her. There's no excuse for it. We aren't together that much anymore. But I get tired of her sometimes when we've barely had two minutes together at some meeting. I feel a rage coming over me. It probably would worry me if I didn't know it's nothing new. They say sudden personality changes should warn of incipient mental illness, but there's nothing new about my getting irritated by Marianne. I can't explain it. I just feel that way about two people, Norma and Marianne. (I'm sure I would have to add my mother-in-law to the list if I were around her much.) But how unfair it is to couple Marianne with Norma who is such an obvious stinker, such an all-black villain-of-the-piece. The only honest criticism I could make of Marianne is that she really is a boring person. But this is not through any fault of her own. It isn't her fault that she simply isn't heavily endowed with brains. Actually her mother isn't very bright. But Mrs. Snyder considers herself endowed in all departments, whereas poor Marianne doesn't give herself much more than a passing grade in anything. I should be ashamed of myself. I am.

Another time I was more collected. "I wish you would tell me just what it is about me that's worrying you," I said.

"I was thinking of it only as prevention, a sort of insurance," she said.

"But what made you think of it at all? You don't mean you go around recommending psychiatric treatment for everybody you know, do you?"

"I'm sure it would be helpful," she said.

"Get down to cases, please. What am I doing that strikes you as being nutty?"

"But nothing, nothing, I don't see how you could even think . . ."

"Something got you started on this tack," I said. "The first time was when we had lunch at that French place in Wally's Village Green, the one that folded practically the day it opened . . . you remember . . ."

"I felt so sorry for them but they did serve the most awful food," she said.

". . . you had been with my mother before coming to the restaurant. Was it something she said? It isn't like Mother to worry about my health."

"Keri, she's devoted to you."

"And I am devoted to her in the same way," I said, "but I don't go worrying about her health unless there's a good reason, unless she has a bad cold or something."

"As I recall she did say something that morning about your having insomnia."

"The doctor must have told her. I didn't. I don't know why I keep on going to him. He's cross as a bear and tells everything he knows."

"That's all she said. I don't know how it came up. I don't remember what we'd been talking about. I might have said I hadn't slept too well the night before . . . yes, that must have been it. I have a restless night once a month if I'm not pregnant. Then she said you'd been having some insomnia but that she was never bothered that way. I'm sure that was all there was to it but on the way to the restaurant I got to thinking you'd been looking tired . . ."

"Who isn't looking tired? Who isn't tired?" I asked. "Tell me who isn't always on the run. Give me ten years and I'll not have insomnia anymore. No, better make it twenty because by then Karen and Andy will both be well out of my hair."

"Oh, Keri, you know they're wonderful children."

"I didn't say they aren't. I am not blaming them for driving their mother mad and according to you it would be, instead of a drive, a short putt?"

"If you and Jock could just take a trip or something . . ."

"But I thought you preferred to have me go in for psychiatric treatment."

"Keri, all I wanted you to do was make one appointment with Dr. Lester . . ."

"Because of my insomnia?"

"Yes."

"And only because of that?"

"It's silly to be dependent on pills if you can solve whatever the problem is."

"As of now I have a big fat sister-in-law problem," I said.

"I know," said Marianne. "But maybe she and David will get married."

"And maybe they won't," I said. "How long do you suppose he's going to think it's cute when she tells him he's an idiot and that all Englishmen are stupes? He's supposed to come back next fall on a part-time teaching and studying basis, but do you think he will?"

Marianne thought he would. At the small dinner party I had just before he was to leave, somebody, bidding him good-bye, said, "Hurry back." In her inimitable way Norma snapped, "He doesn't need to on my account." David didn't sound very amused when he laughed. He said lightly that what Norma wanted was his apartment. The conversation shifted before she could say anything to that, but after the guests had left, I asked if she were taking over David's apartment and she said, "Why should I, just because he wants me to, just because he's too lazy to find a sublet for himself?"

I don't think all was lost until she made it very clear to him that she would not take his apartment for the summer even though she planned to attend summer school. He probably never suspected that she doesn't pay rent here. I heard him say that in order to keep the apartment so he could have it next fall, he would be willing to sublet as cheaply as anybody could get a room in one of the boardinghouses. I'm sure he didn't know what low rent he was competing with. Such as zero.

After I complained to him about it, Jock did tell Norma he expects her to pay for her toll and long-distance telephone calls. She said her long-distance calls, restricted to calls to the farm, were as much his as hers and that she was very sorry if he was worried about the occasional nickel she may have cost him. That was the last of that. Jock seems too tired to think about anything that isn't business. I ask him how things are going at the plant and he says okay. He makes me feel so guilty. I am so relieved to be making a good dent on our debts, but he makes me feel guilty about the relief. It is as if somehow I had sold his soul to Mr. Prentice. Oh, I know Jock surely can't feel this way about it, but I find myself haunted by an uncomfortable impression, when writing checks, of sending out money that isn't rightly ours. Why do I feel this way? Jock puts in more time than anybody else at the plant. He didn't ask for that big raise. Mr. Prentice gave it without being asked. It shouldn't be long before the vice-presidency is announced. I don't expect any further raise but know Mr. P. could do it if he wanted to.

Mrs. Kermit told Gran and Gran told me that David Alstaire did sublet his apartment just before he left for England. A young couple, both in grad school, took it even though it's smaller than they want—the girl's pregnant. But the baby isn't expected until the middle of August and, in any case, David wants the apartment back the first of September. The young couple will continue looking for a larger apartment this summer. So far no letter for Norma has come from England. She's more irritable than ever. I feel sure she and David broke up before he left. Mrs. Kermit thinks so, too. In fact, she thinks he wouldn't have gone home at all this summer if he hadn't wanted to get away from Norma. Naturally she said this to Gran in confidence, but Gran told her she didn't need to worry, that I had been wondering how the affair had lasted as long as it had.

In the meantime, Norma has gone out once with one of the Kermits' other young men. I recognized him when he came for her. He didn't come to the door, but just sat out at the curb until she went out to his car. I imagine she had told him to do this. I wonder where they went. Although the University is now allowing mixed-student visiting, the Kermits won't let their students entertain girls in their rooms. I have such a low opinion of Norma that I can't imagine a man dating her for any reason other than getting some free sex.

It has occurred to me several times that I may indeed be off my rocker and inventing all of this. I did not invent the passionate kiss I saw reflected at the Kermits', but I have nothing else to go on and for all I know Norma never allows anything more than necking. It would seem more in keeping with her type for her to be a tease rather than a girl who allows great liberties because she intends to follow all the way through. Still, as Marianne so obviously believes, something may be wrong with me.

Maybe what troubles her is what is making Jock so withdrawn. Maybe he isn't really so worried about the business as I think. The last time I asked him if Prentice were still sending electronic equipment out to Vietnam he just shrugged and said he wasn't keeping any particular track of what went where. "Not what I'm paid to do," he said.

Well, he is certainly paid handsomely and yet it is amazing how quickly the new money gets absorbed. I can't help hoping Mr. Prentice will see fit to back the rise in title up with at least an added five thousand.

TWENTY-ONE *The Manuscript*

Publication of *The Different One* is slated for September. No book club acknowledged receipt of what Daddy sent, but the *Reader's Digest* is still interested if, they say, Mother will compromise on the matter of format. So far Mother is saying the hell with them, trying to turn my poetry into prose. Wally says this isn't the point, that it is a matter of economics. "Since when did those people ever have to worry about economics?" says Mother. "I've heard *plenty*." No telling from whom or what about, but if she's decided to apply it to the present situation nothing will stop her. Wally is frantic. He keeps saying it isn't the money, it's the general principle of the thing, plus the wonderful coverage the *Digest* would give her.

"But whoever said I wanted coverage?" asked Mother. "As for money, Wally, do you know the book is selling as high as fifty dollars . . . that people who have Daddy's first edition are getting fifty dollars for it now?"

"But Daddy isn't and neither are you," says Wally and on and on it goes.

Well, I hear things too. It's odd what people will say they feel they "have" to tell you because it's something "you ought to know, dear." It seems that according to this self-appointed dear friend of mine, Mother's book is getting a lot of underground publicity about being dirty. Hero is "different" because he's a homosexual, see.

"You mean you actually think that's different these days?" I asked the slob.

"There's more to it than that," she said. "They say it's full of sexual symbolism but of course I wouldn't know, never having so much as seen a copy."

She had already hinted that my good deed for the day would be giving or at least lending her a copy.

"My mother wouldn't ever monkey around with symbols if she wanted to get something about sex across," I said. "Of course some of her writing is a little hard to stick with, being quite complicated, but if she's writing about fornication you know it without ever having to look up your Freud notes."

"I just thought you would want to know," my chum said.

"Why?" I asked. Until then she'd worn a helpful, sort of smiling frown. Now the smile vanished.

"Well, really, Keri," she said, "I didn't think you would be so huffy when all I was doing was preparing you for what you'll be bound to hear anyway."

I wasn't able to shrug it off entirely. I told Wally. I shouldn't have been surprised by his reaction, I suppose, but I was. "Great," he said. "If that's so, we're in, really in. I told Bébé something like this was all we needed, and she said don't be ridiculous because by no stretch of the imagination could even a pervert find anything dirty in the book."

"Evidently somebody was able to."

Again Wally said he sure hoped the rumor would spread. I warned him not to say anything to the folks. "Or to Jock," I added, "if you don't mind."

"What's the matter with the guy?" asked Wally. "He's been

looking like he's lost his last friend. Prentice didn't change his mind about the raise, did he? The bastard wouldn't dare."

"It's just the title he's holding back."

"What the hell? Everybody knows Jock's second-in-command and probably Prentice's heir, too, not that he's about to kick off."

"But you know how Jock feels about the war."

"Who doesn't? And what's that got to do with Prentice Products, for God's sake? Just because they get a few government orders, you don't mean to tell me Jock . . . no, he's not that big a fool."

"He doesn't see it the way you do, Wally."

"I'd better have a talk with him."

"Oh, please don't, please, Wally. He'd think I . . . well, it would just make things worse, honestly it would. He'll stick. He knows he has to, but it would be harder for him if you mixed in, I mean, surely the less said about it the better and I shouldn't have said anything."

"You didn't have to. I had him figured," said Wally. "He sure as hell better stick. He's got obligations."

Although I agreed, I didn't like the way Wally said it, as if he'd march Jock off to jail or something if he didn't toe the mark. But, as I had said, I was sure Jock would stick. However, he didn't. He didn't give me any warning, but just came home early one afternoon last week and said he'd quit.

"My God," I said, " did you have a fight with the Old Man?"

"We didn't exactly kiss good-bye," he said. "He's giving me a three-week vacation instead of requiring me to give him three weeks' notice. And I am accepting it. It's sort of a bribe, I suppose, so maybe he can pretend he fired me rather than that I quit but if that makes him feel good, okay, okay."

"But I don't understand. What happened?"

"Nothing in particular; that is, it wasn't the first time he had practically asked me to congratulate him for getting another contract that we both know would have gone to one of the big outfits if they hadn't already got all they could handle. If he hadn't kept on talking about how he hadn't had to pull any political strings, I might have been able to keep my mouth shut. But in any event, Keri, it couldn't have been much longer. You surely know that."

I knew. Of course I knew. But that didn't make it any easier. "Well," I said after a while, "I guess I'm a good deal like Wally after all."

"There's nothing criminal in wanting to be able to meet your bills on time and have something left over," he said.

"But what will you do?"

"I'll get something. Don't worry."

"But, Jock, it would have to be something pretty great to make it possible for us to stay here."

He looked surprised. "Honey, you wouldn't want to stay on here, would you? In Prentice's house?" He laughed. "I've always felt it was more his than ours. You aren't so crazy about it yourself, are you?"

I said no, I wasn't.

All the same, when Jock began talking about his chances of getting into teaching and about wanting to try for something at the University, I couldn't help thinking about the Kermits' house, which they'd had only after he became head of his department and relatively rich for a teacher. What a poor, shabby old place it was in comparison to our fine house in Elk Run. Saying there was no sense in putting all your eggs in one basket, I suggested that Jock get in touch with the placement people he'd dealt with before. "Just in case there's nothing at the University or nothing you would want. I mean, Jock, there just might be something like with Mirex only with money, too."

He said he would call the agency up, but that he felt this would be the time for him to see if he could get into teaching with some research assignment on the side. "Or the teaching on the side, if possible," he said.

"Do you want to do something about the house right away?" I asked.

He said no, he didn't see why that couldn't wait a little. "Let me sound a few people out first," he said, "not that we would be keeping it but we ought to know a little something first about where we'll be going, don't you think? If we're staying in Maxwell and find a place right away, we could give almost immediate occupancy here . . ." As he talked he seemed to be gaining weight and losing years. I knew I should be glad. And

156

I was. But I was worried too. Who wouldn't be? However, I kept thinking about how crass Wally so often seems and how I would hate for Jock to think I'm that way, too. I tried to be gay and to talk about how this house has been getting me down, as it has.

If there's anything easier to get used to than money, I don't know what it is. Since this house was a great bargain, we could afford to buy it. What we couldn't afford was keeping it up the way houses of this type are supposed to be kept. I should have had a live-in or at least a daily maid in addition to the cleaning woman coming in twice a week. I should have had a gardener. Like everybody else in the neighborhood, I put on a big show of being mad about taking care of the garden but all the other botanical enthusiasts have gardeners. The man I had coming in once a week to do what I couldn't manage was the one who worked for nothing and who had never professed any special skill in flower beds. What he'd been brought up on was haying and milking, plowing and filling the silo.

I've got several big jobs coming up for next year. Each requires me to do quite a bit of entertaining, luncheons and teas for committee people and several bigger deals for boards on which I sit more prominently than I used to. It all not only costs money but it requires a setting not like the Kermits', you can be sure, which is bigger and better than I can aspire to if Jock should be lucky enough to get a job at Maxwell.

I've made a list of the organizations I belong to. The dues don't come to any enormous amount. If dues were all, I certainly could manage to stay on in a few of the groups. But these organizations are fund-raising clubs and a member has got to support the projects. I've never got by in any one of them under a hundred dollars for a year. Usually it's at least twice that in the groups in which I am more active. I can't pretend that I am looking forward to dropping out of everything. It would be less embarrassing, of course, if Jock should get something out of town. I don't know why he's so hipped on Maxwell University. Probably he wouldn't think it so great if he'd gone there.

But there is one bright spot, not counting how it is wonderful, of course, to have Jock cheerful again. Unless he gets some-

157

thing far better paid than either of us anticipates, what about old Norma? We just aren't going to be able to take her with us, are we?

By now she knows that Jock's left Prentice, but I don't think the logical chain of events in which she shortly leaves us has dawned on her. Well, well, well . . .

Good for Jock, good for the worm that finally turned, I have been saying to myself and barely resisting saying to Mr. Kincaid.

I didn't think he had it in him to quit Prentice without getting Keri's permission first. And she wasn't about to give it, not with thirty thousand in the hand and more about to bloom on the money tree. What a blow for her! One ending I could see for this story, if I didn't know the end that must be, is that Mrs. Prentice, invalid, would die, Keri would divorce poor Jock, who wouldn't have gumption enough to see how lucky he was, and then she would marry Mr. Prentice and be rich, rich, rich ever after. Unfortunately for me, though, what that girl is going to be is dead, dead, dead. With animation then supplied by yours truly.

I admit that Norma was a pain in the neck. But Keri should

have been adult enough to know there are things you have to do for relatives whether you like them or not. You're stuck with them, that's all. If you aren't willing to take on in-laws, you shouldn't get married.

I believe the manuscript has now entered the final phase and that I won't be getting any more material from Dr. Leonard or Mr. Kincaid. Since it was written by the lady herself, it can't go much farther now that the acute stage of her illness is approaching. Of course I'm not able to make a medical diagnosis, but I think Keri would have been headed for a nervous breakdown even if a brain tumor hadn't been involved.

The rest of the downhill journey is going to be hard for me. And knowing that it will end before I come into the picture is maddening, too. Will Mr. Kincaid ever tell me what he knows, or are he and Dr. Leonard and the others in the plot sworn to eternal secrecy?

What was I doing when Keri, I mean the Other Caroline, was nearing the end of her autobiography? Was I going to a job, keeping house, teaching school? I have no desire to remember the actual end, the automobile crash or whatever it was that closed the door on my chance ever to be a whole personality again. I could have survived being a cripple far better than I can endure what did happen.

Once I am out of Applewood, I might be able to find out who all were on the medical team that must have had an anxious time, not only when both Carolines lay dying but when the one came back to life and, for all they knew, might have been in a position to embarrass them considerably. Might my body have been rather prematurely ushered from this world? Or might the Other Caroline's brain have been removed when it was obviously not yet entirely done for? They must have been afraid of letting the operation go long enough for the cancer to spread. It occurs to me that I might be able to sue somebody. Might it have been malpractice? But how would I go about it? How could I get a lawyer to take such a case?

My position might be compared to Aggie's. She knows her former friend stole some of her valuables but she's also aware that she would have a hard time proving it. Still, it is conceivable that with that doctor's help she might, if she had the energy, get her belongings back. But I, as I existed before, am no longer available for winners or losers. The person I was before is gone. My being continues, but in another person's body.

Maybe some would consider me lucky or would remind me I could have done worse. The body they gave me is quite good-looking, I suppose. The shape is good. The skin is unwrinkled and unblemished. So what am I griping about? Have I any reason to think I was so great before?

Mr. Kincaid is a fine man and he's doing well at the University where he is so much happier than he was in business. He has two children who seem to be healthy and bright and an old house that's rather nice, somehow. I can't say I think much of some of his relatives and in-laws, not if I take the manuscript's word for them, but I'll bet you I could put up with them a lot more gracefully than the Other Caroline did. So what's the beef?

Just a matter of identity. I can survive even a permanent loss of memory just as I could have survived the loss of a limb. There are things you have to accept whether you want to or not. But how can I accept not being a person, not really, but just existing inside of somebody else's shell? I can overlook the woman's faults easily enough, I suppose. What proof do I have that I was ever any better? But to pretend that I am somebody I definitely am not is unendurable.

Riding beside Mr. Kincaid I sometimes wish history would repeat itself to the extent of removing me completely from the world. But I sure wouldn't want him to be injured. Those kids need him.

And, I am beginning to admit to myself, I need him, too. Life without Mr. Kincaid simply doesn't attract me. However, unless I can establish myself, unless I can find my true identity, I certainly cannot live with him, either. I cannot allow myself to continue in the role of the Other Caroline. The only reason I have tolerated it so long is that here nothing seems real; it is as if everybody were acting a part upon a large, very strange stage. Surely Applewood doesn't seem real to anybody. If such a place, where natural beauty contrasts so shockingly with human degradation, seemed at all real to the real world, could people tolerate its continuation?

TWENTY-THREE *The Manuscript*

*N*orma is taking it hard. Everybody else, with the exception of my brother Wally, the worshiper of the Almighty Dollar, says now is a good time for Jock to look around for something he likes better. "Change while you're young," says Daddy. Mother, ignoring the fact that there is no way to prove, anyhow not for us, that any of Prentice products contribute to the actual destruction of people in Vietnam, says it was high time for Jock to get away from the munition makers. She is writing a book about it. I think she is hoping she will be jailed for it. She and Daddy have been marching for open housing but neither is much stimulated by the demonstrations. It was more exciting a few years back when so many were actively against it. Now almost nobody says anything against open housing and all they've been doing in Maxwell, really, is to argue about the wording of various laws. The real estate people have either changed their minds or decided it wasn't so much their business before as they'd thought it was and so let other people worry.

Gran says she isn't a pacifist but that she admires Jock for his stand and that of course he couldn't work for Prentice now that they are shipping electronic devices to war areas. Wally says that while he isn't a pacifist, either, they would have to come for him if they wanted him in this one. But he thinks we're stuck in a situation and can't very well get out of it unless we fight our way out. He thinks a lot of saving our face. Bébé suggests that he wake up and come to the twentieth century, but he says we must show the world that we aren't kidding when we undertake to do a thing; we go in and do it.

"I have always thought Wally an intelligent person," said Jock. "Smart in many ways I don't understand . . . but I am beginning to change my mind. He makes money, not because he is smart but because he falls into a pattern that seems to please a great many people. They willingly contribute to his increasing fortune because they see him as the bearer of a tradition. The Alger boy."

We had come from Wally's house where we'd all had dinner. It wasn't the first time we'd been together since Jock quit his job and so there hadn't been any news to break. Everyone but Norma was perfectly calm about the fact that Jock had been out of work a month and still hadn't any sure prospect. I knew he was being considered for a new place at Maxwell University, but the job was contingent on the college's getting a government subsidy. It sounded ideal, except for salary. Jock would be teaching two hours three times a week and spending the rest of the time in the lab on pure research. It seemed almost too perfect except, as I say, for salary. But I am trying to turn back the clock to when I thought eight thousand dollars was a terrific salary. If I could just deflate the cost of living back to the same period of my so-called development, I could feel more enthusiastic about the pay. Although there is no guarantee that if they get the subsidy, it will be renewed after two years, the term of the project, the man Jock talked with said that once on the faculty he would be in a far better position to get a regular teaching job. What Jock would prefer would be the indefinite continuation of the combination work but of course he can't control that. He's very optimistic. I keep hearing and reading about the government's having to cut budgets everywhere except for killing people, and so I have no confidence in the University's ability to get this grant. But Jock says it is just a pittance from governmental standpoints.

Norma conducts herself as I would expect her to if we'd informed her that Jock is suffering from terminal cancer. She's very solicitous and uses a library voice most of the time. She hasn't blatted at the children in days.

Although we can't very well decide on a place to live when we still don't know about a job, we've told the agent who handled the deal for this house that we expect to sell it soon. He is studying the case. He has recalled that Mr. and Mrs. Ross Thermer, friends of the people who built the house, once told him they had never seen another one they liked as well. But we have asked him to wait a bit before saying anything to them. In any case, they own property that they would have to dispose of, I suppose, or would want to although, says Mr. Larch, the real estate man, they are too well off to have to sell before buying. I wonder. I just wonder how well off all of the people in all of these fine houses are. Jock and I can't be the only ones who lived always a little, and sometimes a lot, too well for the pocketbook. I blame myself far more than I ever could blame Jock, unless you should blame a man for leaving everything to his wife. Before I married Jock, I knew he wasn't one for keeping track of his finances. He told me what he had and asked if we could live on that amount and I told him we could. I had decided I would marry him whether he was making enough or not. Much as my job bored me, it would have bored me considerably more not to get to marry Jock right away!

He worried about my having to give up my career (he and Daddy!), since the job he was taking was in Chicago and I had said I wasn't about to commute from Chicago to Maxwell. People do, but the motivation must be a whole lot stronger than mine. If Jock had been making say half the salary he got at the lab, I would have found something not far from our apartment in Chicago. There wasn't a Pickalot nearby but there were other chain stores and I doubted if a good checker would have trouble getting a job. I have always been certain of my skill as a checker and feel I could get the knack back in jig time. I certainly never felt that way about the job on the *Monitor*. If I were to go back to work now, not an outrageous thought, I would vastly prefer going to Pickalot than to the newspaper. Good thing—I doubt if jobs are plentiful at the *Monitor*. The poor old paper is fighting what seems to be a losing battle against the Chicago newspapers. Chicago's papers really are no better than the *Monitor* if news is what you are after, but the *Monitor* doesn't have many of the big-time columnists and comics. Daddy says Mr. Good says he is forced to use more and more canned stuff because that's what the subscribers want. "They are more interested in what Alsop has to say than what Good thinks," said Daddy. "It's a damned shame. Television is making everybody talk alike and the newspaper syndicates make us all think alike."

"Not me," said Mother.

"My dear," said Daddy, "you are the first and last of the Mohicans."

Her book is scheduled for October now instead of September. The delay was caused by its finally getting a book club selection, something that has embarrassed Mother. She says there must be something wrong with it that she wasn't aware of. She says the next thing we know the Wirth Foundation will ask her to give the Award back. "To think that I, of all people," she says, "am going to have to start saying that a thing isn't necessarily bad just because it happens to be popular."

"Don't worry so much," said Daddy. "Its being a book club selection doesn't mean that the masses are going to go for it. Cheer up, it may turn out to be quite a flop."

"Let us hope," said Mother, and I honestly think she halfway meant it. She was very calm about the Wirth Award, which has an unblemished reputation for going only to really top poets, but what has happened to her book since then has shaken her. She says it's bound to sell to the movies. Her contract, arrived at finally through Wally's perseverance, squeezes the publishers entirely out of any possible movie sale. The only reason Wally won that battle, probably, was because nobody but nobody can imagine *The Different One* making a movie. But nobody imagined a book club would want it, either. Jock says it has made him hope that the country is better off than he had thought.

Daddy says no, that the Book-of-the-Era people, or whatever they call themselves, just happened to be so fed up on four-letter words and amoral sex that they turned for relief to a decent book of poetry. I didn't say anything about having heard that some people are reading quite wild, very sexy, and abnormal hidden meanings into the book. Evidently no word of this has reached the folks and I hope it never will. I didn't say anything to Jock about it, either.

I had been planning to tell Gran to ask Norma if she's looking for a place to live now that we're on the brink of selling the house. I hadn't said anything to Gran yet, thought I had better wait until I knew a bit more about the University job. There is a chance we'll go to Minneapolis if the Maxwell job doesn't come through. Jock isn't terribly eager about the Minnesota job, but it isn't at all bad and he says the people are fine. He would rather stay in Maxwell, though, and really wants to go into teaching if he can do it along with a chance to do some research. The Minneapolis job is pretty much straight production, plus some selling and installation. The salary is better than he would be getting at the University but not enough more to be the deciding factor, if we were ever going to let money sway us again.

In many ways the idea of moving out of town when you've got to come down several pegs is attractive. I would have such socially acceptable reasons for resigning from everything. Mother advised me just to say I've decided to write a book. "You can't do both, you know," she said. "Writing is a full-time job."

"But, Mother, I don't want to write a book," I said.

"Oh, nonsense," she said, "everybody wants to write one."

"Maybe they want to have written one," said Jock, "but not to write it."

"You have something there," said Mother, always delighted with his every utterance.

However, when the clan gathered at Wally's, "Just because the roses are so beautiful right now," said Bébé when she invited us, Gran evidently decided to work on the moping, grieving Norma. It may be that I should feel very sorry for Norma. Maybe she is moping and grieving for David Alstaire. Word has come that he will not be coming back. He'd got married and his wife

166

wants them to stay in England. (Two bits the wife treats him decently but did not sleep with him before the ceremony.) If Norma felt she must take on about losing David—not that she hadn't lost him before he went back home—she might pretend that it's all because of Jock and about how terrible she thinks it is that we are going to lose our beautiful home. That's the way she puts it. Actually the real estate people think we can get around ninety thousand, not exactly losing it. We wouldn't come out with such a tremendous profit as it sounds, but after everything is paid off we would have enough to make a very substantial down payment on something we can afford. (I should say that ninety is the figure they reached after we'd told them yes, we would be willing to include all appliances, all kitchen equipment, carpeting and draperies. I would like also to sell some of the larger pieces of furniture that decorator stuck us with.)

"Well, Norma," said Gran when everybody was listening, "have you found a room yet?"

"Room?" said Norma.

We were sitting on the patio. It was a delightful late August Sunday afternoon. There would be some bugs later, perhaps, even though Wally had sprayed and would again, but now there wasn't so much as a gnat. The wide, perfect lawn swept between long rows of marvelous roses. Beyond the roses to the north was the swimming pool, forbidden to the small children who splashed happily enough in a very shallow wading pool at the foot of the section of the yard we were facing. Now and then I had to call out or go have a word with Andy, inclined to be too enthusiastic with water, especially around older children. He understands that he must never pick on babies, but seems to translate this into meaning he can pester anyone bigger than himself. I guess he is going through what mothers say is a "stage." Karen was never such a nuisance.

"You are going to stay on next year at the University, aren't you?" asked Gran.

"Oh, yes, yes, of course," said Norma. "It would be terrible to have to drop out now that I have such a good start on the degree."

"Yes, indeed," said Gran. "I was asking the Kermits if they

knew of anything special. Lucy says one of her friends who takes girls may have a vacancy. I have the name and number somewhere in my bag."

Norma's face had gotten quite red. She said she was sure that was very kind of my grandmother. She said it as if she wanted to hit her.

"You haven't put the house on the market yet, have you?" asked Wally.

"Larch knows about it," said Jock, "but we'll have to wait until I hear from the University. It should be early next week . . . well, perhaps not tomorrow. Tuesday or Wednesday."

"There's a darling house for sale not too far from the campus," said Bébé. She described the house and its location, and Jock and I laughed. Even Jock, no expert at judging real estate, knew that house was easily twice what we would be able to pay.

"Bébé dear," he said, "what they are considering me for is a combined job of teaching and researching, not the presidency."

"If it were only in the English department," said Mother, "I am sure John Kermit could do something for you. Don't we know anybody in those new things? How about Paul Nestor?"

"He's zoology," said Daddy.

"Well, that's science," said Mother. "Maybe you should speak to him."

"I don't suppose Paul knows anything more about the electronics people than I do," said Daddy.

"Here it is," said Gran and handed Norma a piece of paper. "I hope you can make it out. Lucy says they are charming people. I've met her but I just can't seem to place her. But I'm sure if Lucy approves of her she must be very nice and the address is only four blocks from the campus. Now if by some chance she's already booked up, be sure to ask her to give you some suggestion. I know that's the way people get places more than they do through the University advertising service or the newspaper. In the meantime I'll keep my ears pricked up in case I hear anything that might be helpful. What you must be sure to do, of course, is have something lined up while there's still some time. I'm afraid that by the middle of September everything will be gone."

"If not already," said Norma.

"But it was just yesterday evening that Lucy was telling me about that place," said Gran. "I would have called you but she said they don't like to show the room or do business on Sunday. So I'm sure it would still be available if you would telephone first thing in the morning."

Norma was spared having to answer. Wally's youngest, a girl a year older than Andy, came screaming that Andy was trying to drown her. Bébé said it was time for the children to stop playing and get wrung out for supper. Wally's coals, out on his barbecue, were judged just right for the steaks and the hot dogs and so there was a general exodus from the terrace to the dressing room and to the picnic area.

That night after we got to bed, Jock said he thought it was wonderful to be rich in money as well as in name. "Being rich in name only," he said, "can get to be a little wearing when hot dogs and steaks fall into the fire and relatives like Andy wreak other general havoc."

"It will suit me just to have a rich relative," I said. "It's comfortable to know Wally really has got it. I mean, this way I didn't have to keep saying to myself that my child's curiosity and awkwardness with a long stick had destroyed at least five dollars worth of meat . . . to say nothing of his cousin's dress."

"Bébé was very sweet about it."

"Why not? We'd had all the meat we wanted and her children have more clothes than they can wear. . . . Do you think Norma will follow Gran's lead up?"

"Yes," said Jock, "I intend to see that she does."

Jock went with his sister to look at the room. They were still arguing when they got back. "It's quite impossible," Norma said to me.

"Not at all," said Jock. "It's decent and clean and has cross-ventilation."

"There's no use talking about it," said Norma. "I am the one who would have to be living there. And when you think of what rent I would be paying . . . well . . ." She drew an under-water swimmer's breath. "Now that you will be needing it, I think it's very strange, really, I don't know what people would think if I walked out and paid somebody else."

So this was the new tack. Jock was too startled to say anything. Or disgusted. Or just tired of Norma's company. Anyhow he said, "Oh, don't be a fool," and left the room. Norma fixed me by bursting into tears, something she hasn't done before, but which I understand from Jock was her way of winning or at least ending all arguments from childhood on through her teens. I was too embarrassed to do more than suggest that she go lie down until time for lunch. The meal was a gloomy session. Norma sniffled continually until finally Karen said, "Aunt Norma, why don't you blow your nose?" Which was no more than Aunt Norma has been saying to her. But of course Norma was irate. She said for the first time in Jock's presence that it was too bad I couldn't teach my children any manners.

"Aunt Norma isn't feeling well," I said after she left the dining room.

As if bound to prove how mistaken their aunt had been, both children asked rather elaborately if they might be excused. Later Jock asked me how I have been able to endure it. "I guess I'm just a saint," I said. "Otherwise I surely would have killed her."

He said he would get rid of her within the next week, that enough was enough. He would go rent the room she had found too inelegant for her use. "It's worth my laying out a month's rent, don't you think?"

"But, darling," I said, "if we buy a house that doesn't have an extra room, the matter is automatically settled without tears or hysterics . . . I mean, we aren't going to afford a big place. So if you can endure it a little longer, I think we could get separated without making it seem that we're more intent on kicking her out than anything else."

"With her type mentality that's what she'll think anyway."

"Well, I'm thinking more of the rest of the family," I said, not that I thought his mother would take a view any more favorable to me than Norma's.

"If that government thing would just come through," said Jock. "The thing's been hanging fire for a year already. I can't wait indefinitely. It's going to have to be Minneapolis if nothing happens within the next few days, don't you think?"

"No," I said, "not if you don't want it. After all, if we get a big price for the house, why not just go ahead, if Maxwell's where we want to locate? Jobs aren't all that scarce, you know. You can get something you like if you don't have to hurry."

How could it be living more dangerously than we'd been doing ever since getting ourselves trapped in this house? Although Jock had got into the habit of leaving everything about running the household to me, he was nervous about going ahead with the house deals before he had any job. However, I began looking in earnest now that I had finally satisfied myself that he didn't want the Minnesota position even though it has a rather brilliant future. Wally would have died if he'd known we were deliberately muffing the opportunity. The agency people who had got it for Jock were infuriated and had as good as said they would prefer not to carry him on their books any more. I knew from what he told me about his last interview with them that they probably wouldn't be knocking themselves out to find something else for him if he flatly refused the Minneapolis opening or dillydallied around until it was gone.

I told the real estate man to go ahead and sound out the Ross Thermers on whether they might be interested in the house but not to put it on the regular listing yet. "Well, frankly, Mrs. Dunlop," he said, "I happened to be seeing the Thermers socially the other evening and I mentioned the possibility to them and they seemed more than a little interested, provided, of course, I could do something about their present place, which I am working on right as of now . . . and I am bearing your future needs in mind, too, in case you decide to remain in the area."

I said we had decided to stay in Maxwell and, crossing my fingers for luck, added that we were particularly interested in places near the University. He evidently hadn't got our picture clearly in his mind yet because he reminded me that the area immediately adjacent to the campus had, as he put it, "pretty well gone boardinghouse, student religious centers, fraternity houses and so forth." I said perhaps the "and so forth" was for us because what we are after is very inexpensive housing. Looking at a list I'd made I mentioned several addresses of houses I wanted to consider. I had a feeling that he would have managed to get rid of me then, perhaps to an underling, if it hadn't been that we still did own this house, or enough of it so that it can't be sold without cutting us into the pie.

You get used to money so quickly and don't think twice, not after the first few times, of how much better you are treated by people who consider you well fixed. When we were buying this house, Mr. Larch just fell over himself being charming. He's still polite, but he has turned the warmest part of his charm way down. When he has gone with me to look at houses, I have felt as if he were counting the minutes and biting his fingernails in impatience to get back to clients interested in bigger deals.

The Ross Thermers, who decided in favor of our house before coming around to check on whether they still liked it, are being wonderfully considerate. They practically tiptoe when they come to look and they speak in lowered tones as if somebody had just died or is getting ready to. Obviously they are terribly embarrassed about the whole situation. I can't imagine what Mr. Larch has told them. I imagine it was easy for him at first and that he said we were being transferred out of town. But now he's had to alter the story and to say, I suppose, that Mr. Dunlop is considering offers locally.

Jock has been talking to some of his old friends at Chicago Mirex, where he has been told he could start September first. About all that could be said for the pay, though, is that it would be better than nothing. He doesn't blame them. It's simply a very unbusinesslike operation, the kind, not incidentally, that he likes. The people at Mirex don't get rich but what I think is so terrible is that other people elsewhere profit by what they turn up, develop, and refine in fields where the general principles are already covered by patents. They are more interested in what they are doing, though, than in doing it with the right kind of wrinkles needed if a patent is to be obtained. "They need somebody to steer them into more practical production," I said.

"Somebody like Mr. Prentice," said Jock.

"Right," I said. And meant it. I did not mean it would have to be somebody who would be so overwhelmed by a chance at big contracts that he would stop thinking about social values or his company's possible contribution to a sound future. But obviously I hurt Jock's feelings. Clearly he thought I was giving him a dig for having left Prentice Products. I was aghast at the look on his face. "Jock," I said, "I hope you aren't getting sensitive like Norma, so sensitive that you don't stop to think maybe what a person says doesn't mean what it might sound like . . ."

"Not at all, not at all, dear," he said. "You're quite right that Mirex would be something for me to consider seriously if it had

173

somebody like Prentice heading it . . . or, if I had something of his ability. Or Wally's."

"Look," I said, "we've never argued about money and I'm not about to begin now because I wasn't brought up to think it mattered unless you didn't have enough to get by on. I don't have to have any twenty or thirty thousand a year if I am not going to live in this house. And I'm perfectly willing to go into an apartment in Chicago if you want to go back to Mirex."

"No," he said. "If I should go back, we'll stay in Maxwell. I can commute."

"We'll see," I said. "There's no use knocking ourselves out about it until we know for sure that the University thing isn't going to come through." I kept myself from saying I didn't want to live in Maxwell if it would be on the Mirex pay. I suppose I have more vanity and foolish pride than I am willing to admit but living in poor circumstances with Jock working at the University would be one thing. However, having him at Mirex and us living in Maxwell on about the same income would be humiliating for me. Yes, humiliating. I can take very nice care of my ego if my husband's income is small because he's in education, but to have him slugging away at a small, not very successful lab that has no prestige of any kind is a horse of another color. I can't be too sure Jock would understand this as a character defect I do not expect to be able to overcome and therefore do not regard with any great shame. To go from a big job into teaching is something really to brag about. To go from that same big job to a piddling one in a small outfit is something else again. I suppose this attitude means that I am a very insecure person. Or shallow. Or more intent upon keeping up with the Joneses or, perhaps, in keeping in their favor, than I will admit.

TWENTY-FIVE

The Manuscript

*A*fter a week of quiet that even then felt like the stillness before a storm, everything began to happen. The Ross Thermers sold their place, a crumbling house on a five-acre tract, and guess to whom? Right. The joke is that Wally had no idea the Thermers were interested in our house. I'd just told him the real estate man had somebody who seemed to be a hot prospect. It worried him that he couldn't handle the deal for us and said he would manage somehow if we could just hang on a couple of months. His partner was in Europe and so Wally was busier than ever. Because, he said, an unexpected opportunity had turned up. People he and his partner had been trying to interest in selling their property had finally begun to smoke up. He said it was a large property not at present zoned for high rises, but that he was willing to take a chance that the modification would be made to permit him and Mr. Faber, his associate, to go ahead with their plans for a large, high-rising and, you can be sure, high-priced condominium complex. I imagine he let the Thermers believe getting the necessary zoning change would be very difficult and, knowing Wally, that it was in the bag before he closed the deal. Anyhow he got the property and the Thermers didn't seem too displeased with what they were paid. I think Mr. Larch was sad about it since he didn't make the sale but everybody else was satisfied.

I don't know if the real estate agent ever told the Thermers what we paid for the house. I'm sure he wouldn't have wanted to. I suspect that he dwelt lovingly upon the improvements we made, actually not much in money. Jock built a new retaining wall at the edge of the ravine, rebuilt the barbecue and widened the terrace. What we did inside was expensive, all right, being under the control of the interior decorator. Her story was that she'd got practically everything for us wholesale, as a favor to Mr. Prentice, I suppose. Mr. Larch remembered this and didn't underplay it.

Jock and I had decided to be delighted to get eighty even if we had to throw most of the furniture in and so of course were very pleased when the Thermers agreed to ninety provided we would leave a half dozen pieces of furniture Mrs. T. had evidently decided the house couldn't do without, plus the complete guest room as is . . . without Norma, unfortunately. So we were able to settle all of our debts and to make a respectable down payment on a house six blocks west of the campus. It's just outside of the rooming house area where property has been going up since there is a rumor that the college will be expanding west eventually and so buying up all the old houses standing in the way of the project. I don't know how true that is. The house we bought is well outside of the neighborhood that has suddenly taken on more value, although it is looking far worse than it did when the owners didn't anticipate being able to sell at all and so kept their places looking nice because they regarded them as permanent homes.

Our little place was never anybody's idea of their permanent home, I guess. People have come and gone, come and gone and, most of them being renters, have not been constructive occupants. The yard has some very old bushes in it that speak of loving hands forty or fifty years ago and a barn, a small one, that needs most of all to be torn down before the next big wind does the job.

The house hasn't been treated any better than the barn but was just sturdier to begin with. It's the kind of house an interested real estate agent could praise as being basically very sound, with thicker boards and better bricks or whatever than are used in today's quickies; but Mr. Larch wasn't interested. Jock and I sold the house to ourselves, primarily, I hope, because we felt it was a homey place. I speak only for myself when I say that part of the house's attraction was that it just didn't seem to have a place for a guest. But I suspect that Jock didn't find the lack of a fourth bedroom any special drawback.

As soon as we'd decided on the house he told Norma she would have to get busy. "It's just got the three bedrooms," he said, "so you'll have to find yourself a place before we give occupancy here."

"There's no reason why I can't room with Karen," said Norma, "if you don't think it would be perfectly all right for her and Andy to share a room. Heavens, at their age I don't see why not."

"Norma," said Jock, "it just wouldn't do. The rooms are small, much smaller than the one you wouldn't take at Mrs. Kermit's friend's house."

"But that was different," said Norma.

"I'll help you find something else," said Jock. "There won't be much choice, not this late. What you should have done was take David's apartment when you had the chance."

This so outraged Norma that she turned off the tears I had seen gathering. Aside from the fact that she would hardly want to live in a place that would constantly remind her of a person who had turned out to be such a false friend, did Jock think she was made of money?

"Well, Norma," he said, "you never paid a dime at home all the time you were teaching. What you didn't spend on your car or clothes, you must have saved, and I doubt if your expenses have been any higher here than they were at home. So I think you could probably manage a small apartment. But I don't blame you for not wanting to go to any unnecessary expense, and so we'll look for single rooms and not consider an apartment unless no other place is available."

Then she went into a tirade about how people never did want her to have anything, everybody just wanted her to be stuck in a small town teaching in a horrible school system all her life and so on and so on. I was too horrified and embarrassed to listen. I decided the best thing for me to do was slip out and hope that she and Jock would forget I'd been in on the beginning of the tantrum. Fortunately the children were outdoors. I went out to join them. I didn't see Norma again until dinnertime when she appeared to have recovered and even to be feeling relatively cheerful. She insisted on going to the house with us the next day and I believe this reconciled her to her lot. She was so pleased to see how far down in the world I was coming that she couldn't conceal her vindictive joy. She managed to point out flaws in the house that I had failed to notice before. She saw nothing good about it and when Jock said, "Well, Norma, at least the price was right," she said, "Oh, do you mean they are giving it to you?"

"That's my girl," said Jock. "Norma, you sure have the knack for making people feel good."

"I just try to be practical," said Norma, "and honest. But, pardon me, if you can't take the truth as I see it."

"You're pardoned," he said.

Karen and Andy, who had been exploring the barn came back to the house then. "Isn't it wonderful, Aunt Norma?" asked Karen. "We didn't ever have a upstairs before."

Andy carefully repeated this statement.

"It is *an* upstairs," said Norma.

Happily the children agreed and all the way home sang, "A nupstairs, a nupstairs . . ." And here I had thought Karen, at least, would be struck by the great difference between her former home and the new one. Well, she is. But, although it doesn't seem that she's right in the head on the subject, she evidently thinks we are going to improve our situation.

I know that we are and that we've been living as if on the edge of a precipice all the time we've been in Elk Run. I welcome a chance to live sensibly for a change. I know that whatever Jock finally gets will pay enough to finance our new way of life. The summer vacation has given me a chance to slip unobtrusively out of most of the organizations I belong to and I plan to write resignations to the other groups before we move. I thought I would be glad to clear these decks because I belonged to far too many things and had become too involved to enjoy anything. However, I find giving up everything more of a sacrifice than I had anticipated. Some, even most, of the organizations not only were fun but really worthwhile. I know Jock would prefer that I continue in some of them. If just the dues were involved, we could manage. None of the dues is high. It's the fund-raising affairs, and the entertaining you become obliged to do, that make the price zoom upward. There is also the fact that I will not have a place any more for even smallish committee meetings. Oh, not that the new house is so small that I couldn't take care of ten or twelve people, but here again my ridiculous and shameful, I admit it, pride stands in the way. After being able to entertain at Elk Run, I simply am not willing to ask those same people to come to West Seventh Street. It will be different for the people we know best. They can take it and so can we—I hope. But for the less intimate friends, the difference in our two places will be too much not to be embarrassing.

I grew up always being the only poor one in a rich crowd and so I am used to it, you might say, but that doesn't mean I liked it or ever will. You hear about people forgetting their old friends when they go up in the world. Well, now I am going to set about forgetting my rich friends as Jock and I go down economically, but let's hope not in any other way. I am having more and more trouble sleeping, even though you'd think what with the house sold and the deal for Seventh Street nearly closed, I would be somewhat more relaxed. Especially now that it is definitely settled that Norma can't under any circumstances stay with us.

She didn't give up easily. She had several more sessions with Jock—I was not present again—before she got it through her head that he meant it when he said if her not getting to live with us meant she would have to drop out of school, he would be very sorry but that's all. Naturally she goes around looking very sad.

All that holds the Seventh Street deal up is getting a lot of papers cleared through various lawyers. The old lady who owns the house is in a convalescent home and her power of attorney is in the hands of a relative who, according to our lawyer, should be under a legal guardianship herself. It will work out eventually, says Jock, and I'm sure it will. In the meantime, what with the University still dangling him, the delay in the sale is annoying. We may have to give the Thermers possession before we're the legal owners of the Seventh Street place. I keep having a feeling we should have asked Wally to help us. Jock simply isn't a businessman. Mr. Larch's interest in us dropped sharply as soon as the deal with the Thermers was closed. He acts for us as if to do us a personal favor, something this young man is not naturally inclined to do. I hate to say anything to Wally at this late date, but wonder what we will do if that quite antic relative of the owner should decide against us. I don't think my barging in would help, indeed it would probably make matters worse because the lawyers would think then that they had two crazy women to deal with. Jock appears to think all we have to do is be patient. That attitude, in itself, is enough to drive me nuts.

TWENTY-SIX *The Manuscript*

"*S*omewhere in the background a string ensemble ought to be playing 'Hearts and Flowers,' " said Jock, "and you really should be carrying a baby instead of those books."

Norma said she couldn't imagine what he was talking about, but she'd got the message. Her face was so red that I felt myself blushing. Jock, however, was cool enough. "It's really time that you grew up, Norm," he said. "You just can't always be leaning on other people."

But she could make a nice try. Suspecting that we might collapse eventually under the strain, she'd started leaning on David Alstaire who, quite sensibly, I believe, had fled for his life. I doubt if my original analysis of how she came to lose David was correct. Although he did seem rather old fashioned, I don't think her willingness to sleep with him without being married was what put him off. I have a hunch he finally saw her for the parasite she is and that whatever he felt for her simply wasn't strong enough to withstand such perpetual draining.

She made her going almost as hard for me as possible. I suppose it would have been more of a nuisance if she'd fixed her moving date to coincide with ours. I'm sure the only reason she didn't was because she knew we would be so distracted that day that we wouldn't pay sufficient attention to her departure. It had to be dramatic, and in a way Jock played up to her need for histrionics. How disappointing it would have been for her if all he'd said was, "Well, be seeing you around." She demands attention. I can see her as a child, intent upon getting everyone in the family to look at her, to listen to her, to place interest in her welfare above that of their own. Did her mother spoil her into being that way because in Norma she saw a chance more nearly to live her life again? If so, is she pleased with what she created? Or, since pleasure would be outside the scope of that woman, fulfilled in some way that was beyond the powers of her good, patient, but ultimately remote husband? I find myself wondering how Jock and his two older sisters, all such outgoing, marvelous people, got that way. Perhaps their father hadn't retreated completely before his wife's continual attack during their formative years. Maybe she herself wasn't such a virago, if that's the word for it, then. There's nothing of the whirlwind character in that woman, which is the sort of thing I feel really should be in a virago. My mother-in-law is quite placid looking and even wears her lips with a slight upward curve, the better to trap unsuspecting daughter-in-law and innocent little children into the belief that kindness could at least occasionally come forth.

I would like to ask Jock what he thinks went wrong. Romantically I speculate, rather hopelessly, that Dad Dunlop might have been caught *in flagrante delicto* . . .

We signed the final papers and moved into the little old house on Seventh before hearing anything from the University except that they also had not heard. Ten days after the move, Jock got the good and bad news all at once. I don't know what he would have done if he hadn't got the good at the same time. He tried to prevent me from becoming aware of it, but I know him well enough to realize that he was getting near the ragged edge.

Maybe I have been the one with the obvious symptoms, such as my insomnia, but I know Jock's mental condition has been quite poor for a long time, perhaps even before Prentice Products began competing with the bigger companies for government business. I rather doubt if that was what brought his decline in health about. It's too easy to say he just couldn't find the strength to face the fact that in life we have to compromise if we are to live. It must have been something deeper than that, something, perhaps, to do with our sexual relationship? I just wouldn't know. It's been perfectly satisfactory, to my way of thinking, but is my way of thinking his?

At the same time I wonder if everything does have to be sexually based, I mean, isn't it ever possible that something else could go wrong? Couldn't you get liver trouble, or something, without having punished that organ for the weakness of your sex life? I should consult Marianne, the great Freudian. She couldn't have got through a psych course in any regular college but she's sure Mrs. Psychoanalyst herself now. But is there anything you can't get if you have enough money?

As I had been expecting them to do, the way things go in Washington D.C., the government turned Maxwell University's request for new research money down after having kicked it around for almost two years. Prospective people for the project had come and gone, come and gone. Jock was perhaps twelfth in the line of hopefuls who had dropped away because they were tired of marking time or who had got better offers or had simply lost their tempers. Jock, the patient Quaker, just waited. Patient Quaker on the surface but underneath dying by inches. I hope when the man told him the news he put it the way Jock broke it to me. "Cara darling," he said, "the project is in and starts on the first." I could hardly believe it. I sensed that it wasn't quite right.

"What's wrong?" I asked.

"Not a thing," he said. "We're more certain of having a free hand than we would have been if the government had come through."

"Oh, they turned it down . . . I knew they would . . . I just knew . . ."

"Well, evidently you weren't alone because for months several of the department people have been looking around for private money and just about the time the government turndown came through they had a grant all lined up from the Dynamics Foundation. I guess the Foundation had got the word of the probable turndown and being antiadministration anyhow, they decided here was a chance to show Washington it can't always call the tune . . ."

I had thought it might mean more money, but evidently the Dynamics Foundation people are as chintzy as the government when it comes to paying for brains. Under the agreement, Jock will have to teach two more hours a week than he'd thought but this doesn't seem to bother him or anyway he's not letting me know if it does. I keep feeling he isn't as overjoyed as he pretends.

We are still in a mess. Although we sold what seemed like practically everything to the Thermers who appeared to think most of the furniture had been designed especially for them, what we did move has crowded this house until I think I'll surely have to sell a few more things even though what I retained are what seem basic. I keep telling myself that I grew up in a family of five that managed in a house no larger than this without ever feeling cramped. But that was before I'd had a chance to expand, before I knew any better. It is far worse, once you've had enough room, to fit yourself into small quarters. Jock says we might consider adding a room downstairs later on. What we should do first is take out the partition between the two miserable little parlors. Even thrown together they won't make a very large living room. The way they are now is impossible. Daddy says he thinks he and Jock could do the job. The prospect simply makes me sick. Either it must be done professionally and properly or not at all. But as it is, of an evening when we are just sitting and reading I feel as if one of us should be in the other room rather than both huddled into one.

The children continue to have no sense at all. Karen brags disgustingly about having two living rooms, quite as if we hadn't had a gigantic family room, as well as a rumpus room, in addition to a large living room at Elk Run. Of course I wouldn't want her to be grieving for the old house, but I do think she could show a little judgment. Now that she's started kindergarten, she also brags about going to public school and refers to her old days in private school as if it had been a sort of prison term she'd had to serve. "You're awful lucky," she tells Andy, "because you won't have to go to private school at all."

There hasn't been time for me to find out whether I'll have time on my hands now that I don't belong to anything except a faculty wives' thing that apparently isn't terribly demanding. Gran is trying to involve me in the church women's group. I went once with her and found it pretty dull though I suppose educational. I keep wondering if I should get a job but if I had to pay for more help at home and didn't get a very good job, what would be the point? I understand that well-paid part-time positions are very scarce. Oh, I could probably get a few hours a day checking at Pickalot but I don't think that's the thing for me to do. I mean, I just wonder how that would sit with the faculty wives. I'll bet you there's as much politicking going on in the faculty as there ever was in Prentice Products but, thank God, so far the head of Jock's department hasn't asked me to entertain anybody. That's a laugh. If I should ever get well enough organized to entertain anyone it will have to be just that . . . one. I'll have to ask the family one at a time, of course after clearing with Norma about when I may use the place she has nailed down for herself at our "new" table. (We couldn't have got both the table and chairs of the Elk Run suite in this dining room and anyway the Thermers "just had to have it." So I bought what is really a dinette set at a secondhand store.)

Yes, Norma gave us a one-night vacation from herself. She did call up. The telephone was in but the gas hadn't been turned on. I heard Jock telling her that on the phone. "Tell her if it were turned on, I'd be sticking my head in the oven right now," I called from the kitchen, where I was preparing a feast in my electric frypan, a wedding present Mrs. Thermer had not insisted upon buying because I'd hidden it from her.

Next night Norma was Johnny-on-the-spot. She arrived just as we were sitting down to dinner. "I thought I'd better come around to see how you're getting along," she said and pulled up the fourth dinette chair. Andy still occupies his junior chair. He is growing fast, even faster mentally, and will not be happy much longer in a baby chair. But lack of a chair won't keep

185

Norma from gracing, I should say haunting, our table. She'll take the junior chair herself if nothing else is available because, believe it or not, "restaurant food just doesn't agree" with her. When did she give it a chance? The first night we were in the Seventh Street house? No, she sneaked milk and crackers into her room that night. This came out when Karen was trying to make a fine tale of adventure out of our frypan dinner of the night before. Norma topped her with the milk and crackers.

"No cheese?" asked Jock. But I am sorry to say he sounded more amused than sarcastic. Naturally he is like a new man.

I keep thinking he's bound to find that the job isn't all that ideal, I mean what is? Of course I'm delighted that he finally has work he really likes even more than he did the Chicago job he had when we were first married. He never got tired of Mirex. The job was okay, but we really had to have more money. And we wanted to get away from the congestion and smog, things I guess city people who have grown up in it don't mind but which Jock and I find almost unendurable. Of course there isn't any great future in the present job; that is, he can never expect to make anywhere near what he knew was his potential at Prentice. As Wally said when Jock left Prentice, "It's kissing good-bye to a fortune, but of course it's only money." And I think, hard as it might be for some people to believe, he meant that literally. I don't think money means much to Wally; it's the making of a success, the process of working, of pulling off big deals that he loves.

Marianne drops in a lot. She's always wanting to run errands for me or help in some other way. It would be a help if she would keep her nose out, but of course I can't or anyway don't say this. She is so damned patronizing, although I'm sure she doesn't realize it. She goes on and on about this "sweet Victorian house." She speaks of the fancy wood trim around the roof and windows as if it were splendid sculpture worthy of a museum. "Oh, you have a gem, Keri," she says, "a real gem."

She talks about the garden I should have as a setting for this gem and says she will help, she would love to. She is studying all her garden books in preparation. Well, she got on my nerves when we were girls, but it was nothing then to what it is now. I want to scream when I hear her "You-hoo" at the door. By

186

recounting how much I am missed and how deadly dull the meetings are, she manages to keep reminding me of how I've come down socially as well as financially. She speaks as if enviously of the "brainy" types she assumes I am now associating with in that dumb faculty wives' club. The only generalization you could make about those women that wouldn't be too far off the mark would be that they just don't look as good as the gals who have more dough to spend on their hair, faces, and figures. If they compensate for not being able to afford hundred dollar sports dresses and two hundred dollar suits by being especially intellectual, this is something I have not as yet been able to observe.

Frankly, if I had to choose between spending an afternoon with the rich women or the poor, I would choose the rich. In any case you will be bored and so you might as well have something interesting to look at instead of chain-store bargain-rack clothes. But I definitely don't want to be with the wealthy when I cannot afford a hundred dollars for a dress or two hundred for a suit. I plead busy when Marianne, out of the greatness of her goodness, invites me to be her guest at this or that fund-raising affair. She says I will be doing her a favor. This I know. This I am not willing to do. I am tired to death of doing Marianne favors in exchange for what amounts to her cast-off clothing. Boy, I'll bet she's trying to think of some way to offer me her last season's outfits. Too bad I didn't marry a missionary. How Marianne would have delighted in sending me barrels. I wonder if she ever tells her psychiatrist (or maybe he has told her?) that fundamentally she hates my guts and always has.

She is harping on my health again, but is cautious about identifying what branch of it most concerns her. I'm looking too thin to suit her but of course she knows moving is such a chore. (She knows anything about chores?)

Today she asked if I'm sleeping enough. Just when did my sleep become her business? "A little insomnia goes a long way with me," I answered. I don't know what I meant but she seemed to take it as encouraging news. Anyway she answered, "Good."

Before she left, though, she put in another pitch for a good night's sleep, as if I had been arguing against it. Of course

Marianne's coming out in favor of sleep makes me regard my insomnia with less dread. And I figure that it's like with a child that won't eat—give him time and he'll finally get too hungry to keep on holding out. So I figure I can just starve or ignore my insomnia out of existence. I won't let myself get hysterical about it. So I don't sleep more than maybe four hours a night anymore? So what about Edison? Who minds being like him? I said that to Jock the last time he began to stew about my being nearly out of sleeping pills again.

"Maybe Edison didn't sleep much at night," he said, "but I'll bet you he catnapped during the day."

"Well, I will," I said. "Once I get things straightened around, I'll catnap . . . but in the meantime I wish you'd stop by Dr. Griswold's for a refill prescription for me . . . I've got so much I have to do here. . . ." The truth, though, was that I didn't want to lay myself open to what Dr. Griswold would say. He was snotty enough the last time he gave me the refill prescription. Honestly!

"Honey," said Jock when he came home for lunch, "Dr. Griswold says he'll have to see you before he can renew the prescription."

"Oh, the old fool, does he think I've become addicted? Didn't you tell him we've been moving?"

"Yes, but you can't blame him for feeling he ought to check now and then before renewing. So I made an appointment for you . . . as long as I was there."

I was too mad to say anything for a while. Then, before I'd calmed down enough to deliver some scathing comment on people who decide when other people should go to the doctor, Norma arrived for her usual free meal. But to her it isn't free because she often brings something, like a pint of ice cream when it's on sale at the chain drugstore. "If it isn't enough, just give it all to the children," she says. And Jock divides it into three pieces . . . for our three children. Norma's protest is brief.

I'll be relieved when she takes up with another man as I am sure she will do when one comes close enough to be trapped. At least David took her off our necks now and then.

When we were getting ready for bed, I remembered what Jock had said about making that appointment with Dr. Griswold for me. "I'm just surprised that while you were at it you didn't make an appointment for me to go to Marianne's psychiatrist," I said.

"Keri," he said, "it's only sensible to do what you can to get back to normal sleeping habits. If a doctor can help, why not give him a chance?"

"You mean Dr. Griswold?"

"Not necessarily," he said, "but it seems logical to see him first since he's always been your doctor."

"He's an irritable old goat," I said.

"If he doesn't come up with anything, then let's think about somebody else," he said.

"Like for example Marianne's Dr. Lester?"

"But what's so terrible about him, Keri? Is it because he's Marianne's doctor or because of something you hold against him personally or just because he's a psychiatrist?"

"Don't you go putting everything I say into a false light," I said, "and making me sound worse than just a fool, making me a crazy one. Because I know that the crazier people get the saner they think they are and so you'll never hear me saying I know I'm in perfect mental health, not me, because, after all, who is?"

It was a good question, too good a one for him to answer. "Suppose I suggested that *you* go to a psychiatrist, how would you feel?"

"Like I had to go to one, I expect," he said and laughed. "Oh, come on, honey, all I'm asking you to do is keep the appointment I made for you with old Doc Griswold who just doesn't like the idea of keeping on writing sleeping pill prescriptions without giving the patient a little checkup now and then."

"You make it sound so simple, so really casual," I said.

And, not having any more sleeping pills I stayed awake all night. I got up around four and went downstairs to read. I must have fallen asleep at about six but I woke up before Jock came down. Well, actually my only objection to keeping the appointment with Dr. Griswold is that it will cost me ten dollars and not be worth a damn thing. Even if I needed a psychiatrist, he would be the last person on earth to say so. He's one of the last know-it-all family doctors. And a good thing.

TWENTY-SEVEN *The Journal*

Without thinking and certainly without remembering, I reached into the right-hand drawer for the next chapter of the fictionalized autobiography of the woman I had hated so easily and come by now to pity. I knew how her story ended, though not, of course, in any detail, but I certainly hadn't expected my contact with her to be terminated so abruptly. I groped under the typewriter paper I'd had under the manuscript in the drawer but it was all gone.

Mr. Kincaid had brought me the last batch shortly before Dr. Leonard took off for a month in Europe. When the doctor asked me if I had enough to keep me busy, I said I thought so, but that I would ask Mr. Kincaid for more of the manuscript if I needed it. "What you have is all there is," said Dr. Leonard.

"Are you sure?" I asked. "The last batch doesn't seem very thick."

"That's all there is, though," he said.

"Well, I can always improvise," I said, "or copy the newspapers or something."

"Have you got your regular speed back, would you say?" He tacked that last on to prevent me from reminding him that I didn't know what my previous speed was or much of anything about myself except what he and Mr. Kincaid had told me, hardly testimony to be accepted by me if I did not intend to bow to their will and simply accept Caroline Kincaid as my past and, did they ever think of this, as a future from which I couldn't escape. I don't suppose it would be such complete torture, in the absence of an alternative, to accept for your personal use, the past of a woman who was something of a fool but probably harmless, at any rate until what I believe was a tumor distorted the poor girl's thinking to the point where she was obviously beginning to drive everybody, including herself, nuts.

I glanced over the last few pages I had typed. What had happened next? Had the old doctor not been the stupid stubborn nincompoop she considered him? Had he seen right away that her problem called for specialized study? Had he referred her to a neurologist, perhaps, or even to her friend Marianne's psychiatrist? Whatever happened next obviously didn't inspire her to take it to her book.

In view of what I could guess must have happened next, what should my opinion of the people she wrote about be? Obviously, if Marianne weren't the idiot her friend considered her, Keri Kincaid was ill when she started her book and so nothing she wrote could be accepted as factual. The faintly discernible type of distortion is probably the most dangerous and I imagine what she said about Marianne toward the beginning influenced me against the friend more than what she said there toward the end when it was pretty obvious that her friend really couldn't be quite the mess she considered her. Nor Jock quite the weakling. Really, I'm surprised that Mr. Kincaid was willing for anyone to see this manuscript, least of all me, I mean, if he really does expect me to take the Other Caroline's place and keep it the rest of my life.

I am positive he was the one who changed the names but of course don't know if the idea originated with him. He and

Dr. Leonard might have decided that since I wouldn't accept any of the memory they sought to impose on me, I just might take what I could decide I had worked out for myself. There wasn't enough alteration for me to have remained unaware of what was going on as long as I did. The names were changed, but not drastically. Maxwell was kept Maxwell and once or twice Jock called Keri "Cara." This might be an endearment, but it could also be short for Caroline. He's called me that a couple of times but I have pretended not to notice.

It is embarrassing to let him and Dr. Leonard think I am so stupid. Did they actually believe I wouldn't be able to figure out the puzzle they set up for me as a form of psychotherapy? Oh, I'm not ready to accuse them of working up this silly plot. But I do have a feeling that I am on the edge of discovery. It is as if they had meant it when they said my memory would come back. I think maybe it will. I mean the real thing. What a shock it will be to everyone, especially the doctors who are convinced the memory of my prehospital life is gone forever! I can imagine how they will look when I suddenly confront them with my real name, my address, and other facts about my pre-Caroline Kincaid life. It is perhaps silly of me to feel that I must have some evidence. The look on their faces will be evidence enough, I am sure. Just the same, I do wish I had some scrap of identification . . . my driver's license, if I ever had one, a credit card . . . anything. But I am afraid they have been thorough in their determination to exterminate the real me and that when the time comes, I will have nothing (!) with which to fight them except my memory. But how could I ask for anything more? And how can I be content ever again, even if I live to be a hundred, with anything less? You probably have to lose your memory before you can appreciate how valuable it is.

Now and then from what Miss Hazel says, I gather that she thinks I should be contented to operate indefinitely on whatever scraps of the past are thrown my way. She doesn't know about The Manuscript. If she did she would say, "But there you are, dear, just what you've been wanting, a nice little history of yourself." She is always telling me that when people get old they lose their memory and therefore, presumably, I should regard what has happened to me as simply occurring prematurely.

"Let that sweet man do your remembering," she says. "I can't imagine anybody complaining about their past if it included being married to him."

Well, maybe that's what gripes me. Maybe knowing I was not and am not married to him is hardest for me to take. I won't say I have fallen in love with him because surely I haven't. I just couldn't, not under such circumstances. But he is a very wonderful person and he's been so kind and thoughtful . . . not counting whatever part he played in the transplant, of course. That was hardly kind and thoughtful. But I shouldn't blame him for being persuaded by professional people who no doubt convinced him they knew a lot more than he did about the brain. Still, the fact that he couldn't continue to work where his ideas were constantly violated, proves he is a person who has strong ethical beliefs. So how could he have brought himself to condone what the hospital people did? They simply couldn't have operated without his consent.

Who, if anyone, signed me away? I am sure the Other Caroline, or Keri, and I were both out of the picture mentally when the possibility of a transplant was suggested.

Everywhere at the hospital people I encounter either tell me or hint that I won't be staying at Applewood much longer. I am supposed to be very pleased about this. I am complimented on how well I look and repeatedly asked to show pictures of "my" children. Because it finally got so tiresome to be regarded as something of a monster in regard to those children, I asked Mr. Kincaid for a snap of them which, poor man, he joyously provided. He didn't know that it was only because I wanted to be able to shut people up by showing them a picture. They are satisfied now after ohing and ahing, evidently to please me. I won't say I couldn't care less. Mr. Kincaid has become a very good, a very dear friend. I am deeply concerned about his welfare.

How dreadful it is that after poor Keri died, or anyhow was taken away, the sister-in-law she found such a pain moved in with the family. Mr. Kincaid seldom mentions her but it sounds as if she doesn't lift a finger to help out. I am sure she doesn't pay any rent, either. There is the one thing that makes me almost wish I could continue this masquerade after I leave the hospital

—I would certainly like to see to it personally that Norma Dunlop, as I keep thinking her name is in real life as well as in the altered autobiography, gets the hell out of her brother's home. I don't suppose Mr. Kincaid can see it, but there's something really rotten in that girl's determination to live with him. It goes beyond the mere desire to save money. And still I suppose she considers herself quite a proper person . . . even while sleeping around, I bet, with anybody she can get. How dreadful to have her with those poor little innocent children. My only consolation is that evidently the woman can't stand them and so they are spared any intense devotion from their aunt.

Dr. Leonard is expected back next week. I gather that they have been more or less waiting for him to return before kicking me out. I feel rather frantic when I think about it, when I contemplate simply going out cold into the world without any idea of what I am going to do. However, I am in good health and am young, or anyhow I am accepting the Other Caroline's age as near enough. I can type quite well and although I will have to borrow money at first, I see no reason why I can't soon be self-supporting. I can't go off from Mr. Kincaid, however, without telling him why I can't come and take his wife's place. He must understand, if nobody else does, that my having his Caroline's body does not mean I have become his wife. I am not saying I never want to see him again, because I do want to. I intend to keep track of him and I hope he will want to hear from me even after I have repaid the loan which I intend to ask him for. If he hasn't got the money, perhaps he could get it from his rich brother-in-law or even his parents-in-law. I understand that they are getting quite prosperous. Mr. Kincaid says his mother-in-law's book is selling like hotcakes. Although a movie sale isn't in the bag yet, it looks as if the publishers made quite a mistake when they "humored" her (meaning Wally) by letting her have all the movie rights. Well, whoever thought they would want to film a narrative poem or is it more an epic poem? But either one hardly seems Hollywood.

However, all that concerns me is that it shouldn't be impossible for me to borrow about five hundred dollars from these people. I'll go to Chicago, I think, and get a room at a YWCA— or might I be too old? Does the Y still stand for Young? No matter, I'll get a room somewhere, preferably in a place for women only. Then I'll find a job. It won't amount to much at first, I suppose, but I am prepared to work hard. If I were the Other Caroline, I suppose I would hurry to some supermarket. Her idea of a fine job evidently was checking in a supermarket. Or a dime store. How perverse it was of her not to care for that really very good job she finally got on the newspaper.

Not having Keri's talents, I have no hope of getting a newspaper job and really don't want one. I'd rather work in something less personally demanding. I think it's going to be a while, memory or no memory, before I feel exactly robust mentally. I wonder if I'll have trouble getting a job, incidentally, if I tell my medical history, that is, that I was a patient at Applewood. I'll have to ask somebody if the reluctance people used to have about hiring former mental patients still exists. I believe what Aggie has told me but think her information on that subject may be quite out of date.

There are many things I think I should take up with a doctor, preferably a psychiatrist, but naturally I am reluctant to talk frankly with Dr. Leonard. Even if I had access to the other doctors in the case, I wouldn't be able to trust them. I am not saying the plot was wicked. But it certainly forced me into a life I didn't ask for. People sometimes whine about how they didn't ask to be born. Well, I didn't ask to be born twice!

In my absorption with myself, I haven't been much affected by the gradual turnover in our ward. Some of my best friends have gone home. We parted with promises to get together later on, but even at the time I am sure nobody believed we would ever meet again unless by chance. I know it seems very paranoid of me to say some of these women weren't in as good mental health as I am; this is what I believe. It's what Miss Hazel tells me, too. But surely she is the most nonprofessional hospital employee in the world. When I tell her I still can't remember the past, she just shrugs and says, "Who don't forget?" She goes into great detail about how much she forgets. She is a good woman, anyway, she's been kind to me, but I am weary of her company. I wish I could get acquainted with some of the younger attendants, but the ones I think would interest me are very standoffish. They aren't exactly rude, but they make it clear they are not going to hobnob with a patient on an equal basis. I wonder if this feeling I sometimes have when repulsed by these people is the way members of minorities feel most or all of the time. In a way I would guess that the mentally ill and the former mental patients are the worst off of any of the minorities because they have nothing they are willing to accept as a rallying point. Indeed, I shouldn't wonder if they all tend to discriminate against each other. The chief thing is to hide the present ailment and to conceal, of course, the past one.

Of course it was different with me. I know this is what thousands of other people must say but I think it would be unbalanced of me not to believe my case highly unusual. I am not claiming that the operation didn't damage my brain in other ways. I know they planned to destroy my memory. Maybe they did other injury. But an injured brain is rather different from a sick one, even if the overall effect is about the same kind of nuttiness.

Miss Johnson, in the outer office, has finally taken pity on me and given me some typing to do. It is against the law or maybe just against the Applewood rules for a patient to take a pay job on the grounds and so of course I am not being paid for the records typing I am doing just now. Miss Johnson worries about this. She knows nobody will reprimand her for giving me something to do as long as I can do it properly. What troubles her is that she can't afford to pay me out of her own pocket since the hospital cannot or will not. How ironic it is that an institution trying to persuade industries and businesses to hire former patients is unable to pay those able to do satisfactory work.

I haven't discussed this with Miss Johnson but got it from a woman on our ward who has been in and out of the hospital for the past thirty years. She is quite rational most of the time and not especially offensive, except, obviously, to her family, when in one of her spells. Maybe I should feel as if my nose were out of joint. She and Miss Hazel are old friends and spend a lot of time talking. I'm glad enough not to be included and get tired of being teased about no longer being teacher's pet. "But it will be different when your paramour gets back, won't it?" says that dreadful Leona who, sadly for us but happily for the rest of the world, is still among us.

I am too tired of Leona's accusing me of being Dr. Leonard's "paramour" to bother with a denial. It wouldn't do any good. When I deny it she reels off what she calls proof. She uses obscene language that is astounding to hear coming from a woman. Of course when I don't try to argue with her she screams in triumph. She runs around shouting that the "Scarlet Woman" has finally confessed.

We have been told that Dr. Leonard will meet his psycho-therapy group day after tomorrow. There is nothing I wish to take up with him and the others in class but plenty I would like to discuss with him privately. I am not ready to spring my knowledge of the plot on him yet, though. I just don't feel steady enough on my mental pins yet. But I don't have much time left for coasting.

TWENTY-EIGHT *The Journal*

In group psychotherapy, as I understand it, the professional person in charge is supposed to keep out of the discussion as much as seems to him possible while maintaining a therapeutic atmosphere. But Dr. Leonard, just home from a month in Europe, wasn't in any mood to remain silent. He seemed very young in his response to our questions Friday morning.

I don't know why I felt so sophisticated. As far as I know, my knowledge of Europe is limited to what I've read and seen in movies or television newsreels. But inasmuch as I dislike being drawn into the regular sessions, I was glad enough for him to spend most of the hour telling about his travels. The rest of the time was given over to the most talkative of the ladies telling him how rough it was Friday mornings under the leadership of the damned psychiatric social worker. Actually, while we had the substitute, the group developed a harmony and a sense of being a group that we certainly had never experienced before. It's sad, I suppose, but true that sharing a common hatred will bring people together. Just why we hated that social worker, I couldn't say. She was competent, brisk, polite, and rather handsome. If she seemed a bit masculine, this undoubtedly was because she thought we would respond better if she didn't appear too feminine. But according to Miss Hazel, there's a professional handicap that is felt by all social workers. She says they are afraid they won't be given their due respect.

We didn't worry about whether we respected that woman. We simply hated her. Instead of feeling gratitude about getting attention that so few mental patients get, we acted as if we'd been insulted. We were in the habit of being in a group led by a psychiatrist. Now we were all prima donnas.

The reason my occasional "private sessions" with Dr. Leonard are resented by those who could be objective, is that each patient longs for more psychiatric help. So Leona Carson isn't the only one who speaks harshly of my relationship with the little doctor. I tower over him as we walk slowly through the hall. We do not make an attractive couple. I am envied, though, because I am being given what certainly is "private" psychiatric attention.

I didn't improve things by defending the few minutes of private conversation with Dr. Leonard by explaining that he had been my doctor Outside. Leona threatened to have him kicked off the Applewood staff, which would be a neat trick. Even if he were engaged in some questionable practice, I doubt if the hospital is interested in hearing charges against doctors serving them for free. Or against any doctors, for that matter. Miss Hazel tells us the budget allows for twice as many professional persons as are actually employed here. She says if they could take half of the unused money to raise salaries they could get more help and be in a better position, too, to hold the professional employes. But no, the funds have to be used the way some politicians have said while other states taking a more realistic view are hiring our people away. "As a newspaperwoman you'd ought to do something about it," she says. Maybe the Other Caroline would have tried. It didn't seem in line with her character, though, to do any socially beneficial work that wasn't Social. Little did she know it, apparently, but she was a great climber. A weaker man than Mr. Kincaid would have been broken to her harness, would have stayed in the hated job to earn thirty-five, forty, and so-on thousands a year. They would have got a still bigger, still more fancily decorated house and perhaps eventually been able to shine almost as brightly as her brother and his exotic wife. To say nothing of pal Marianne.

If I hadn't already decided on the brain tumor interpretation, I would think the Other Caroline's, or Keri's, decline was caused by her inability to survive the removal of her dream of grandeur. She probably always had it, always aspired to be the one to give away the clothes rather than to be the recipient. Writing her page in the *Monitor*, how she must have longed to see her own name listed among Maxwell's elite. Well, a crumbling of the personality might well have been caused by a combination of physical and mental difficulties. Many of the diseases we've always thought of as being entirely physical are believed by some quite rational people to be at least sometimes if not always in the psychosomatic group. Even cancer. I wonder if I could sound Dr. Leonard out on the subject without making him suspect that I have finally hit upon the truth about my own case. I still go carefully and slowly through my hair in search of a scar but I find nothing. Of course I can't see the back parts at all well in a mirror but I should think a scar, however skilfully made, would be noticeable to the touch if nothing else.

Since we'd given him the chance to go into a regular orgy of reminiscing about his trip, I didn't feel obliged to add anything on the subject as I accompanied him through the building after class. I told him I was doing some typing for Miss Johnson now that the manuscript was finished. "That is," I said, "I came to the end of what Mr. Kincaid brought last. It certainly didn't seem finished, though."

"No," said the doctor, "it wasn't."

"I assume that from the way things were going, she became ill."

"Yes."

"Seriously?"

"Seriously."

"Well, I got over hating her, by the way."

"I'm glad," he said.

"She's not a type I could ever like," I said, "but I became sorry for her."

"Yes."

Evidently he had talked himself out. We were almost to the parking lot when he said he saw no reason why I should stay at the hospital much longer.

"Do you mean you consider me well?" I asked. "I still don't remember . . ."

"It's been slow," he said. "I wouldn't be able to guess how much longer it could be. I wouldn't even be able to guarantee that it would all come back although my opinion is that it will. When, I don't know. Or how. It could be sudden, the way it seemed to go. Or it could be gradual, the way the illness itself, apart from the total amnesia, developed. Part of the memory came back very quickly, you know, that is, along with the return of awareness."

"If you can call it memory," I said. "To be able to translate a scrap of Latin and to know that Dickens wrote novels . . . to know that when you were handed a bowl of stew and a spoon, you were not being provided with the kind of food and service you'd been used to Outside. . . . Oh, great!"

"Yes, great," he said. "Haven't you ever stopped to think how it would have been if no memory at all had come?"

"No, thanks," I said. "It's been bad enough without my imagining how it could be worse. I have never thought it was so comforting, when you have a headache, for instance, to contemplate the fact that some people probably have no heads."

He laughed. "But the main thing is that I am recommending a conditional discharge, conditional not because I have any idea that you won't continue to improve but because this way there will be less staff reluctance. They won't feel obliged to probe into how much of your memory has come back, but will just take my word for it, I believe, that there is enough to provide a basis for ability to function in the normal world."

"Do you think I could get a job if I told the prospective employer I just had a conditional release from a mental hospital?"

"Your job will be at home, Mrs. Kincaid," he said. "Time

enough to think of resuming your career later on if you should decide that is what you want. For the present, though, you're needed at home. Having you gone over a year, nearly a year and a half now, isn't it, has been hard on the children, you know."

I went back to the Ward in a sort of daze. The doctor had finally washed his hands of me. It was useless to pretend that he would ever try to help me recover my past. He's thrown that Mrs. Kincaid at me as if he never wanted to bother about me again. In all fairness, though, I had to admit he hadn't turned away without giving me a chance to speak. But what could I have said?

Had they won? Must I never recover even a small glimpse of my past? Mrs. Kincaid. The children. Mrs. Kincaid's relatives. Mr. Kincaid's relatives. These must be accepted as mine?

It was difficult to pretend to Aggie that I was feeling fine. I agreed with her that it was good to have the doctor back. "You'll be leaving soon," she said. "Oh, how I will miss you!"

I told her she would leave Applewood before I did. "But no matter which of us leaves first," I said, "we'll be getting together."

She said it was nice of me to say that, but not necessary. "I'm getting tougher," she said. "I no longer expect my life here or elsewhere to be easy."

In my depressed mood there was nothing I could say to cheer her up. I actually was relieved when another patient came between us and said, "All right, all right, no more secrets. If you've got anything to say, tell all of us." She held up her hands and called for attention. "Aggie," she said, "wants your attention."

There was some booing and some laughter. Aggie was a good sport. "Okay, girls," she said, "how would you like to have me lead you in a spelling drill?"

"How do you spell Applewood?" one of the girls shouted.

Then another who liked to sing and did have a fair voice began to croon: "A—P—Double—L—O, A—P—O spells Applewood, Applewood. That's a funny kind of candy. The man who makes it isn't Sandy. . . ."

We all laughed then and clapped. And I gave the impression of having snapped out of my bad humor. Aggie said it was good to see me cheerful again.

The next day Mr. Kincaid was practically turning handsprings. He said he had been talking with the doctor and had been told that there was every reason to believe the Applewood staff would be receptive to Dr. Leonard's request for my conditional discharge on or before September first. "How long before?" had been Mr. Kincaid's first question. This had amused Dr. Leonard who had said he mustn't expect anything connected with government to happen overnight. Maybe the last day of August, he said. Mr. Kincaid spoke of this as if it were a year away. To me it was all too close. I still didn't know how I could tell this very nice man, of whom I had grown so fond and whom, I was beginning to admit to myself, I might even love, that I would take nothing more from him, upon my discharge, but the loan of five hundred dollars to tide me over until my first paycheck.

"But I told Ellen it might be any minute because, well, how do we know when someone in charge of red tape may suddenly decide to cut through a lot of it?" He was so gay that I felt I had to pretend to be pleased, too. Certainly I couldn't let him get the idea that I wanted to stay on indefinitely at Applewood. You would have to be crazy, all right, to want that. Still, when you don't know where you are going or how you will support yourself when you get there, the hospital doesn't seem the worst possible place in the world.

He continued to speak of his sister Ellen's great reluctance ever to let go of a dollar. She has evidently never been frugal when other people's money is footing the bills but hates to spend any of her own. "But even Ellen can't quite figure out how to fit herself into one of the little bedrooms with Kathy," he said. "I told her she would have to get out of the big bedroom before the end of next week because I have things to do to the room before you and I take it over again." He took one of my hands and squeezed it. I could hardly bear to look at him. I found myself thinking what difference does it make if I'm not really his wife because if she's dead, if everybody who doesn't know what actually happened is going to think I am she and that all she had was a nervous breakdown, all right, why not take her place? Is it because I think there's something so great about somebody's asking you a few questions to make a relationship legal? Or is my reluctance to accept what is being thrust upon me due to a kind of eroding jealousy of the woman whose husband and children I have inherited along with her body?

Resolutely, like the heroine in a soap opera, I made myself think about five hundred dollars, looking for work in Chicago and a YWCA room or a room in a hotel for women. I tried not to hear Mr. Kincaid's eager talk or to feel the pressure of his hands. It was a relief when we decided it was time to start for the Country Kitchen where we had decided to have dinner. Dr. Leonard had got permission for me to stay out until ten thirty and so we were going to a movie. Mr. Kincaid said he'd thought about asking me to go dancing but that there was no ballroom near enough. I remembered then that Jock and Keri Dunlop had danced, that they had, indeed, met at a dance hall. Although I hoped to avoid putting it to the test, I wondered if having the Other Caroline's body would automatically bestow upon me the ability to dance as well as she had done. I found the dislike of Keri creeping back and distorting the blurred image I had of the Other Caroline. If Keri and she were the one and same person, I could hardly hate one without giving up my carefully tended neutrality about the other.

At the restaurant I decided the hell with the Other Caroline's tastes always being imposed upon me. "I'll have a glass of wine, too," I said to the chummy hostess who was already writing down a Martini on the wine check. I half expected her to say that since I'd always had a Martini, I would have to continue. "They're simply too strong for me," I told Mr. Kincaid when he commented that probably it was not the drink for warm weather, even in an air-conditioned place. "I don't think the weather has anything to do with it. It's the gin."

He said he had never cared for gin or for whiskey, either. I said it was probably a religious thing with him and he said maybe so but that if he'd been going to interpret religion in his parents' way he wouldn't have been having wine, either. I asked how they explained the wine drunk by Jesus and the Disciples and he laughed and said they seemed honestly to believe that what the Bible calls wine was in reality just grape juice. "Year-around grape harvesting?" I asked, "Or did they use preservatives to keep it from fermenting?"

"It would be futile to try to argue with my mother on any

subject," he said. "She bolsters all difficult arguments up with Biblical quotations so subtly connected with the subject that it's impossible for the ordinary person to get the drift. Or there is the chance that what she quotes is whatever pops into her mind at the moment. That's a consideration I didn't think of until after I was away from home and no longer so intimidated by her quotations."

"How come your sister Ellen was apparently so untouched by the family religion or your mother's preaching?" I asked.

"Ellen's only five years younger than I," he said, "but the folks thought they couldn't have any more family and so my mother, especially, took her birth as something of a miracle, I guess. Anyway, none of the rules ever held for Ellen, which perhaps gave my mother some pleasure she had always missed in her life before but which I believe was very tough on Ellen. She's a difficult person . . . as you know all too well."

I knew Ellen only as she was Norma in the autobiography I had just finished typing. From it I knew that the woman was more than difficult. I reminded myself that although I felt I could have handled Jock's problems far better than Keri had done and not gone to pieces when he threw up a big career in the electronic industry, I wouldn't have found dealing with that sister-in-law simple. "Will she drop out of college?"

"It's what she threatens, of course," he said, "but what could she do but go back home and try for another teaching job somewhere in the area? She's evidently decided that can't be the life for her. I don't know what she will do. I feel sure she will hang on in Maxwell as long as she can and maybe even try to get some kind of job when her money gets low."

"But isn't she getting near the end of her Ph.D.?"

"Most of the class and seminar work, yes, but if she has started on her thesis I don't know anything about it."

Remembering Norma's David, I asked if Ellen dated at all. "I think there's somebody," he said, "but she doesn't tell me anything and she doesn't bring anybody around. All the same, I think she's seeing somebody."

"Then let's hope it's serious," I said.

He said for me not to bank on it. "I think it was very serious, at least on her side, with the English chap," he said. "Ellen's trouble seems to be with getting serious too soon. At any rate there were a couple of boys down home, you know, that we thought for sure she was going to marry. Obviously she thought so, too. Ellen's greatest obstacle, of course, is that she can't believe everybody isn't always panting for her company. My mother led her to think she was conveying favors when she gave anyone some of her time."

Well, if I am right in thinking the Other Caroline wrote the manuscript I have just finished typing, what Mr. Kincaid's sister conveyed to the boys, or anyway to one at least, was a considerable favor.

The dinner, as usual, was delicious. I am aware of the abundance of food at the Country Kitchen but Mr. Kincaid is mistaken when he thinks my comments on the bountiful servings means I don't get enough to eat at the hospital. There we get more than we want, not because there is such a lot, really, but because it simply isn't good. I believe it probably starts out being all right, not choice, but perfectly decent. However, by the time it has steam-tabled its way to us, it all tastes, somehow, of long-cooked cabbage even though cooked cabbage is seldom served. I perhaps libel the honest flavor of cabbage. What destroys the good taste of the hospital food, and surely much of the nutritive value, is steam. Our desserts and biscuits are all made with the heavy-handed flavoring of a bitter baking powder. Pies have this flavor, too, but probably get it from rancid shortening. I don't tell Mr. Kincaid any of this because why worry him? And am I really protecting him by delaying what I must tell him within the next two weeks?

We have movies now and then at the hospital. They used to have them oftener but that was before each ward had its own television. To me, a movie on television is quite a different form of entertainment and one I just don't think I could ever learn to enjoy. I know you can get so you neither see nor hear the commercials but I wonder if cultivating this ability is worth the effort. I would rather see a movie in a theater and just not see so many if time and money were a factor. I don't suppose the one Mr. Kincaid and I saw Saturday was any masterpiece but I enjoyed every minute of it. It was a sort of Western, I guess, although happily there wasn't any shooting, and the colors of the mountain and desert scenery were wonderful. "We'll go there next year if you'd like," said Mr. Kincaid on the way back to the hospital. "The kids will be old enough to enjoy the trip, don't you think? We might get a camper . . ."

Poor, poor man. I hadn't the heart to do anything but agree, nor to pull myself away when, before I realized it, he was kissing me as we stood beside the car in the parking lot. I felt very dizzy but managed to laugh as he let me go. "If you don't watch out, I'll be expelled," I said.

"Then what have we been waiting for?" he asked, but I hurried off toward Martin House and was signing in by the time he caught up with me. "Did you have a pleasant evening?" asked the nurse.

"Very pleasant," I said and felt myself blushing.

TWENTY-NINE *The Journal*

*W*hen Miss Hazel and I were discussing my approaching departure, I asked her why my friend Aggie, by now surely as mentally well as I, wasn't being given a conditional discharge. "Is it because she doesn't have any Outside doctor pulling strings for her?" I asked.

Miss Hazel, always a great critic of the hospital and prone, in my opinion, to say quite libelous things about it, sometimes ruffles up if somebody else criticizes Applewood. She snorted at my question and said nobody ever pulled strings in this place. "I agree that Aggie's perfectly able to get along Outside, or would be if she had a husband and family to go to like you, but we can't turn her out when she's got nowhere to go, can we?"

"Can't she go where she was before?"

"She shared an apartment with two girls who vanished from her world when she got sick, which is par for the course, in case you don't know it. And believe me, not all husbands stick either. Or wives. I've seen plenty abandoned out here, plenty who could have left if there had been somebody to take responsibility for them. You can't just walk out of here and start living like nothing had happened. You may think you can but you can't, no, ma'am; what you've had is a major sickness and you have got to convalesce from it like from anything else. Aggie can't just rent a room and start working right off the bat."

"But what will happen to her?"

"She'll have to stay until she can make it on her own, I guess. What else?"

"In our Friday morning group we've been talking about the part-time patient projects. I thought Applewood had some."

"A few of the men go into town now to work," said Miss Hazel. "For maybe twenty years they've been talking about how this part-time project is so great but they can't seem to get it off the ground, not in any big way. Oh, I suppose if one of the doctors could find a job for Aggie not too far from here, there'd be no staff objection to her going and coming for a while to see how it would work. But who's going to find her the job? Not them fellows, always breaking their necks to get away and into private practice where they can make fifty thousand a year without hardly doing anything but listen to a bunch of rich women talk about theirselves. But don't you worry about Aggie. She'll get away eventually in spite of them, in spite of everything because she's got guts."

And the implication was that I hadn't? But I had been wondering. It had been so easy, as long as it seemed in a very distant future, to think about starting out on my own, but now I found myself cringing not just from the embarrassment of asking Mr. Kincaid for a loan but from the prospect of being out in the world all by myself. I began to wonder if maybe I would be better off looking for a job in Maxwell, where I could continue to see Mr. Kincaid or at least to know I had a friend available if I needed one. And it crossed my mind, too, that he might feel he would have to notify the hospital if I refused to go home with him. I mean the conditional release might name him as a sort of guardian held accountable for my welfare.

I have told Miss Johnson that I will be leaving soon. She has said for me not to come to my office just to type for her, not unless I want to. "But of course I expect these last days will be going very slowly for you," she said. "I know how it must be."

She didn't at all. I have never known time to go so fast. I have decided, though, to have done with this shillyshallying. I will speak frankly with Mr. Kincaid next Saturday. I will not say anything to Dr. Leonard because I feel it is only right to talk to Mr. Kincaid first. Dr. Leonard is involved but not personally . . . except that I do feel that if I wanted to I could get him jailed. Oh, not that I intend to threaten anybody. What is done is done. Some medical procedures are definitely irreversible. The only thing I could do to get out of having Caroline Kincaid's body would be to have another transplant or, of course, die. I expect that what my subconscious was trying to do during my catatonic period was exactly that, to reject the Other Caroline.

Friday I will clear out my desk here, so I won't have to be dashing over to Administration at the last minute. Still, I might let it go until Monday and then spend my office time writing how, if I can bear to do it, I broke my news to Mr. Kincaid who, in turn, will probably take it to Dr. Leonard. Yes, I had better leave things here until Monday at least because it is possible that after I have spoken my piece, Dr. Leonard will influence Mr. Kincaid to withdraw his sponsorship of my conditional release and, like Aggie, I'll just have to wait until they consider me up to making it entirely on my own. Maybe Aggie and I could take a small apartment together in the event that they decide not to release me September first.

It is Monday now and I am going to close up shop here at Administration after I have written about what to me has been an historic weekend. Although the original plan was for me to leave next Saturday, Dr. Leonard has got permission for Jim to get me late Friday afternoon. They agreed that it would be simpler then when no visitors are cluttering up the scene. How ridiculous it seems that I started to write "Mr. Kincaid" instead of Jim. I mean, how crazy can you get! Well, if I'm the example, there's really no limit.

Saturday afternoon my gentleman visitor, whom I really should refer to as Mr. Kincaid because at that point he still was that to me, looked so triumphant that I thought surely he must have got a big raise, but what had happened was better than that to him and even though I was still such a nut, I could see that it really was wonderful for him and would have been for me, too, if I'd been who he thought I was. I had decided to lay my case on the line for him, put my cards on the table, talk turkey or whatever, anyhow tell him it simply wouldn't be possible for me to be his wife because I wasn't, I just wasn't. But his news so completely absorbed him that I could tell he wouldn't half listen to me until after he got his story told. So I asked him what it was and he said, "You'll never guess . . . you'll just never guess who got married."

My heart sank. Of course he had a perfect right to get married. Why not? His wife was dead. But I pretended to play it cool.

I said I couldn't remember anything sensational in the morning paper. How about the waitress at the Country Kitchen? No. Then maybe Dr. Leonard? But, unless he had abandoned her in Europe, Dr. Leonard had a wife.

How about Miss Hazel? That would be staggering news, all right, but Mr. Kincaid wouldn't have heard that before we did. But then I knew I'd just been afraid to say what I hoped. "You mean Norma—" Quickly I coughed and substituted his sister's real-life name before he could notice the slip. "You mean Ellen has actually . . . ?"

"Yes, Ellen, Ellen of all people," he said and gave me a hug. "She evidently did have a beau because now she's got a husband and what's more, he has a job and an apartment."

"Where?"

"In Chicago," he said. "That's really about all I know because she's mad at me. Last night she came home at about ten o'clock and said all she wanted to do was pick up a few of her things so they wouldn't be in your way and I said she didn't have to do it at that moment, but she said she was leaving. I asked where she was going and she said to her husband's apartment in Chicago, that they had got married a couple of hours ago."

Later in the afternoon he spoke more soberly about his sister's marriage and said he hoped his telling her she had to go live somewhere else hadn't made her rush into something she would regret. "Well, it isn't as if she were seventeen instead of twenty-seven," I said. "And don't blame yourself anyhow, no matter how it turns out because I expect she's glad she was given the impetus or whatever it was she needed . . . I don't know, I think probably all that girl ever needed to get a husband was to stop acting so pleased with herself for about two minutes." Of course Norma was the one I was thinking of, and how she surely could have married David Alistaire if she had treated him with a little respect. I felt I couldn't or shouldn't judge Ellen Kincaid too severely on the basis of evidence provided in The Manuscript.

We dined at the Country Kitchen again but didn't go to a movie. Maybe we would have if Mr. Kincaid had thought to sign me out until last bell but in his excitement over his sister's marriage, he had neglected to ask for the special late pass. Again I let him kiss me goodnight or, rather, didn't pull away from him. I had about decided to go home with him because whether it was legal or moral or not, it certainly would be the most convenient and expedient thing for me to do. There was a good chance, for example look at Aggie, that I wouldn't be allowed to leave unless I went along to Mr. Kincaid's house and let the hospital authorities believe that there is where I intended to remain. I must admit I would have felt easier in my mind about going with him if I'd thought I could have a separate bedroom. But I'd learned that the little house had just three. Of course I could do as Ellen had done, share the big bedroom with the little girl. This and many other thoughts that whirled through my mind that evening were obliterated by the way I felt when Mr. Kincaid kissed me. I found myself thinking why not, why not just forget what was inconvenient to remember, why not just go ahead and take the Other Caroline's place?

The night nurse who gave me a pill said she knew how it was. "They talk a lot about how tough it is here at first," she said, "but it seems to me almost everybody finds the last week or so the worst. The place I worked before, a private hosptial, never told the patients more than a few hours ahead, but I always thought that was treating them like they really weren't able to take it yet. I think it's better to know, to be treated like you're one of the team even if it does make you jittery."

I said yes. I was falling into the habit of saying yes, it seemed to me, to just about everything that was mentioned. I wondered if I should ask Dr. Leonard to let me have The Manuscript again. I hated to give him the satisfaction of knowing the experiment had been successful and that I was wanting it so I could bone up on what would be a memorized history rather than a remembered one, but I felt I must have the diary in order to help me get through what would be bound to be difficult encounters with the Other Caroline's relatives. I couldn't bear the thought of having them think I was completely blank as far as the past was concerned. I don't know why I felt ashamed of the amnesia, more ashamed of that than of the attendant mental illness. Maybe it was because it seemed as if it must be at least partly deliberate. I could see them asking each other why it was I had "decided" to wipe the past from my mind. I could imagine them saying I could remember if I wanted to, if I would just try. And so on. I dreaded my return to the world because of my conviction that it would be such a new one to me, except for what preparation I had got from Mr. Kincaid's remarks and from his wife's book even though it was one written during a period when her mental health was deteriorating.

But I finally slept.

Saturday morning I helped one of the aides in the linen room. We hadn't quite finished our job of taking inventory when it was time to quit for lunch. Afterward I went back but she said she could finish alone and since it was nearly time for visitors, anyway, it would be foolish for me to start anything more. "You go along now," she said. "If I know Mr. Kincaid, he's already there in the visitors' room. It's okay for you to go on in." She grinned. "You're practically a visitor now yourself, you know."

So I went back into the hall and toward the visitors' room. I didn't like to enter it ahead of time if other people were there, because it would look as if I didn't think the rules applied to me. But, looking through the door's glass, I saw that Mr. Kincaid was the only person waiting. It was a quarter to one, fifteen minutes before the visitors' bell. The room would be filled by then.

He wasn't facing the door but I could get a clear view of his profile, a very good, strong one, I thought, not pretty or handsome even, but strong. His hair, blessed with a wave, was closer to the color of mine in this light than it was when we were out of doors when mine would blaze if touched by the sun. He was reading a magazine he'd taken from the stack on the table in the center of the room.

I believe this was the first time at the hospital that I had looked at him when he wasn't also looking at me. I thought that although he looked different, the man I was watching now was rather more familiar than the one I was accustomed to see standing facing the door to greet me as I entered. It is hard to explain just how what happened then happened, because I don't know. It was something that wasn't present in me a moment before and then, quite suddenly, it was there as if it had never been away. Why, it's Jim, I said to myself as if this were some great revelation.

As it was.

I must have stood leaning against the wall and not looking into the room for at least five minutes. You read about how his whole life passes through the mind of a drowning person. I assume that this testimony has been obtained from people who have been resuscitated. What I experienced certainly wasn't like drowning but as I leaned against the hall's darkened tan wall, the entire life, not just what she put into her autobiography, of Caroline Brown Kincaid passed before my inner eyes and became my property. I knew then, without thinking of how absurd it had been, that I was not the product of some sensational transplant, that I was simply Caroline and that there had never been any Other except in my sick mind. I told myself then that I must be well or practically, and as I pushed the door open, I thought how fortunate it was that I had kept all that transplant fantasy to myself. What I apparently dread more than being found foolish in somebody else's eyes, is the feeling that telling on myself would lower my estimation of my worth. It seems to me that maturity obliges a person to keep a great deal of his personal gripes to himself. I don't want to tell anyone "all," not even my beloved husband. Maybe my "everything" doesn't amount to much as confessions go, but I would like to keep it my own.

Jim didn't hear me enter but he looked up as I approached his chair. Before he could rise, I said, "Are you tall standing up?"

He put the magazine on the chair next to his. For a moment he leaned back with closed eyes and I wondered if I had been too abrupt in telling him I'd got my memory back. But how could I have led up to it? Either I remembered or I didn't. Before I didn't; now I did.

Then he sprang up. "Let's get out of here," he said.

But I shouldn't brag too much about my memory. I don't have a very clear idea of what we did yesterday afternoon. We walked and walked. Here for a while and then in town. We talked about going to Gran's where the kids were, but I decided it would be too hard on me to see them only briefly. Not hard on them. What will probably be hard on them is having a stranger around all the time. But I flatter myself that they will get used to me and prefer me to Mrs. Brent and their happily departed aunt.

Mrs. Brent wants to depart, too, but says she will stay a few more weeks if I can't get along without her. Her daughter keeps insisting that she stop work. I told Jim to tell her to make next week her last because a big strong woman like me can certainly take care of that little house. "Ye gods, who do you think did the housework at home?" I asked. "Surely not the poet!"

It's almost four. If I wait for the bell I can meet Aggie and we'll walk back to Martin together. Now and then I run into the Pink Lady who always tells me how much "everybody" misses me in Maxwell and looks forward to my return. She has promised me that I won't have to feel in the least bit "nervous" because she will "look after" me whenever I "feel timid." Unfortunately the return of my memory has restored this ridiculous woman to her small niche in my past. So it isn't all roses.

And it seems that like it or not I will have to go regularly to Dr. Leonard for an indefinite period. "Couldn't we find somebody cheaper?" I asked Jim. "You know he's all for the rich, like Connie. I suppose she's still running to him."

"Oh, Connie's okay," said Jim. "She's been quite a help, believe it or not. Yes, I guess she still goes to him, but he doesn't charge us anywhere what he does her. You went to him maybe six times before he had you hospitalized and I didn't think the bill was bad. Less than I had expected, in fact."

"Then I don't remember everything," I said. "What I can't remember at all is about where that manuscript stopped. Then there's a blank until I came to at La Salle House."

Jim said I hadn't missed anything worth remembering. Will Dr. Leonard want to probe into the past? Beyond preferring to keep it to myself, I've no interest in it. Might the man stray far enough from Dr. Freud to analyze my future? That's all I am concerned about.

Just now Miss Johnson popped her head in to say they are cutting a birthday cake next door in fifteen minutes and I am invited. I am one of the girls again, it would seem, not just another of the patients.

I've been looking out as far as La Salle where the Other Caroline's illness became malignant. Beyond that are barns, then fields, and then a forest. You can't see it from here but Miss Hazel has told me that beyond the woods is a cemetery where they bury patients whose bodies aren't claimed by anyone and for whom the books show no one who can be held legally liable. That's where I am leaving the remains of the woman who finally expired while looking into the visitors' lounge of Martin House last Saturday afternoon.